WHISPERS
ON THE DOCK

POSTCARDS
from
MISTY HARBOR INN

WHISPERS ON THE DOCK

EVANGELINE KELLEY

Guideposts
New York

Postcards from Misty Harbor Inn is a trademark of Guideposts.

ISBN-10: 0-8249-3259-5
ISBN-13: 978-0-8249-3259-6

Published by Guideposts
16 East 34th Street
New York, New York 10016
Guideposts.org

Distributed by Ideals Publications, a Guideposts company
2630 Elm Hill Pike, Suite 100
Nashville, Tennessee 37214

Guideposts and *Ideals* are registered trademarks of Guideposts.

While Nantucket is a real place, please note that we have taken poetic liberties with aspects of Nantucket history, organizations, landmarks and geography for the purposes of our story. The characters and events in this book are fictional, and any resemblance to actual persons or events is coincidental.

Library of Congress Cataloging-in-Publication Data

Kelley, Evangeline.
    Whispers on the dock / Evangeline Kelley.
        pages cm.–(Postcards from Misty Harbor Inn; 3)
    Includes bibliographical references and index.
    ISBN 978-0-8249-3259-6 (alk. paper)
1. Bed and breakfast accommodations–Fiction. 2. Nantucket Island
(Mass.)–Fiction. I. Title.
    PS3552.E6999W45 2013
    813'.54–dc23

                                                                                    2013018272

Cover and interior design by Müllerhaus
Cover illustration by Marilyn Chamberlain
Typeset by Aptara, Inc.

Printed and bound in the United States of America
10 9 8 7 6 5 4 3 2 1

WHISPERS
ON THE DOCK

CHAPTER
One

Sam Carter had her hands coated with flour when she heard a loud "*Helloooo!*" trumpeting from the entrance foyer of the inn. Sam was sure it must be Trish Montgomery, a guest they were expecting to arrive today.

From where Sam stood in the inn's kitchen, she couldn't see her older sister Gracie Gold, but she knew Gracie was out tending to the garden. A violent squall the night before—not unusual for July—had caused some damage to the roses, so Gracie had gone out to apply a few agricultural Band-Aids, so to speak.

Sam's oldest sister Caroline was out with her fiancé George, looking at yet another house to buy. The wedding was set to take place in mid-September, so they had to find their new home soon or they might be bunking in the inn's guest bedrooms.

"Hello? Anyone here?" Trish called. She had a loud voice with full, rounded tones. Sam wondered if the woman had spent time on the stage or as an opera singer.

Caroline had said she'd be back in time to greet their new guest, but if Trish's wall-shaking decibels hadn't brought Caroline to the front foyer, it was likely she was late. Which didn't exactly surprise Sam—Caroline's vivacious love of life often led her on distracting side paths wherever she went, whether to the grocery store or to visit a potential new home. She could imagine Caroline losing track of time quite easily.

Sam stared at her floury hands and then moved to the sink to rinse them quickly in cold water. The inn had only been open for two months, and while it had enjoyed enough business to keep it bustling, they couldn't afford to offend a guest who would be staying for an entire month.

Sam hurried to the foyer with what she hoped was a professional smile on her face. "Hello, Ms. Montgomery. I'm so sorry to have kept you waiting." Sam touched her apron and was appalled to see a faint cloud of flour rise in front of her. "Oh. Um … maybe I shouldn't shake your hand."

Trish raised red-gold eyebrows at the cloud of flour before glancing down at her magenta silk top and black slacks. "*Hmm.* Yes, good idea."

"I'm Sam Carter." Sam went to the antique wooden bookstand podium that Gracie had discovered and brought home. They hadn't wanted a big, formal front desk for the inn, so this gleaming four-foot-high walnut podium was perfect because the flat top was only a little over a foot square and there were convenient shelves set in it to hold the guestbook and other essentials. The entire thing tucked away neatly against the wall of the foyer, blending in nicely with the warm patina of the cherry wainscoting.

Trish handed over her credit card. "I have to say, it was immensely easy to find this place. And what a view."

"It's one of the reasons my sisters and I decided to buy the Misty Harbor Inn. We love living right along the beach."

"I set my fourth book in the Bahamas." Trish had a dreamy smile on her face. "The research for that was *such* a chore." She winked a bright blue eye at Sam and chortled.

"Your…fourth book?"

"Oh, I forgot. Most people don't realize I wrote under a pen name for my first two."

Sam blinked and tried to follow the conversation.

Luckily, Trish seemed not to notice her confusion. She went on, "People always think of *Passion in the Sand* as my second book, but I wrote two American Colonial romances as Tisha Parker before I switched to Trish Montgomery."

"Oh." Sam hoped she didn't look too clueless.

"One of the reasons I chose this place was because it was a bit outside of the main part of town." Trish lowered her voice. "It's so hard to get any privacy when I go away to write. Fellow guests at the hotel are always interrupting me for an autograph or wanting to talk about writing." She sighed.

"We don't have any other guests at the moment, but if other people do arrive, we can ask them to respect your privacy." Was this woman famous? She sounded like a romance novelist, perhaps, except that Sam had never heard of her. She mostly read biographies and history, although Gracie had recently introduced her to Debbie Macomber.

"No, that's all right." Trish waved a hand. "I've learned that the fame comes with the territory. But I must say it was nice not to be greeted with a squeal and a request for an autograph as soon as I came in. That happened at the last bed-and-breakfast I stayed at."

"Oh. I'm sure I would never do something like that. I wouldn't want to scare you away."

Trish gave a full, deep laugh that rang throughout the foyer. "You're such a sweet young thing."

At fifty-three, Sam was gratified to be referred to as young. Trish looked to be about Caroline's age, although Trish's red-gold flyaway curls revealed not a single strand of gray.

At that moment, Caroline sailed through the front door with a breathless "I'm so sorry I'm late." Her short blonde hair was more windswept than normal, but she looked charmingly young as she smiled at Trish and held out a hand in greeting. "You must be Trish Montgomery. I'm Caroline Marris, and this is my fiancé George Wright."

George had followed Caroline through the front door with less haste. He nodded at Trish.

"Let me take care of checking you in," Caroline said. "It looks like Sam was in the middle of baking something yummy."

"Scones," Sam said. "I thought it might be fun to have tea this afternoon in the front parlor."

"I love scones," Trish said. "Before I wrote my Pounding Scottish Hearts series, I hadn't even tasted a real scone, but the research trip for those books was fabulous. I had the most wonderful tea in Edinburgh."

Caroline had a slightly startled look on her face, and Sam quickly said, "Romance novels like yours must be so much fun to write." She gave her sister a meaningful look.

"It's the research I love the most. I'm here writing my next manuscript, which will be set in Colonial Nantucket."

"How wonderful," Caroline said. "How many books does that make for you?"

"This is the last in a three-book series, so that will bring me to forty-four," Trish said.

Sam had to fight to keep from choking in amazement. She gave a pleased, surprised look instead. "I had no idea you'd written that many."

Trish rolled her eyes. "It's like having forty-four children you have to keep track of. Most readers don't notice it, but I made a mistake and named the heroine in *The Sheriff's Sundered Heart* the same as the heroine in my third book, *Breathless Barbados Belle*." She winked conspiratorially. "My editor didn't catch it either."

Sam needed to escape back to the kitchen before she did something horrible and laughed out loud. "Now that you're here, Caroline, I'll let you take care of Trish. It was nice meeting you. I hope you enjoy your stay."

Sam had shaped the scones into little soft triangles and popped the tray into the oven by the time Caroline entered the kitchen, a mock frown on her face. "How could you abandon me like that?"

Sam gave her an innocent look. "Abandon you?"

"It was so hard not to react to *Breathless Barbados Belle* that I thought my face would turn purple." Caroline grinned. "Does she really have a book with that title?"

"We should go down to the bookstore and find out." Sam set the timer for the scones. "She thought I knew who she was. I was too embarrassed to admit I had never even heard of her."

"She seems like quite a character, which would explain how creative she is. Now I'm interested in reading her books."

"We should get a few titles for our library. Maybe Trish will do us a favor and autograph them."

"We can tell our guests that a famous author stayed here." Caroline spotted a flyer on the counter that Sam had been given that morning when she went grocery shopping. "They were passing this out at church last Sunday when you filled in for the preschool teacher."

"Stan Wildes gave it to me. I bumped into him at the grocery store this morning."

"Yes, Pastor Stan told me the town puts on the Summerfest event every year at the end of August, and Harvest Chapel always has a booth set up. But this flyer is for the baking competition at the festival. Are you going to enter?"

"I was thinking I'd like to enter my blackberry cobbler recipe. It's Mom's special recipe, but I've been tweaking it. I can't believe the number of wild blackberries that grow in the wooded areas around the island, and they're so sweet."

Sam would have expected Caroline to be enthusiastic in her encouragement, but instead a look of concern clouded her sister's face. "Are you sure you have time to enter the contest?"

"What do you mean?"

"You're already baking for our guests' breakfasts every day, and you've just started substituting in the Sunday school too. You're not taking on too much?"

"Of course not. I love baking—I never really realized how much until we bought this inn. It's not work, it's fun for me. And this contest is perfect for me to hone my skills." Sam gave Caroline an interested look. "I would expect this kind of cautious advice from Gracie, not from you."

"I just…don't want you to get overwhelmed."

But Sam had a feeling Caroline was talking about herself, not Sam. "Overwhelmed? What's up? Is the wedding planning going okay?"

"Oh, it's fine. Well"—Caroline ran a hand through her hair—"there just seem to be so many decisions to make."

"Can't George help? Where is he, by the way?"

"He's helping Trish carry in her bags."

"I thought she only had that one small one she brought in with her."

"She apparently had a few more stashed in her car."

Sam bit back a laugh. "So why can't George help you more with the wedding plans?"

"Oh, he is. He's taking care of the honeymoon—which he wants to be a surprise for me—plus, he's looking for houses in Nantucket for us to buy."

"I remember looking for my town house. It took forever just to sift through all the listings and visit all the ones that looked promising."

"He's doing all that, and he's only bringing me along for the ones he has already looked at first and thought I might like. So I hate to ask him for help when he's so busy."

"I thought you were planning a simple wedding?"

"I am. But there are still an awful lot of decisions." Caroline's hands fluttered in frustration. "Who'd have thought a simple wedding involved things like how many people to invite and where I can have it and what food to serve and what time it should be, and the entire time I'm just not happy with any decision I make because it seems too…" She stopped and then laughed to herself. "Here I am complaining, when most women have dreamed about their weddings since they were little girls."

"I can assure you that mine wasn't all that wonderful," Sam said drily. "I hadn't even realized yet how controlling Gerald was, but he had wanted certain things for our wedding and I'd blithely let him make all the decisions, so certain parts of my wedding weren't really what I would have preferred."

"I should be even more grateful that I can make all these decisions for myself," Caroline said. "But all I can think about is that I don't know what I want."

"Well, you have some time. And if it'll be a small wedding, you won't need a huge amount of planning."

"I guess."

Caroline's voice was strangely colorless, which Sam wouldn't have expected from her energetic sister. But before Sam could ask her about it, Caroline straightened up. "I'm going to head to town to the bookstore and look for some of Trish's books. Did you need anything?"

"Nope. Now I'm interested in reading her books too." Sam's scones timer went off. "If Trish's books are anything like Trish herself, they're sure to be very entertaining."

CHAPTER
Two

*G*racie snipped away the base of a stripped rose blossom and added it to the pile of trimmings destined for the compost pile. *What a shame the storm last night ruined these lovely blooms,* she thought. The season had brought out the best in the roses and was turning them into riots of full-blown color. Caroline's cocker spaniel Max was enjoying rooting around the downed petals on the ground.

She worked her way closer to the birdbath—a weatherworn cupid holding a scalloped shell over its head, who seemed to look a little sad, too, that the roses had been damaged. She clipped away some twigs that partially blocked an edge so more birds could perch on the bronze shell.

She heard someone walking along the side of the inn, someone with a firm tread that couldn't be one of her sisters. Bill Dekker appeared, carrying a metal structure that looked something like a spiderweb. His smile when he saw her made his blue eyes twinkle.

"What's that?" she asked. "Did you make it?" As a metal sculptor, he usually created things like animals or beach scenes, not something utilitarian like this.

"It's for your roses to climb on." He frowned at the bush behind her. "But they don't look so perky today."

"They took a beating from the storm last night. But thank you. If I can't use it this year, I can use it next year." She fingered the delicate metalwork. The roses would climb into beautiful shapes on this frame.

"Where do you want me to put it?" The wind ruffled Bill's long hair.

Gracie tried not to *tsk* at that shaggy mane and instead scanned the backyard. "Right here, in front of the garbage cans. When the roses climb onto it, they'll screen the trash bins."

"Good idea." Bill set up the climbing frame for her. "Looks good?"

Gracie nodded. "That's perfect."

He didn't respond, and she caught him staring at her. Heat rushed into her ears and up her cheeks, and she turned away toward the roses to hide it.

"What have you been up to?" She snipped a rose head with a little more force than was necessary.

"I finished a sculpture a couple of days ago—a commission from a collector in New York. It was a reproduction of his father's yacht, which had apparently burned twenty years ago, so all he had were some grainy photos. But I think I did a good job on it. He seemed pleased."

"You're so talented and creative. You're a lot like Caroline."

"We're creative in different ways and have very different personalities."

Gracie wasn't so sure about that. Despite being in his late fifties, Bill still had the carefree outlook on life of a much younger man. He was also still physically strong and fit, and he had a playful side to him. Caroline also had a youthful zest for life that sometimes made Gracie feel like a stick-in-the-mud. Bill's youthfulness had the opposite effect.

"How are you settling in, now that you've decided to move to Nantucket?"

"Oh, I love it." Gracie swept her arms around at the colorful garden. "I have plenty here to keep me busy, and talking to the guests at the inn is so much fun. Plus I'm helping Caroline put together a cookbook of Mom's recipes that will feature pictures of the inn and anecdotes about its history."

"How's that going?"

"The pictures and the recipes aren't hard, but we're still looking for more stories about the inn." Gracie went back to clipping at roses. "It's pretty exciting because we've already discovered so much about Hannah Montague. But there's still so much we don't know yet, like who really stole the money from the lighthouse, and why the coins were in the chest of drawers in the secret room, and what really happened to Hannah."

Gracie stopped for a moment and looked at Bill. He smiled, a dimple appearing in his cheek. "Sounds like this is all right up your alley."

"Well, I was a little slow to get caught up in it, believe it or not. I kept trying to keep my sisters on track to get this place up and running. But now we're all very curious about Hannah and what really happened to her. You probably find it tedious."

"I don't think it's tedious. I like that you're so excited about it."

The tone of his voice made Gracie turn away from him again and focus on the rosebush in front of her for a minute or two.

"Did you decide what you're going to do about your house in Portland now that you've moved here?"

"I think I'm going to sell it." But even as she said it, Gracie's heart stuck in her throat. She knew she couldn't maintain her home from so far away, and it didn't make sense for her to keep it, but this had been the house she and Art had bought when he'd come home from Vietnam in 1975. It was their first house. Her two children had been raised in it, and now strangers would live there who didn't know its history and the love saturating its walls.

"Are you sure?" Bill asked gently. "Sounds like you might still be undecided."

"I'm just being sentimental. I need to sell it. There's no point in keeping it if I won't be living there."

"Speaking of homes, I saw that the Nantucket Garden Club's Annual House and Garden Tour is in a week." Bill paused and took a breath. "Would you want to go with me?"

Gracie bit her lip. "I'm so sorry, Bill, but I already told David Starbuck I'd go with him." The local gardener had been helping her restore the inn's back gardens to their former glory, and he'd asked her to go with him only a few days ago.

"Oh?" Bill asked, his voice neutral.

"David's on the planning committee, so he offered to take me on the tour early before it starts."

"That should be fun for you." His smile seemed a little strained.

The silence between them grew awkward, but then Sam's voice from the back door rescued them. "Gracie?"

"Yes?" Gracie asked, grateful for her sister's timing.

"Could you help me for a minute? Trish Montgomery is having problems with her sink faucet, and Caroline has gone to town with George, and my hands are coated with sticky scone dough."

"Certainly." Gracie stripped off her gardening gloves.

"Do you want me to come take a look at it?" Bill asked.

"Thanks, Bill, but I'm sure it's nothing too serious."

"Well, okay. I do need to be going," Bill said. "I'm starting on a new sculpture for one of my longtime clients in California."

"Thank you so much for the rose trellis. It's beautiful." She realized with a start that she'd been so flustered by his gift, she had neglected to tell him that when he presented it to her.

"I'll see you around, Gracie." He headed around the house, the way he'd come.

Gracie hurried into the house and was met with the delicious scent of baking scones. "I didn't realize Trish had already arrived."

"I didn't get a chance to tell you." Sam's voice dropped as she went back to her scones. "She's a famous romance writer."

"I didn't recognize her name. I don't think I've ever read her books."

"Caroline is rectifying that right now. I hope she buys the one Trish mentioned, *Breathless Barbados Belle*."

Gracie blinked.

Sam went on, "Trish came downstairs a few minutes ago and said she doesn't know how to work the taps on the sink."

"Maybe she's never seen antique hot and cold taps. I'll go up and see."

She tapped on Trish's room door, which was immediately opened by a short, plump woman with copper hair that made it look like her head was aflame, especially in contrast to her magenta silk blouse. "Hi, Trish. I'm Gracie Gold."

"Ah yes. The third sister! Yes, I read about you on the inn's Web site." Her voice had a loud, rolling quality—like that of a Shakespearean orator.

"Sam said you had problems with the taps?"

"I feel like a complete idiot." Trish led the way into the small bathroom attached to her room. "I can only get hot water."

Even though the sink had been installed in the fifties when the inn was renovated, it had been fitted with old-fashioned double faucets—one for hot water, one for cold. A person was supposed to mix the two waters in the porcelain basin. Gracie turned the cold water faucet, but no water came out. "That's not supposed to happen." She tried to keep her voice light, but inside she worried about yet another problem they would have to fix in the inn. She had hoped that the worst of their issues had ended before their grand opening, but she supposed it was wishful thinking for an old colonial home to be trouble-free for longer than, say, a week.

And now she wished she hadn't sent Bill away.

"I'll get our handyman to look at the faucet. In the meantime, did you want a different room? There are two others free right now."

"That would be lovely. Luckily I haven't unpacked much yet." Trish gestured toward the six—*six!*—suitcases scattered around the room. Only one had been opened and a few toiletries removed from inside.

"Let me help you move your things." Gracie grasped the handle of the closest suitcase. "*Oomph!* That's heavy."

"That's my computer and my research books." Trish picked up another suitcase that was apparently much lighter and followed Gracie to the next room.

Gracie wheeled the suitcase to the room and opened the door. "How's this one instead?" The Periwinkle Room was almost the same size, only a tiny bit smaller.

"Do the sink taps work?"

"Oh, good point. Let's check." This bedroom's bath had a more modern sink tap, and when Gracie tested it, the hot and cold water flowed. "It's working fine."

"Then this room is perfect." Trish plopped her suitcase down on the bed.

They went back for more of her things. "What brings you to Nantucket?" Gracie wheeled a slightly lighter suitcase to the new room.

"I'm writing a manuscript set in Colonial Nantucket."

"How exciting. I love Colonial history. It's one of my favorite subjects, and Nantucket is chock-full of interesting people and events from the past."

Trish gave her a wide smile. "A fellow history lover. You must have read my books."

"Er…" Gracie remembered what Sam had mentioned. "You wrote one set in Barbados, right?"

"Two, actually. But you should read my Revolutionary War series, the Cannoneer's Captivated Cousins. You'd love it."

"Oh. Sounds fascinating."

"It's out of print now, but you can buy used copies online or you can buy them on eBook."

They went back for more luggage. "Where do you live?"

"Minnesota." Trish rolled her eyes. "I know, a rather unusual home for a best-selling historical romance author who's best known for her Confederacy novels. It's where I grew up. Luckily, I only have to see my family once or twice a year."

Gracie thought that was quite sad. She loved being with her sisters and had mourned the fact that they hadn't been able to see each other as often as they'd liked—that is, before they'd decided to buy the Misty Harbor Inn. Now they were bonding more than ever before. "I'm sorry you don't have a good relationship with your family," Gracie said gently as they dragged the last of Trish's stuff into her new room.

Trish sighed. "They just don't quite approve of my career."

"But…you're a best-selling author."

"I'm a best-selling *romance* author. They look down on that."

"But why? Debbie Macomber writes romance—"

"I'm not sure I'm in the same league as Debbie, but even if I were, they'd still feel the same."

"I'm sorry." Gracie reached out a hand and touched Trish's shoulder. "I couldn't imagine not having my sisters' support. It must be very hard on you."

Trish was silent a moment, her face unreadable, but then she gave Gracie a bright smile that didn't seem too forced. "But I get to travel for my book research, and that is much more fun. I've found the best ideas for my novels from obscure little tidbits I uncovered during my research."

"Elizabeth Adams at the historical society building here has been very helpful to us."

"What have you been researching?"

"My sisters and I are putting together a cookbook of our mother's recipes, with historical anecdotes about the inn." She hesitated to say too much about their research on Hannah Montague. "We've been trying to find out more about its history."

"Then I'll start with Elizabeth. Thanks for the tip."

Gracie headed toward the door. "If you need anything, just let one of us know."

She went downstairs to the front foyer and changed Trish's room in the guest register and then headed to the kitchen, where Sam was slipping another pan of scones into the oven. "The cold water tap in Trish's room is out."

Sam groaned. "We'll have to call Bill again."

The thought of speaking to Bill after the way their conversation had ended made Gracie squirm. "Could you call him?"

Sam didn't speak, but stared at Gracie with raised eyebrows.

"Well…he was just here a little while ago. He invited me to the Nantucket Garden Club's Annual House and Garden Tour—"

"Ah, the same one David asked you to a few days ago?"

Gracie nodded.

Sam grinned. "So Bill was a little jealous, was he?"

Gracie tried to glare at her sister. "Sam, really, I'm not interested romantically in either of them."

"I'm sure that's true, but that doesn't mean Bill or David feels the same way about you."

"I am going to ignore you because you are obviously speaking nonsense." Gracie bent over some scones cooling on the wire rack on the counter.

"Hands off. Those are for tea."

"Tea?"

"Today at four in the parlor. Just like civilized Englishwomen." Sam adopted a British accent, but dissolved into giggles, ruining the effect.

Gracie giggled too. "I think Trish will like that, since she's a historical romance writer."

"How did you like her?"

Something in Sam's voice made Gracie guess that she might have been put off by Trish's loud voice and novel-centered conversation. "I actually had a nice chat with her."

Sam looked at her sister with admiration. "You're always so good at that."

"I like talking to people. I have to admit, when I went back home the last time, it had been a bit lonely rattling around my home all by myself. I was so used to talking to Art, and before that, I had been used to talking to Paige and Brandon. But here at the inn, there are always people to talk to, and they have such interesting things to say."

"Trish is certainly interesting. I can't wait to read her books."

"Me too. She apparently does a lot of research for them."

"You would love the historical aspect of it."

At that moment, the telephone rang. "I'll get it." Gracie headed to the foyer. She picked up the phone resting on the antique podium. "Hello, Misty Harbor Inn."

"Hello," said a quavering female voice. "I'd like to make a reservation."

"Certainly." Gracie got out the guest register. "When did you want to arrive?"

"This weekend, if you have anything available."

"Oh yes." The Emerald Room was available now that Trish had been moved. Like the larger room of the suite, it faced the ocean. "How long will you be staying?"

"Oh, I'm not sure."

Since they didn't have any other reservations until later in September, she supposed it would be fine. "No problem. Could I please have your name?"

"Doris Waverly. And would it be possible to have one of the rooms facing the ocean?"

Gracie blinked. How did she know about the orientations of the rooms? "Have you stayed here before?"

The old woman chuckled softly. "In a sense. You see, I used to live at Montague Manor as a child, and I wanted to see it again."

Gracie's heart stopped for a second and then began thumping out a big band beat. *Doris must know loads about the house.* "Did you really? That's wonderful."

"I heard about the reopening of the inn from one of my cousins who lives in Nantucket. She mentioned you had put on a 'mystery night' or something like that."

"Yes, we talked about the disappearance of Hannah Montague in 1880." *Will Doris know anything about that?* she thought.

She almost asked, but then Doris said, "I remember that story. My cousins and the other children would tell stories about Hannah's ghost haunting the lighthouse and Montague Manor, until I pointed out that Hannah couldn't haunt two places at once, and that I lived in Montague Manor and hadn't seen hide nor hair of a ghost."

Doris sounded like she'd been a feisty child.

"I'll arrive on Friday," she said.

"We'll get one of the ocean-view rooms ready for you."

"Thank you. Good-bye."

Gracie felt like it was Christmas Eve and she was six years old. Doris had actually lived in the inn. Granted, she'd probably lived there long after the Montague brothers had sold the house, but perhaps she knew something about them and the disappearance of their stepmother.

Gracie couldn't wait to meet her.

CHAPTER
Three

While waiting for George to arrive to pick her up, Caroline flipped through the latest book she'd picked up, *How to Plan Your No-Frills Wedding While Keeping Your Sanity*. She'd spied the title the day before while at the bookstore looking for Trish Montgomery's books, and she hadn't been able to resist picking it up. It sounded exactly like what her frazzled brain needed.

But the book itself suggested an awful lot of list-making. While Gracie would have reveled in it, it gave Caroline the heebie-jeebies. She flipped through it more, hoping for some inspiration.

She still hadn't decided how many people to invite, much less who, and she had no idea if she wanted an outdoor wedding— at the risk of bad weather—or an indoor wedding, which seemed somehow claustrophobic to her. She wasn't sure if she wanted a new dress or even if she wanted to wear a dress, but somehow a pantsuit didn't seem right either. She had no idea what her wedding colors would be, which would determine the flowers she chose, and maybe she should figure that out first because some flowers wouldn't be available in mid-September. But she had no clue what blooms she'd prefer. Which again made her wonder if she should pick her colors first.

She normally wasn't this indecisive, but she also realized that it seemed like nothing about the wedding planning excited her. It all seemed a bit…boring. And this event wasn't just any event. It was her wedding. It was for George and her family as well as for her. She wanted it to be special. She wanted it to be perfect. That was pretty much all she had decided about it.

She tossed the book onto a walnut lamp stand and decided that the title lied—just skimming through it was driving her insane.

Luckily, there was a knock at the front door and Caroline had just risen from her wingback chair in the parlor when George opened the door and stepped inside.

"Ready to go? I think you might like this one."

Caroline tried to return his smile, but inside she felt a heaviness, like a bundle of clothing soaked with water. George had his heart set on finding them a nice house to live in after the wedding, but she had fallen in love with the Misty Harbor Inn, with the rooms her mother would have delighted in walking through, and she'd rather live here after they married.

But she had a feeling it would be hard for him to live in an inn with guests and her sisters always around. He was a private person, and living with so many "housemates" would be a challenge.

They drove to a snug cottage along Rolling Hills Drive, which was lined with trees that shaded the street. But as soon as Caroline saw the cottage, she knew it wasn't right.

She slowly got out of the car, and they walked up the flagstone walkway, but she could see that there was only perhaps ten feet between the two sides of the house and their neighbors' houses.

"It's really closed in on each side, isn't it?" Caroline said to George in a low voice.

He looked at either side. "I didn't really notice that the last time I came. I was too impressed with the house and the backyard."

Curious, Caroline followed him inside, where Deborah Greenleaf, the Realtor who had helped them buy the Misty Harbor, looked up from some papers she was scanning at a hall table. "How nice to see you again, Caroline," she said heartily. "George."

The foyer was wide and bright, although not deep, and there was a hallway that ran through to the back of the house. On either side of the foyer were large rooms with fireplaces.

They walked down the hallway to the back of the house, where they found a spacious kitchen, a laundry room, a small office, and a short flight of stairs to the second floor. The kitchen was full of light and looked out into a deep backyard. The home rested on the edge of a slight hill, and the land fell away at the edge of the property line, giving a lovely view of the main part of the town and the ocean beyond.

The rest of the house was just as lovely, with two large rooms on the second floor and plenty of windows.

But even as they traversed the house, Caroline could faintly hear the sounds of the neighbors on either side. On each floor, there was only one window on each side that faced the two side neighbors, but those four windows collected the sounds of the two teenagers in the house on one side and the blaring television of the house on the other side.

"Well?" Deborah asked as they finished the tour, smoothing an auburn strand of hair in her sleek chignon.

Caroline hesitated in indecision. The house in general had been very nice.

"No pressure," Deborah added. She held placating hands in front of her. "You don't want to settle for a house you're not one hundred percent happy with."

"Well, I'm uncomfortable with the neighbors being so close on either side," Caroline admitted.

"They did seem louder this time than the first time I came to see this place," George said.

"It's actually a great neighborhood if you have kids, because there are several families down the street," Deborah said. "But that may not be right for the two of you."

"I like kids. I love my sister's grandchildren. But only when they visit, not when they live next door." Caroline gave a sheepish smile.

"I understand perfectly," Deborah said. "I'll keep looking. We'll find you the right house, don't you worry."

As they drove away, Caroline turned to George. "Am I being too picky?" She bit her lip.

He gave her a reassuring smile. "If I were less secure in my love for you, I'd think you didn't want to live with me."

Caroline laughed, because she knew he expected her to, but a part of her wanted to cry. How could she possibly tell him she'd rather they live at the Misty Harbor Inn? She could imagine their argument, and he might call off the wedding. She didn't want that—she loved George and wanted to marry him.

But she hadn't realized how marriage could make a good relationship so complicated.

Some of her thoughts must have shown on her face, because he gave her a questioning look. To distract him, she asked, "So what are you planning for our honeymoon?"

"If you're trying to get me to tell you, that's not a very subtle approach." His blue eyes twinkled.

"Do you know yet what you're going to do?" she asked as he parked in front of the inn.

"I have a few ideas." He walked her to the front door and opened it. "But I'm still deciding what would be exactly right."

"Someplace romantic," Caroline said, getting into the swing of things. "Hello there," she said to Sam, Gracie, and Trish, who were seated in the parlor around a small round table. Sam had cooked up a scrumptious-looking tea—the charmingly mismatched china teacups circling the large teapot, and in front of each woman a small plate with scones, Devonshire cream, reddish jam—probably strawberry— and tiny sandwiches. Sam had also whipped up some little cookies.

"Looks yummy," Caroline said.

Sam had already risen to her feet. "You'll join us, right?"

"I'd love to. Er…" Caroline looked at George.

He grinned. "Set a place for me too."

They rearranged the chairs and brought two more around the table while Sam brought back two more teacups, and then two plates of goodies. "The cookies are a new recipe. Earl Grey cookies."

"With real tea in it? How neat." Caroline sat down.

"What were you talking about when you came in?" Trish asked eagerly. "Did I hear the word *romantic*?"

"Oh, our honeymoon," Caroline said. "George is planning it and he wants to surprise me."

"Well, it's a good thing I'm here," Trish said triumphantly.

Caroline wasn't sure how to answer that until Gracie spoke to Trish but with a subtle look at her sister. "Didn't I read that *Romantic Newsweek* called you the 'reigning queen of romance'?"

Oh, that must have been what Trish meant by her comment. Caroline wasn't entirely sure she wanted Trish's opinions on her wedding, though. She'd glanced through *Breathless Barbados Belle,* and Trish's idea of romance seemed to be a lot of long, flowery speeches and public declarations of love.

Trish preened at the title. "I was so honored they called me that, especially when there are so many other romance authors who deserve the title." It sounded like false modesty to Caroline, but Caroline also figured Trish couldn't exactly go around crowing about it. And Gracie had been the one who brought it up.

"So what's the theme of your wedding?" Trish asked.

Theme? A wedding had to have a theme?

Sam saw Caroline's expression and saved her. "I think at this point, she's open to ideas. Have any suggestions?"

"Well, you're in this wonderful inn steeped in history. Maybe a historical wedding?"

Gracie laughed. "I'm probably more of a history buff than Caroline."

"What do you do?" Trish asked Caroline.

"I'm a travel writer."

"*Oooh,* maybe an exotic wedding. Something that brings back your favorite memories from abroad. A celebration of all the best parts of your travel experience."

"Best parts." Caroline liked the sound of that. She had been so happy during her travels and had a favorite memory from so many places. But her favorite had been the trip on which she met George. "George and I met inside the Hagia Sophia in Istanbul, Turkey. We were looking at a mosaic of Christ. It was a magical place, but it was even better sharing it with someone fun and interesting." She smiled at him.

"Now that's romantic, a Turkish wedding. Exotic and festive. And it will be even better because everything will remind you of one of your favorite trips."

Caroline liked the idea of aspects of the wedding representing things special to her.

"How many people are we talking about?" Trish said.

"Oh, probably not many," Caroline said.

Trish's eyes widened. "What? But it's your wedding. God willing, you won't have more than one of those in your lifetime."

"My favorite people are already here." Caroline glanced fondly at her sisters and George. "I don't want strangers there."

"Oh, I don't mean strangers. But if you're going to have a wonderfully creative wedding with a Turkish theme, wouldn't you want to show off a little? Go all out in terms of your creativity and imagination."

The wheels of Caroline's mind began to spin as she started to see the possibilities. She didn't have many outlets for true, unbridled creativity—her travel was fun, but she had to stick to certain guidelines for her articles and books. Here was something she could do completely the way she wanted it. Now she understood why brides got so excited about planning their weddings—because there were no rules. She hadn't realized that before this moment.

"You want to make your wedding a day none of you will ever forget," Trish said. "That's my philosophy for my weddings."

Caroline choked on her tea. "How many have you had?"

Trish suddenly gave a peal of laughter. "Oh, I'm not married. I meant in my books."

"I read about that online," Gracie said. "*Romance Today and Yesterday* mentioned that no one does weddings like you do."

Caroline thought Gracie must have spent a large part of the afternoon looking for information on Trish online so she'd know a little more about her.

"I probably shouldn't tell you this," the novelist said, leaning in, "but I spend more time trying to come up with a truly unique wedding for my books than the plot and the characters," Trish said. "I have a reputation to uphold. If I had a mediocre wedding in a book, people would say I'm starting to lose my edge."

Caroline thought that the author's priorities were off-kilter, but then again Trish had to have something unique about her books in order to compete with other romance authors.

"In fact, I have the perfect idea," Trish said. "I had an Italian wedding in my book *The Irredeemable Italian Count*. It's close enough to Turkey, right?"

Caroline had been to both Italy and Turkey, and she knew that weddings in the two cultures weren't similar at all.

Trish continued, "Anyway, the wedding's for an older man and woman, so it will be perfect for you."

Trish's face had no guile or slyness, only eager helpfulness, so Caroline couldn't really fault her for the "older man and woman" remark. Trish didn't look much younger than Caroline herself, to be honest. "Er…that's a good idea. I'll read the book to see if it sparks any ideas."

Trish looked at her watch, a decadent affair awash in diamonds and rubies. "This has been lovely, but I need to get to work. This is a working vacation, after all." She laughed heartily and then left them to head upstairs.

"I had better head back to my boat. I still have some business calls to make." George rose and kissed Caroline's cheek. "I'll see you tomorrow."

After George left, Sam rose and asked, "Want more scones?"

"Yes, please," Caroline said quickly. Sam's blackberry scones, a tweaked version of their mother's blueberry scones recipe, was wonderfully crispy on the outside and buttery on the inside.

When Sam returned with a platter of scones, she sat back in her chair with a fresh cup of tea and looked at Caroline with a cat-in-the-cream expression.

"What is it?" Caroline asked her.

"I haven't seen you this happy about your wedding in a long time."

Caroline considered the strange conversation with Trish. "I suppose Trish made me realize that the decisions I have to make about the wedding can be fun rather than confusing. It didn't occur to me that this would be a chance to do things I haven't had a chance to do."

"Yes, I liked how she described it." Gracie grabbed another scone. "Planning your wedding should be like planning an adventure, not a production."

"An adventure…" Caroline's imagination was going full-steam ahead now. "I think I'll read Trish's book, even if it is set in Italy."

Gracie's eyes were dancing. "An Italian-Turkish-themed wedding. I can't wait."

CHAPTER
Four

Oh no, you don't." Sam caught up with Gracie as she was heading out the back door to the carriage house and the 1941 Packard station wagon.

"I wasn't sneaking out," Gracie said.

"I meant you're not going to pick up Doris Waverly without me."

"Or me." Caroline hurried up from behind them.

"We can't all three go. Who will stay at the inn?" Gracie pointed out.

"I twisted George's arm," Caroline said. "He's in the dining room with his laptop, looking through house listings."

"But we'll crowd Doris in the backseat." Gracie climbed into the station wagon.

"There's plenty of room for us *and* Doris in this big ol' car," Sam said. "We all want to meet her."

"I want to ask her about Montague Manor," Caroline said. "Can you imagine what kinds of stories she might be able to tell us? I can't wait."

Gracie passed Sam, who sat in the backseat, holding the thermos of cold lemonade that she'd brought with her. "That's for Doris," she warned Sam.

"You told me that twice when I was making it this morning." But Sam only grinned as she tucked it into the backseat.

They drove to the wharf, and Sam took a deep breath of the sea air, which was cooler and brinier here. The wharf was dotted with half barrels planted with summer flowers, the petals fluttering slightly in the breeze from the ocean.

Gracie brought out the sign with Doris's name written on it, and they stood waiting as people disembarked from the ferry. They saw Doris almost immediately, a very tiny old woman with a wispy cloud of hair peeking out from a dark green cloche hat. She looked to be in her late eighties, and she leaned heavily on her cane. Her brown eyes alighted on the sign, and her soft smile peeked out. "I'm Doris Waverly." She had a gentle, lilting voice that was nearly drowned out by the surf and the raucous cries of the seagulls circling above them.

"Welcome to Nantucket. I'm Gracie, this is Caroline, and Sam, and we own the Misty Harbor Inn—or rather, what used to be Montague Manor."

"Can I help you to the car?" Sam asked. Doris walked with a delicate step, despite the cane, and looked like one of the ocean gusts would sweep her out to sea. The porter standing behind her had his hands full with two small suitcases.

"Oh, thank you," Doris said.

Sam took her arm, which felt fragile, and helped her to the station wagon. Caroline helped the porter swing the suitcases into the trunk.

Sam slid into the backseat next to Doris. "You don't mind if I sit here, do you?"

"Goodness, no. I wouldn't want you to squeeze into the trunk."

Sam couldn't help but laugh. "We've been so excited to meet you. We can't believe we're meeting someone who actually lived in our inn."

"Of course, it was a regular house back then," Doris said. "I haven't been in the best of health for the past few years, not since I fell and broke my hip, but I so wanted to see the house and Nantucket again."

"We'll take you on a tour of the town." Gracie fired up the engine. "It's a beautiful day for it. Or would you rather go to the inn and rest?"

Doris did look very weary. "If you don't mind, I think I'd rather go to the inn."

"Coming right up." Gracie turned the big red car toward home.

Home. How quickly the inn had become home to Sam. Once again she felt that giddy rush of pleasure that she was actually living in the Misty Harbor Inn and running it the way their mother had dreamed of doing.

Sam offered some lemonade to Doris, who sipped delicately. Then Caroline, sitting in the front seat, twisted around to ask Doris, "So when did you live in Montague Manor?"

"I was only a child, but it was one of the most wonderful places my family lived." Doris's eyes were focused someplace distant. "However, we didn't actually live in the Manor. My mother was the cook, and my father was the chauffeur, gardener, and general handyman for the house. We lived on the second floor of the carriage house."

"We haven't really explored the second floor much," Caroline said. "When the previous owners were renovating the house, they just used it to store a bunch of things from the house up on the carriage house's second floor, so it's crammed with furniture and boxes."

Doris seemed a little sad. "It was such a cozy apartment. There were large windows, so it let in lots of light, and the Fortescues had installed a modern heater so it kept very warm in the wintertime."

"What were the Fortescues like?" Gracie's voice was alive with curiosity, and she looked in the rearview mirror at Doris.

"You know about Ezra and Mabel Fortescue?"

"A little."

"They were from Philadelphia, and they bought Montague Manor from the Montague brothers as a vacation home."

Caroline said, "They must have been very successful artists."

"Oh, they were. But also, Mabel's family was wealthy. I remember the Fortescues as being cold and unfriendly, but I was also just a child, and probably not very well behaved." Her eyes twinkled. "Mabel always gave me a freezing look that made me feel like I had done something very bad, even if I hadn't been doing anything at all."

"We had an aunt-in-law who was like that," Caroline said.

"The Fortescues weren't on Nantucket much during the years we lived at the house," Doris said. "They'd bought it as a vacation home, but almost immediately Mabel grew ill and couldn't travel much, so my parents and I had the house to ourselves quite often. I used to pretend it was ours." A mischievous look appeared in her brown eyes, and Sam could almost see her as a precocious young girl.

"What years did you live in the house?" Sam asked.

Doris thought for a moment. "I believe it was from 1932 to 1937. I was about eleven when Ezra Fortescue closed up the house and took his wife abroad for her health. I believe they went to Italy. Oh, is that the Old Mill?" They spied the historic windmill in the distance.

Gracie, being the history expert, chatted with Doris about the sights as they drove closer to the inn.

As they drove up to the Misty Harbor Inn, Doris gave a soft cry and put her hand to her mouth, like someone seeing a very good friend for the first time in years. She stared at the house as Gracie circled the car in front of the door.

Sam helped Doris out of the station wagon and up the stairs to her room. She seemed very frail and she walked stiffly on her right hip, which might have been the one she'd fallen and broken. Doris was breathing quickly by the time they reached the head of the stairs, with Caroline and Gracie behind carrying the suitcases. George was following, trying to take one or both of the suitcases, but the sisters insisted they were fine, so he went back downstairs.

They entered Doris's room—the Emerald Room, the largest room other than the suite—which had been Trish's before the faucet problem. Bill Dekker had taken only a few minutes the day before to fix the broken cold water faucet. He'd helped them do so many of the repairs and renovations around the inn that he knew it perhaps even better than they did. Sam didn't know what they'd have done without him.

Doris sat on the soft bed and stared out the window at the ocean. She breathed deeply. "It's so nice to be back here."

"I'm sure it's much less grand than when you stayed here." Gracie set the suitcase she carried down in a corner of the room.

"The layout of the rooms is a bit different," Doris said.

"The inn was renovated in the fifties." Caroline set the other suitcase next to the first one. "They tore down some walls and added the en suite bathrooms."

"I wonder if the old passage is still there," Doris murmured, as if to herself.

"Passage?" Sam and Caroline said at the same time, and Gracie's mouth had become a large O.

Despite the tired lines around them, Doris's eyes sparkled. "Do you know about the secret passage in the house?"

"We didn't find any secret passages," Sam said, "but I found a secret room."

"In the basement?" Doris asked.

"No," Sam said in surprise. "Here on the second floor, in one of the other guest bedrooms."

"There's a secret room in the basement?" Caroline asked, her voice pitched higher than normal.

"There's a secret passage down to it from the library," Doris said. "Next to the fireplace, a panel in the wall swings inward and you enter a narrow hallway that follows behind the fireplace. It leads down to some stone steps to a room full of bookshelves. I always figured old Jedediah Montague might have kept his valuables down there."

"Did you find anything there?" Gracie asked.

"No, there were only old newspapers there when Mother and I discovered the room."

"It's in the basement?" Caroline asked.

"One wall of the room is wood, and we figured out it was one of the walls of the basement, but we never did find a way into the room from the basement."

"How in the world did you find it?" Sam asked.

"Mother found it. She was cleaning the library and discovered how to open the panel. You have to turn one of the wall sconces, and then you can push the panel open like a door."

The sisters looked at each other. Caroline's and Gracie's eyes were alight, and Sam knew hers must be too. *A secret passage!* Sam could hardly wait to try to find it.

"But tell me," Doris said. "What was the room you three found here on the second floor?"

"We found it by accident." Sam grinned. "And nearly broke down a wall when we did it."

"*You* nearly broke down a wall," Gracie said to Sam.

"I went into the closet of the Emerald Room to put some hangers on the rod. I leaned against the wall, and one of the wooden panels moved. When I looked inside, I saw a small room filled with old furniture. Later, when Jamie and I investigated, we found that most of the things looked like they had belonged to Hannah Montague."

"I always sort of thought she was just a made-up person because no one knew much about her except that she disappeared." Doris then let out a ladylike yawn. "I'm so sorry. It was a long ferry ride and I don't have as much energy as I used to."

"What in the world are we doing?" Gracie looked appalled. "We'll leave you to rest."

"Thank you for telling us so much about the house." Caroline paused by the door. "We hope you'll be able to talk to us more later."

"Oh, I'm looking forward to it. It's so nice to have the opportunity to talk about the old days with you three."

Caroline was almost bounding down the stairs after they had closed Doris's door and were heading back to the first floor. "This is so exciting. A secret passage in the library—let's look for it right now."

"I'm game," Sam said, but then the phone rang.

"You better not start looking without me." Gracie headed to answer the phone. "Hello, Misty Harbor Inn."

Her brow lightened for a moment. "Oh, hi, Brandon. How—" She suddenly grew grave. "Are they all right?"

"What's wrong?" Caroline and Sam crowded closer to Gracie and the phone.

"I perfectly understand." Gracie looked a tad less worried. "Yes, we'll be ready for her. I'll pick you both up at the last ferry."

As soon as she hung up, Caroline burst out, "What's wrong?"

"The twins have scarlet fever."

"Both of them?" Sam asked. Jamie had had scarlet fever when she was six, and while the antibiotics helped her recover in less than two weeks, she had still been a very cranky little girl for that period of time, mostly because she'd been kept to the house so she wouldn't spread the illness to anyone else.

Gracie nodded. "They both have it, but Evelyn hasn't gotten sick yet. Brandon doesn't want three children with scarlet fever, so he asked if we would take Evelyn so she can get out of the house."

"Of course," Caroline said quickly.

"When is she coming?" Sam asked.

Gracie winced. "Tonight. We'll have to scramble to get the Amaryllis Room ready before she and Brandon get here. Caroline, do you mind sharing with Sam? Evelyn can sleep in our room, while she's here, just in case we get another booking."

"I don't mind," Caroline said. But then she sighed. "But I guess we won't be looking for the secret passage today."

CHAPTER
Five

The next morning, Gracie woke up early in order to take Brandon down to the wharf so he could take the first ferry back home. Evelyn had been tired and cross the night before when they arrived and had barely spoken a handful of words to her grandma. Gracie also suspected Evelyn wasn't entirely happy to be away from her friends during these weeks in the tail end of summer vacation.

A firm tread down the stairs signaled Brandon coming down, but she didn't hear Evelyn's light step with him.

He appeared in the kitchen, inhaling deeply. "Is that fresh ground coffee?"

"Of course. Aunt Sam wouldn't let us serve anything else." She poured him a cup, resisting the urge to ruffle his straight blond hair like she used to when he was a boy. She'd have to reach up quite high now, since he towered over her at six feet tall, an inch taller than his father had been. "Where's Evelyn?"

"She's"—a look of concern flashed across his face and then was gone—"she's in the bathroom. She'll be right down."

"She's all right?"

"Oh, she's fine. No symptoms." He sipped his coffee and began rummaging in the muffin basket on the counter.

That hadn't been what she'd meant when she asked the question, but Gracie didn't push the issue. This entire trip for him was difficult because he taught classes and had preseason training for his team, so he had to take time off from his summer work in order to bring Evelyn so last-minute. He must also be worried about the three-year-old twins, sick at home with only Stacy to take care of them.

"Any offers on the house yet?" He bit into a blackberry muffin and leaned against the counter.

"No, although it's only been on the market for a week. The Realtor said not to expect it to move quickly because it's somewhat older than the other houses for sale now in the area."

"You're not regretting putting the house on the market, are you?" Brandon looked down at his mother somberly. "I don't want to have pushed you into doing this—"

"Oh, you didn't. I'm truly happy here in Nantucket, and I know I need to sell the house. It's just... I never thought I'd be selling it. I know that must sound silly, but the idea never occurred to me. It seems strange to me, now. I've lived in that house for so long...."

There were so many memories there—of Art and the kids. Though she had gotten used to the idea, a part of her rebelled at the thought of strangers invading that space and erasing all those memories.

"Well"—Brandon paused, as if weighing his words—"don't sell it to anybody just to sell it, okay? Wait for a really good offer."

"Well, I'd like to do that, but I'm not sure if I can—"

"No, I'm serious, Mom. Wait for a really good offer."

He had placed an odd emphasis on the words. *Does he know something about the house that I don't?* Gracie wondered if he was saying this because he didn't want his family home being sold either. "I'll hold out as long as I can afford to. The only problem is that it will take a while for the inn to start making much of a profit."

He seemed satisfied with that answer. "Let me go see what's keeping Evelyn—"

But at that moment, Gracie heard her granddaughter's slow steps on the stairs. "I think that's her now."

In a few minutes, eight-year-old Evelyn appeared in the door to the kitchen, her eyes red and puffy. *Poor thing*, thought Gracie, *misses her family*. Gracie hoped staying with Grandma would partially make up for it.

"Ready to go?" Brandon asked heartily, trying to boost her spirits.

She shrugged and bent her head so all Gracie could see was a crown of straight brown hair.

"We'd better go," Gracie said, "or we'll miss the ferry."

Evelyn and Brandon were quiet on the ride to the wharf. While they waited for the ferry, Evelyn clung to her father, looking much younger than her eight years. Gracie stepped away to give them a little privacy. Evelyn, torn from her home so suddenly, must be a bit confused by it all.

Gracie's cell phone rang and she recognized the number of her Realtor in Portland. "Hello, Burt."

"Hi, Gracie. Good news, I have an offer for the house."

"So soon? That's wonderful."

But then he rattled off a number that was 60 percent of the price she had listed it at.

"What did you say? I must have heard you wrong."

"No, I'm sorry. The buyers looked at the house and thought it was sort of...run-down."

Run-down? She and Art had taken meticulous care of the house. There were no leaks in the roof, the pipes had been replaced only a few years ago, and while the kitchen was small, it had an updated electrical system to handle all the appliances. And the garden was award-winning. "So they gave a lowball offer because the house isn't new like the houses in the development on the other side of town?"

"I'm sure they didn't mean that."

"I'm sure that's exactly what they meant, Burt. Tell them no."

"Why don't we try to negotiate—make a counteroffer—"

"Absolutely not. If they're going to insult me with an offer like that for a perfectly fine old house, then they're not going to respond with a decent counteroffer at all."

"Well…" Burt's voice dropped. He sighed. "Gracie, the house is over thirty-five years old."

"It's also been kept in excellent condition. It just hasn't been renovated with things like a Food Network kitchen and plush carpeting."

"You might want to consider giving it a paint job," Burt said hastily. "And maybe replacing the toilets."

"They work fine."

"But they're not the new water-conservation ones. Just adding a new toilet might raise the price a few thousand."

"But it'll cost money for that, and I've just bought a third of an inn," Gracie reminded him with asperity.

"Could you get a loan from the bank?" Burt said matter-of-factly.

"Yes, I suppose so." But Gracie didn't really want to do that. It would require more effort, and she'd need to increase the asking price to cover the cost of the bank loan. Plus, there was no guarantee that the house would sell for that much if she did make all those improvements.

"So, you won't take this offer?" Burt said.

"Absolutely not."

He sighed again. "Okay. Let me know if you decide to get that loan. I can advise you what kinds of improvements you might want to make."

After she hung up, she took a few deep breaths to calm herself. What a horrible offer. She couldn't believe Burt wanted her to try to negotiate.

Doubt also began to creep up on her. Would she be able to sell the house? If she couldn't, she might need to pull out of her share of the inn, or worse, accept another lowball offer. Was moving to Nantucket a mistake?

The ferry was starting to load, and Evelyn clung to her father. He bent to say something to her, and she nodded slowly. Then he kissed her.

Gracie came up to give him a hug. "Have a good trip back. Call me when you get home."

"Sure thing, Mom. Have a good time, Evie." He gave Evelyn another hug, but she sniffled noisily in response.

She stood quietly beside Gracie as her father walked onto the ferry and as the boat pulled away from the wharf, waving frantically back at her father when he appeared and waved good-bye. Gracie put her arm around her granddaughter, who leaned closer to her as the boat became a dot on the ocean.

"How about some ice cream before we head home?" Gracie asked as they headed to the car.

Evelyn gave a wary look from her brown eyes, which were still a little red. "Mom doesn't like me to have ice cream in the morning."

"I think just this once won't hurt," Gracie said. "It might cheer us both up."

But the forbidden treat didn't seem to improve Evelyn's mood much as they sat in the Sweet Dreams ice cream parlor with banana split sundaes in front of them. Evelyn played with the hot fudge while her ice cream melted.

"What's wrong, sweetheart?" Gracie asked in a gentle voice.

Evelyn shook her head, looking down at her banana split, and didn't answer.

"You're going to make me think you've become allergic to ice cream," Gracie said with a smile.

This got a small smile from Evelyn, but she still didn't say anything.

"Miss your dad?"

Evelyn nodded.

"He'll be back soon to take you home."

But at her words, Evelyn's face crumpled, and a tear rolled down from the corner of her eye to her nose.

"Oh, sweetheart, what's wrong?"

"Will"—she gave a short gasping breath—"when will Daddy come back?"

"In two weeks. No longer than that, I'm sure."

"But"—Evelyn scrubbed at her tear with the back of her hand—"he didn't want me at home."

Gracie suddenly understood why she was so upset. "Oh, Evelyn, he does want you at home, but your brothers have a...a bug that's really easy to catch, and your parents don't want you to get sick too."

Evelyn raised worried eyes to Gracie. "Will Zach and Jake be okay?"

"Oh, they'll be fine. It's very easy to treat with antibiotics, but it's also very contagious, and the last thing your daddy wants is for you to get it too."

"So…Daddy is coming back to take me home?" Evelyn asked in a small voice.

"Of course he is, sweetheart." Gracie put as much emphasis and encouragement as she could into her voice so Evelyn would be reassured. It had been so long since Brandon and her daughter Paige had been eight years old, and she had forgotten about the kinds of fears children had.

Then she hit on the most brilliant idea. Gracie leaned in closer to Evelyn and whispered. "Can you keep a secret?"

Evelyn's brown eyes grew round. She slowly—and maybe a little warily—nodded.

"Your Aunt Caroline and Aunt Sam and I talked to Mrs. Waverly, who's staying at the inn." Gracie lowered her voice to a near whisper. "And she told us this secret about the inn."

Evelyn's eyes narrowed slightly. Gracie could tell she was intrigued, although she was trying not to show it.

"Mrs. Waverly used to live in the inn many, many years ago. It used to be the home of a very rich couple then, not an inn like it is now."

"Was Mrs. Waverly rich?"

"No, she was only a child at the time, and her parents worked for the people who owned the house. But she got to roam around the house a lot and you'll never guess what she found." Gracie leaned in again and paused.

In spite of herself, Evelyn leaned in too.

"She found a secret passage."

Evelyn let out a breath. "Oh, Grandma. You're just making that up."

Gracie sat up straight. "I am not. Are you calling your grandma a liar?"

Evelyn looked sheepish. "No, but it sounds like you're just trying to fool me like Grandpa used to when I was little."

Unexpectedly, tears pooled in Gracie's eyes but she didn't want to alarm or upset Evelyn, so she just smiled and tried to blink them away. She'd forgotten how much Art had loved to tease little Evelyn with his tall tales. "Well, this is for real. We didn't get a chance to try to find the secret passage yet. What do you say you and I look for it today?"

Evelyn's eyes lit up, although her response was a dignified, "Okay, cool."

She reminded Gracie of Paige at this age, although Evelyn might be terribly embarrassed if Gracie were to tell her that.

Evelyn finished her ice cream quickly after that, and Gracie drove them home. When they entered the kitchen, they found only Sam there, looking serious as she consulted a sheaf of paper on the counter with fierce concentration.

"Where's Caroline?" Gracie asked. "And Max?"

"Max was underfoot too much so I banished him to the backyard, and I sent Caroline to the store for more butter."

"We need more already? I thought I just bought some."

"That was before I almost tripped over Max and dropped four sticks onto the floor." Sam had a distinctly sour look.

Gracie tried not to smile. "Poor Max."

"Caroline was appalled so she immediately volunteered to go pick up more for me. When did you want to eat lunch?"

Gracie bit her lip. "The later, the better. I kind of spoiled ours." She and Evelyn exchanged looks.

Sam's eyebrows rose. "With what?"

"Ice cream."

Sam tried to frown but Gracie could see the laughter in her eyes. "Gracie! If this were your daughter, you'd say, 'No way,' but because it's your granddaughter, you spoil her rotten."

"Grandma's not spoiling me rotten," Evelyn said. "She's spoiling me sweet."

Both Gracie and Sam laughed at that.

"Evelyn and I are going to look for that secret passage," Gracie said. "Want to join us?"

"You two go ahead. I'm still working out the kinks in this cobbler recipe while I wait for Caroline to come back." She turned back to her scribbled notes.

"Before we go exploring, let's change." Gracie remembered the dust from the secret room on the second floor. "This secret passage is supposed to lead to the basement, so let's dress accordingly."

They donned old long-sleeved shirts, despite the warm weather, and Gracie tied a handkerchief over Evelyn's smooth brown hair. She threw an old gardening hat over her own head.

She also grabbed two flashlights and stopped by the broom closet to grab a broom in case there were any creepy crawlies she didn't want to walk into.

They entered the library, which was well lit by light from the tall windows. On the wall hung the sampler stitched by Hannah Montague and a few gilt frames with pressed flowers that Caroline had found at flea markets. The bookcases gleamed with a recent polishing but looked forlorn with only the few books the sisters had been able to find to populate them. Some of Trish's books had been discreetly slipped in, next to a few by Jane Austen.

But it was to the wall against the side of the house that Gracie headed, followed by Evelyn. What had Doris said about the secret passage? Something about the ornate brass wall sconces on either side of the fireplace that dominated the wall.

"There's supposed to be a secret passage near the fireplace," Gracie said. "I think it opens by turning one of the wall sconces, but I'm not sure which one, and I don't know if you need to turn it like a doorknob or twist it like a lightbulb."

Evelyn approached the left wall sconce, and Gracie went to the right one. Each one was a heavy bronze affair with lots of curves and twists to the metal that had been very tedious to clean, but it was very beautiful and matched the "English gentlemen's club" feel to the library.

Evelyn could barely reach her wall sconce, so Gracie pulled over a small footstool Caroline had found at an estate sale. It was a solid gold color that was a close enough match to the gold swirls in the brocade of the wingback chairs. Evelyn hopped on top of the footstool, which brought her up to the right height for the wall sconce.

Gracie went back to the right side sconce and began tentatively turning it, but it wouldn't budge. She was a little afraid of breaking it or causing damage to the wall if she worked it too hard, but she turned and saw Evelyn pulling rather violently on her wall sconce.

"Careful you don't damage the wall," Gracie warned her.

"I won't." Evelyn tried twisting the sconce, but it wouldn't move.

Gracie applied herself to the bronze fixture, but nothing she did would make it move. She tried turning it every which way, but the heavy sconce remained firmly fixed in the wall.

What had Doris said? A panel had opened in the wall next to the fireplace like a door. Gracie switched to searching the wall carefully for any cracks that might be the edges of a panel. She ran her hands along the brick-red walls. They hadn't repainted or papered the walls when they were renovating because the color had still been rich under all that dust. The surface felt a little uneven under her fingers, but at the time she'd been washing the wall, she hadn't remarked upon it because the house was so old. Now she felt every bump, trying to see if she could find any sort of line or straight crevice.

She was about to give up and try the other wall when she thought she felt a shallow vertical line that lay about eighteen inches away from the right edge of the fireplace. She ran her finger down. Yes, it was roughly straight, although it could simply be a crack in the wall.

She followed the line upward and tried to see if she could find a horizontal line that intersected it, but couldn't quite feel anything. But the vertical line was a good sign, she figured.

She stared at the wall and the sconce. She couldn't feel any hinges on the wall, so if it was a flat panel in the wall that was a door, it probably swung inward instead of outward, with the hinges inside the wall.

She tried to picture the other rooms in the house and their doors. The doorknobs were on the doors, and she would turn them and then push the door inward.

But here, the wall sconce was directly above the edge of the fireplace mantel, so it was possible it wasn't like a regular doorknob that was set in the door. It looked like the sconce was set outside the door. So what did that mean?

If she turned the sconce like a knob, perhaps it pulled back the latch that connected the door panel to the wall. Whoever had made the secret panel would have tried to make it difficult to find. Otherwise a maid cleaning the sconce could open the door by accident—though, come to think of it, that was how Doris's mother had found it.

Evelyn had followed her lead and was feeling the wall on the other side of the fireplace. "I don't feel anything, Grandma. Are you sure it's here?"

"Feel this side and tell me if you can feel the edge of a door."

Evelyn did so and immediately found the vertical line that Gracie had thought might be the edge of a door. "Grandma, I think I found a door." Her fingers scrabbled at the wall. "Do you think it's been painted over?"

"I hadn't thought of that. I hope not."

"So how do we open it?" Evelyn pulled the footstool over and began feeling along the wall to try to find the top edge of the door.

"Good question." Gracie stared grimly at the wall sconce. How would she make a secret doorknob that opened a secret door that wouldn't be easily detected by the wrong person? Did she need a key? But Doris hadn't mentioned anything about a key. Her mother had figured out how to open the door while they were cleaning in this room. So she must need to fiddle with the sconce somehow.

Gracie went back to the sconce just as Evelyn said, "I found the top edge." She ran her finger along the wall, going from the vertical crack toward the fireplace.

"If that's the top of the door, it must be a very small door."

"We can squeeze through," Evelyn said blithely. Apparently nothing was going to deter her from this secret passage.

Gracie studied the sconce. It wouldn't just turn like a doorknob or it would too easily open the door. Same with twisting it, probably. But what if she did two things at once?

She pushed at the wall while trying to turn the sconce. Nope. She tried twisting it. Again, no luck. How about pushing on the sconce itself?

She pushed on it but met with resistance. Then she pulled on it...and the sconce moved.

It was rough, from years of disuse, but it did move. While still pulling at it, Gracie turned the sconce counterclockwise. It moved like before—roughly but easily.

"Grandma," Evelyn breathed.

"Push on the panel."

Evelyn gave the wall a hard shove, and a panel broke away to swing inward a few inches. From inside came the high-pitched screech of old metal hinges. Perhaps because of the dark color of the wall paint, the seam of the panel in the wall had been so perfectly hidden that if Evelyn hadn't felt for it, they would never have seen it.

A puff of stale, moldy air hit them, and they both coughed. But despite the dank smell, Evelyn looked ecstatic. "We found it, Grandma!"

"We certainly did." Gracie couldn't resist a tremor of excitement in her own voice. After arming themselves with flashlights and the broom, they squeezed through the tiny opening.

They entered into an equally narrow passageway that ran the length of the wall along the side of the house. Just to be sure, they peeked behind the panel door, but there was only a dead end there, so they headed the other way, behind the fireplace.

The passage had been very carefully built, with sturdy beams running across the top and down the sides. However, the beams also were excellent for web-building, and the passage seemed to be clouded with cobwebs. Gracie attacked them with the broom and sneezed as dust rose in the breeze from her vigorous fanning.

"Let me do that, Grandma."

Gracie handed her the broom, and Evelyn pulled down the webs with aplomb. Apparently dark, cobwebby passages didn't frighten her at all. Gracie was grateful she hadn't seen any live spiders in all the webs she pulled down, although she kept her eyes open for them as they slowly headed down the narrow hallway. She searched the walls and ceilings not just for spiders, but also for anything left behind by whoever had made or used this passage. But the walls were bare except for some water stains, and the stone square that was the back of the library fireplace was a smoky black color from years of use.

They reached the end of the passage, which would have been the corner of the house, but to their left was a steep flight of narrow stone steps heading down.

"Where do they go?" Evelyn whispered, her eyes wide with excitement.

"Doris said that the passage goes down to a secret room in the basement," Gracie caught herself whispering back.

The air cooled as they descended the steps, which were very steep and even more cramped than the passage. The smell of mold also grew stronger, and Gracie was glad they discovered this passage in the summertime and not the cold dampness of winter. She was also thankful that the stone walls of the steep flight of steps weren't conducive to spiderwebs.

They reached the bottom of the steps and shone their flashlights around the room. Three of the four walls were stone, and the fourth was water-stained wood. Gracie knew that the walls of the basement were wood and guessed that the wooden wall was one side of the inn's basement utility room where the new commercial-grade washer and dryer sat.

Against two of the stone walls were old, heavy wooden bookcases, their shelves warped from time and damp. Gracie and Evelyn eagerly peered at the shelves, but they were empty of anything but dust and a couple of dead bugs.

Against the stone wall where the steps came down stood a squat wooden table that resembled a bedside table, with an additional shelf underneath. However, both surfaces were also depressingly empty.

The excitement of the room apparently began to wane for Evelyn. "It stinks down here."

"It's the mold." But even as Gracie said it, she looked around. If there was mold, where was it? She hoped it wasn't the dangerous black mold she'd read about. The mold wouldn't be on the stone walls, which left only the wooden furniture and the wooden wall as the culprit.

Against the fourth wall, the wooden one, stood a table, although this one was significantly larger than the table against the stone wall. Gracie swept her gaze over the empty top before peering at the base of the wooden wall behind the table. As she grabbed the edge of the tabletop, the surface wobbled.

She grabbed Evelyn as the table started to lean drunkenly sideways, continuing with the momentum, but it did no more than stand there lopsided.

"I thought it was going to crash," Evelyn said.

"Me too." Gracie shone her flashlight on the legs of the table and saw that they were rotted through. "Let's be careful."

She squatted down to look at the base of the wall and saw that the wood panels were also rotted like the table legs. Perhaps water had leaked into this section of the hidden room, causing the wood to degrade, since the bookcases and the other wooden table seemed relatively undamaged. She didn't see the black mold she'd read about that could be dangerous to young children and elderly people— although she hoped she wasn't quite yet in the latter category.

Evelyn sat on her heels and shone her flashlight at the wall. Her beam suddenly made something flash white in the crack between two rotted panels.

"What was that?"

Gracie hesitated a second, not wanting some creature to come scurrying out if she prodded the wood, or, worse, for the wall to come down entirely. She shone the flashlight on the wall above and around the rotted section and saw that the wood was solid. Apparently the water hadn't dripped from the roof but had come from the basement— maybe from the decrepit washer that they'd replaced last year.

"Stay back." Gracie grabbed the broom handle. She prodded the soft wood with the hard end of the handle, and the two panels shifted farther apart.

Evelyn shone her flashlight at the space between the two wooden pieces. "There's something behind the wall." She thrust her hand forward and plucked out a yellowing piece of paper, which she held out to Gracie.

"This paper isn't wet. How strange." The paper was relatively dry, only a tiny bit damp from sitting behind the moldy wood pieces.

She could immediately tell from touching the paper that it was also very old and fragile. The paper was thicker than modern commercial paper, but it also had a crackly feel to it that reminded her of the old paper in historical archives.

"Is there anything else down there?" Evelyn immediately shone her flashlight and the light flickered off of something else behind the wall. She reached in and pulled out an envelope.

Gracie shone the light while Evelyn opened the envelope and pulled out a small folded page. Evelyn and Gracie read the faint print on the page. "It's a ticket."

They shone their lights at the wall again, and Gracie poked at the boards more with the broom handle. Behind the rotted boards was another wall, probably the one in the basement. The wooden boards of the other wall also felt soft, so Gracie didn't poke at them very hard. They'd have to make sure to look at the wall from the utility room side to see what had to be replaced.

Gracie and Evelyn searched as much as they could through the small gap in the rotted boards but couldn't find anything else in the space between the two walls.

"Let's take these two things upstairs so we can see them better." Gracie led the way up the stone stairs, down the passage and back into the library.

Gracie immediately took the handkerchief off her head and grimaced at the dirt stuck to it. Evelyn did the same, but she obviously wasn't as disgusted as her grandmother.

"These go into the trash." Gracie dumped them both into the woven basket trash can in the corner of the library. She would empty it and clean up the broom later.

She set the two items on a small side table between the wingback chairs, and she and Evelyn sat to examine them in the bright light from the library windows.

The paper had the handwriting she was so familiar with by now, William's bold hand. But instead of a postcard, this looked like a letter, and instead of a picture and Scripture references, it was filled with letters in no discernible pattern.

"This looks like some sort of code," Gracie said.

"Like a secret? How are you going to find out what it says?"

At the top right was what looked like a date that hadn't been encoded. Gracie pointed sharply to it. "That's the date Hannah Montague met William at the Brant Point Lighthouse."

Evelyn looked at the strange letter with renewed interest. "Dad told me and Mom that you found some moldy old diary about Hannah."

"It was Isaac Elliott's, Hannah's father."

"But how are you going to figure out what this says?"

"I'll have to ask Sam. She's the one who figured out the postcards."

Gracie laid the letter aside and picked up the ticket. It was for a ship, the *Blue Star,* leaving Nantucket to Massachusetts. "The date of passage is two weeks after the date we think Hannah Montague disappeared from Nantucket."

"Was this her ticket?"

Gracie noted the name scrawled in the line under the section printed, "Names of Intending Passengers": Emmaline Nickerson, aged thirty.

"Who's Emmaline Nickerson?" Evelyn asked.

"I haven't read anything about an Emmaline or a Nickerson. But it might still be Hannah." Gracie frowned at the faded handwriting of the ticket agent. "Hannah was twenty-six when she disappeared, not thirty. But she could have lied about her age and her name."

"Wouldn't that get her in trouble?"

Gracie had to repress a smile at Evelyn's comment. "Yes, you're right. But it also makes me realize that if this ticket is here, it means she didn't use it."

"Oh. Yeah."

"It's just so strange. The date is such a coincidence. Not to mention finding it here at Hannah's house."

The rest of the ticket spelled out the name of the ticket agent— John Rivers—and the price, twelve dollars. But the line next to "Purchased by" was blank.

Who bought it? Gracie wondered. *Emmaline Nickerson maybe? But if this Emmaline was actually Hannah, then she intended to travel under a false name. But why? Was she running away?*

A chill ran through Gracie. Perhaps Hannah had been running away under a false name because she had stolen the money from the lighthouse.

"If she was running away, she never got a chance to use this ticket. But if she didn't use it…" Gracie stared at the ticket. "Then what happened to her?"

CHAPTER
Six

Gracie, this is so exciting." Caroline leaned over the paper her sister had found.

"It also means we need to get that basement wall checked for rotted wood," Sam pointed out.

"Spoilsport."

"I want to see that."

Caroline slid the paper across the dining room table to Sam.

At that moment, Evelyn entered the dining room, but Caroline was surprised to see her looking downcast. She would have expected Evelyn to be excited about their adventure. "Hey, pumpkin, what's wrong?"

Evelyn didn't answer.

"Evelyn, what is it?" Gracie sounded worried.

Evelyn shrugged and then handed the cordless phone back to her grandma. "I'm done talking to Daddy."

Gracie, Sam, and Caroline exchanged perplexed looks with each other.

Gracie stood up. "Why don't we go for a walk on the beach? The fresh air will feel good after that dirty passage."

Evelyn shook her head. "I don't want to go to the beach." She leaned against the doorjamb, her hands in her shorts pockets. She wasn't petulant or whiny, she was just...unnaturally quiet.

Gracie looked like she wanted to fold Evelyn in her arms and hug away whatever was bothering her. "How about you join us? I think Aunt Sam made cookies."

Evelyn shrugged again.

Not sure what to say, Caroline said, "Max is out in the backyard. Did you want to help me out by keeping him company?"

Finally a spark of interest appeared in Evelyn's eyes. She glanced toward the back of the house. "Okay." She left the dining room.

Caroline and Sam turned to Gracie and at the same time, both of them hissed, "What's wrong?"

"I don't know." Gracie looked completely flummoxed. "Brandon called a few minutes after we came out of the passage. After I talked to him for a few minutes, Evelyn got on the phone with him. Then I came in here to show you what we found." She gestured toward the empty doorway. "You saw exactly what I saw. Maybe I'll go outside to try to talk to her."

Gracie got up to leave, but she came back inside only a few minutes later. "Evelyn won't talk to me." She sat back in her seat, but her brows were knit together and her palm rubbed the knuckles of the other hand.

"Maybe she'll talk to you a little later," Sam said.

Gracie nodded, but she looked as melancholy as Evelyn had been only a few minutes ago.

To try to cheer her up, Caroline said, "Both of you are brave for going in there with only flashlights and a broom."

Gracie surprised Caroline with a smile. "After reading so many books about people finding antique treasures in secret rooms in old houses, there was no way I'd let a few cobwebs keep me from exploring."

It was fun for Caroline to see Gracie being so bold and adventurous when she was usually so reserved and cautious. Misty Harbor Inn had become a place of new steps for all of them, it seemed.

"The one thing that baffles me is how the page and the ticket are both dry when the wall was falling apart with water damage." Gracie turned the ticket over in her hands.

"Let me feel that."

Gracie gave Caroline the ticket. It was a little bit damp and cool, but it was much drier than she would have expected from something stuck in between two water-damaged panels of wood. "Well, we know the water damage had to have happened before we moved in, right?"

Gracie nodded. "The damage must not be too bad on the utility room side of that wall if we didn't even notice it when we were switching out the old washer and dryer."

"The only thing I can think of is that these two things fell in between the walls sometime after the water damage," Caroline said. "If they fell there before, they would have been stained and probably unreadable."

"Fell...?" Gracie had an intense, faraway look on her face. She twisted in her seat and looked up at the ceiling.

"Gracie?" Caroline asked. Sam, who had been studying the paper, glanced up at Gracie.

Gracie was tracing something on the ceiling with her eyes. She then turned and seemed to be trying to look through the walls into the library. "I think that the wooden wall in the secret room in the basement is directly below the secret room in the Emerald Room closet."

Now it was Caroline's turn to stare at the ceiling as she pictured the layout of the second floor rooms. "Which wall in the Emerald Room?"

"The one closest to the trunk." Gracie's finger traced an invisible line from the second floor down to the basement. "I think the wall goes all the way down to the basement room."

"That would help explain the paper and the ticket being in the wall." Caroline also traced an invisible line from ceiling to floor. "If the two papers were originally in the secret room in the Emerald Room, maybe they fell through the floor, or through a crack in the wall."

"Or maybe Hannah stowed them in the wall to hide them," Gracie said. "She hid the money in the dresser drawer, remember."

"And then at some point the paper and the ticket fell down the wall into the space between the two walls in the basement, sometime after the water damage had been done."

"So maybe Emmaline Nickerson really was Hannah. But if she was, why didn't she use that ticket? Why was she leaving under a false name? And why Massachusetts?"

Caroline and Gracie stared silently at each other, equally perplexed.

"I don't think it's a difficult cipher," Sam said, although she didn't look up at Caroline or Gracie. She ran a finger across a line of letters. "The problem is that there's usually a key that indicates which number corresponds to which letter of the alphabet, and we don't have the key,"

Caroline's feeling of excitement deflated slightly. "How would we get the key? How would we even know where it is?"

"It would probably be something Hannah had," Sam said.

"Can you crack the code without the key?" Caroline asked her.

Sam hesitated, chewing absently on her bottom lip. "Maybe," she said slowly. She reached for her coffee cup, but it was empty.

"I'll go for refills." Caroline got to her feet and picked up all three cups. "Back in a sec."

As she was pouring coffee in the kitchen, she suddenly heard George's baritone voice out in the foyer. She hadn't known he would be by today. Caroline continued to pour Sam's coffee. She'd drop these off in the dining room and then see if George wanted a cup too.

But then she heard steps on the stairs, and soon Trish's clarion voice carried through the walls. "Hello there, George. I'm glad I caught you without Caroline. I wanted to talk to you privately for a moment."

Without Caroline? What was Trish up to? Caroline froze, listening.

"Caroline mentioned you're planning the honeymoon?" Trish asked.

George said something Caroline didn't understand.

"That's all well and good, but you want to really wow her," Trish said. "How about a castle in Scotland?"

Caroline's jaw dropped. A castle in Scotland for her honeymoon? That sounded wonderfully romantic, but would probably be expensive.

George must have echoed Caroline's thoughts, because after he said something that Caroline again couldn't hear, Trish replied with a jovial laugh. "But it's your honeymoon. Don't you think it's worth splurging for something so special? In one of my books, *The Anguished*

Outlaw of Comanche County, I had the couple ride out to some hot springs where the hero had arranged to drape silk curtains around the spring and scatter rose petals up to the entrance, and they dined on French champagne and strawberries."

Caroline reflected that for an anguished outlaw, he had rather modern, extravagant tastes.

George said something and then Trish said, "I know just the castle for you. It's a fabulous place where they put on jousts and medieval dinner nights. It's tons of fun. I know the owner and can probably get you a really good rate."

Caroline was frustrated she couldn't hear George's answers clearly, but she had no problem hearing the higher tone of his voice, which seemed to indicate that he was interested in Trish's suggestion.

Caroline bit her lip. A castle in Scotland could be very romantic, but not if it was noisy and specialized in touristy things. She'd prefer someplace quieter, not someplace that sounded a bit like a theme park. Maybe she could give George hints about what she wanted for their honeymoon trip.

But what if he liked the idea of this "fun-filled" Scottish castle? Caroline thought about it for a moment. To be honest, she would be happy anywhere as long as she was with George. That's why she didn't mind that he wanted to keep their honeymoon plans a secret from her. She liked the idea of a surprise.

But now the surprise might be taken from her too. Caroline sighed.

Well, even if her honeymoon didn't turn out to be the romantic, secluded place she had hoped, she could at least make sure her wedding was exactly what she wanted. Trish's words about "creative expression" had fired Caroline's imagination as she reveled in the fact that she had free rein to make her wedding anything she wanted it to be. She could create a miniature of the Taj Mahal if she wanted to.

Well, maybe not the Taj Mahal. But certainly something unique and exotic.

Nantucket had never seen a wedding like what hers would be.

Sam paused at the stall in the farmers market with her shopping bag slung over her forearm. She peered at the baskets of elderberries, their dark purple skins appearing almost red in the bright sunlight. She'd never baked with elderberries before, although she had read lots of recipes with them in her mother's books, in some Nantucket cookbook collections, and online. The plump jewel-like berries tempted her to buy them and experiment with a few pies, jams, desserts…

No. She was here to buy groceries for the inn and more blackberries so she could work on her cobbler recipe. She didn't have time to be distracted by experimenting with a luscious new berry. Maybe later, if the elderberries were still in season after the Summerfest baking contest.

"Are you going to enter the Summerfest baking contest?" a woman's voice behind her echoed her thoughts.

Sam turned and started to say yes, but then she saw that the woman was talking to her friend. The two women stood in front of a vegetable stand inspecting the lettuces. Sam turned back to perusing the berries, but she couldn't help overhearing the conversation.

The second woman made a scoffing sound. "Why bother? Everyone knows it's rigged."

Rigged? Sam frowned so fiercely that the berry stand owner asked her, "Is everything all right?"

"Sorry. I'm fine," she said quickly.

"There you go again with that nonsense," the woman was saying to her friend.

"It's true and you know it."

"I know no such thing. Just because Eloise Meyer won it three times doesn't mean it's rigged."

"Eloise Meyer won it five times, not three, and some of the Meyer aunts have won it a couple of times each before Eloise, and Eloise's daughter Betsy won it for the past four years. You can't tell me that's a coincidence."

The woman had apparently heard this litany from her friend several times before, because she sighed. "And you can't tell me that Betsy Carlisle isn't a good baker, which is why she won the past four years. Or maybe the Meyer women share recipes and tweak them and that's why they always win."

"Share recipes? That clan? Ha! When pineapples start growing in Nantucket."

"Come now, they're not that bad—"

"The only people they're more competitive with are the other contestants in those baking contests they love to enter."

"Oh, hurry up and pick a lettuce and let's get going. I want to buy some tomatoes."

"Ma'am, did you want to buy some of those?" asked a voice in front of Sam.

She realized she'd been staring at the blackberries as she strained to listen to the women's conversation. "Oh yes. I'd like an entire flat."

"Planning on making jam?" asked a querulous voice at her elbow, and Sam turned to see Shirley Addison, the inn's next door neighbor. Today, Shirley had on a lavender seersucker pantsuit and a camel rhinestone pin on the lapel. Her snow-white hair, usually piled atop her head, had fallen loose and now hung lopsidedly over her left ear.

"Hi, Shirley. Nice to see you."

"*Humph.* I needed lemons so I decided to brave the crowds." She gestured with her cane to the sparsely populated market, which had been quite busy an hour earlier when it had first opened.

"How did you get here? Do you need a ride home?" Shirley was stout, but sometimes she tottered a bit with her cane when she walked.

"Got a ride from Stan Wildes. He was going to pick me up, but if you could give me a ride, that'll save him a trip."

How like the Harvest Chapel minister to go out of his way to give Shirley a ride to the farmers market. Sam would have him over for dinner again some night this week to thank him.

"You never answered my question. Making jam?" Shirley nodded to the large flat of blackberries that the stand owner handed to Sam after she paid him.

"No, I'm working on a cobbler recipe. I'm going to enter it into the Summerfest baking contest."

"Well, you might do well at that." Shirley's cantankerous tone didn't hide the genuine compliment.

Sam smiled. "Thanks, Shirley. Assuming the contest isn't rigged," she added before she could stop herself.

"Rigged?"

"Oh, never mind me. I overheard some women talking."

Shirley made a dismissive sound. "Of course it's not rigged. I even judged it one year. I picked the three winning items in cakes, pies, and breads. Why would anyone say it was rigged?"

"It might have just been sour grapes. The women were saying how a Meyer kept winning the contest each year."

Shirley's eyes shifted sideways, and her mouth was grim. "Let's head to the flower stand." Her grip on Sam's elbow was surprisingly strong.

"Is it true?"

"Well…it's true that Betsy Carlisle won the contest for the past four years, but even I have to admit her desserts are always good. I got to judge her bread pudding three years ago. And it wasn't rigged," Shirley added defensively. "I didn't know it was hers until it won."

"It was that good, huh?" Sam's heart felt heavy in her chest. Who was she kidding? She was only a novice at this baking thing, and she didn't have a chance of winning any sort of ribbon with her pathetic little cobbler.

"Your cobbler's pretty good too, you know, missy."

Sam had to laugh at Shirley's fierce expression. "Thanks, Shirley."

They crossed the market toward a large stand of flowers, some grown in local greenhouses so that a variety of blooms filled the air with their scents.

"You have to understand something," Shirley said quietly. "The thing about the Meyers is that they're one of the richest families on the island. Close-knit, proud, and competitive." She *tsked* and shook her head as if it was a criminal offense.

"One of the women I overheard also mentioned that they were competitive."

"I'm not a family friend or anything, but there are rumors. They compete with each other at family gatherings, people say. And they enter baking contests a lot."

"Maybe they just like to bake."

"I think they just like to win. One of my friends, Lorna, told me she caught Betsy snooping around her kitchen one year when Lorna was going to enter her pumpkin muffins."

"Snooping?"

Shirley nodded and then *harrumphed*. "Lorna said Betsy seemed pretty furtive, and when Lorna confronted her, Betsy had a pretty flimsy excuse for being there. Lorna suspects Betsy was trying to steal her recipe. Or worse." Shirley *tsked* again. "One thing I do know—Betsy Carlisle is even more competitive than her mother, Eloise. Eloise Meyer won five Summerfest baking contests in a row about a decade ago and to hear her talk, she's prouder of that fact than her own children," Shirley said.

Sam had a hard time believing that. Still, if Shirley heard the story of Betsy snooping directly from her friend Lorna…

Sam bought some flowers to brighten the dining room table and then she drove Shirley home. Evelyn had a lemonade, and Caroline and Gracie were enjoying a cup of tea in the kitchen when she entered the house.

"*Mmm.*" Caroline snatched up a blackberry and popped it into her mouth.

"Don't eat too many. I need them for my cobbler." But Sam also dropped a few berries into Evelyn's cupped hands.

"You've been working hard on it," Gracie said. "How's it going?"

"I still think I'm missing something." Sam began putting away the fruits and vegetables she'd bought at the market. "The crust isn't quite right."

"Have you had time to look at that encoded page?" Caroline got a vase out from under the sink and filled it with water.

Sam winced. "No, sorry. I've been working on my recipe instead."

Caroline began trimming the stems of the flowers Sam had bought and dropped them into the vase of water. "Do you mind if I take a look at it?"

"Don't you have wedding plans to make?"

Caroline rolled her eyes. "I can only look at fabric samples for so long. I'm thinking of an Indian sari instead of a wedding dress. What do you think?" She struck a pose like a Bollywood dancer.

Evelyn smiled, her eyes alight for a moment.

"I think you'll look beautiful, whatever you wear," Sam told Caroline.

Caroline gave her a smacking kiss on the cheek. "That's why I love you. Gracie was a wet blanket and said I wouldn't be able to find anyone on the island who could make one for me."

"That's exactly what I was going to add." Sam grinned.

Caroline sighed. "The problem is that I know you're both right." But then she recovered her spirits and began circling around the kitchen in a dance that was half-swing, half-Indian. Max gave a little yip of encouragement. "So you'll get me the encoded page later?" Caroline asked Sam breathlessly.

"Sure thing."

As Sam put the blackberries away, she remembered what she'd overheard at the farmers market and gave an involuntary sigh. "You don't think I'm being foolish in trying to enter this baking contest, do you?" she asked her sisters.

"Of course not," Gracie said.

Caroline stopped dancing to look at her with surprise. "What makes you think that?"

"Oh well…I heard there's a lot of competition this year."

"I think that in a small town like Nantucket, there would be a lot of competition every year. Did you hear something at the farmers market?" Gracie asked Sam quietly.

Sam hesitated and then said, "I overhead two women say Betsy Carlisle is expected to win this year like she's won the past four years."

Caroline made a *pffft* sound. "She's won because she's never faced off against you."

"I appreciate the vote of confidence, but who am I kidding? Apparently Betsy's entire family are good bakers. They're like a baking dynasty."

"You come from a family of good bakers too. Mom was fantastic. Just because she didn't enter baking contests doesn't mean she wasn't great. Same with you."

Sam had to admit their mother had been a terrific baker. She'd loved tweaking recipes and seemed to only make them better each time.

"You make the best chocolate chip cookies, Aunt Sam," Evelyn chimed in, her eyes solemn.

Sam smiled at her. "Just for that, you can have some for dessert."

The girl's expression perked up a little, which both encouraged Sam and broke her heart. What had happened to the carefree little girl she had been? She glanced at Gracie, who gave a shrug and a small shake of her head to indicate she hadn't been able to get Evelyn to talk to her about it yet.

But then Evelyn said, "But I can't have cookies. I made Grandma mad today."

"I wasn't mad, I was just worried about you," Gracie said.

"What happened?" Sam asked.

"Evelyn disappeared for a little while. I didn't know where she was."

"I told you I was only in Mrs. Addison's yard." Evelyn's lower lip looked a little pouty.

"But I didn't see you, Evelyn. I wasn't mad, I was worried." Gracie's expression seemed anxious, which Sam could understand. With Evelyn being so uncharacteristically quiet lately, none of them wanted to upset the girl further.

"I ran into Shirley Addison at the farmers market too," Sam said. "She said that Betsy might resort to snooping and stealing people's recipes, although it's only what she and her friend suspect."

Gracie burst into laughter.

"I just read a book a few weeks ago," Gracie said. "A cozy mystery. A new competitor in a small-town pie baking contest was poisoned with cyanide in her ice cream sundae."

"That's terrible," Caroline said.

"You'd better be careful," Gracie said with a laugh.

Sam grinned at her. "I'll be sure not to eat any ice cream sundaes."

CHAPTER
Seven

*G*racie entered the historical society building and breathed deeply. The antique colonial house smelled like old parchment, aged leather, beeswax, and lemon polish—thanks to the antique chairs sitting along the edges of the foyer.

Though she loved her granddaughter, Gracie was relieved that Evelyn had opted to go with Caroline to the library. While there, they'd make photocopies of the encrypted page they'd found so they'd have plenty of copies to try to decode.

As Gracie had left the house, Evelyn had been sitting in the parlor, waiting for Caroline so they could go to the library. She'd been staring out the window with a sad, anxious look on her face. When Gracie called good-bye, Evelyn had started and then quickly waved good-bye. Gracie had hesitated, wondering if she should try to speak to Evelyn, but then Caroline had bustled in and swept Evelyn away to the library.

Evelyn worried her. What was going on with her? Why was she so quiet? Gracie had spoken to Brandon on the phone but he'd seemed perplexed. He hadn't been able to speak to her very long because he'd been at work, but he promised to call her later.

Gracie stared up at the lovely molding in the ceiling, basking in the beauty of the house and the quietness around her. Evelyn would definitely have been bored if she'd come with Gracie, so she hoped her granddaughter was having fun with her aunt Caroline.

Summoned by the ringing of the bell over the doors, the historian, Elizabeth Adams, ran lightly down the stairs from the second floor. "Hello, Gracie. How are you doing?"

"Oh, busy. Evelyn, my eight-year-old granddaughter, is visiting for a few weeks."

"You'll have so much fun, I'm sure. And how is your niece… Jamie, isn't it?" Elizabeth tucked a lock of straight dark hair behind her ear. She was dressed today in a vintage dress of a soft peach color that looked like it was from the sixties. It fit her slender form to perfection.

"You have such a good memory. How do you do that?"

Elizabeth laughed. "I've always had a good memory, but I really had to hone that skill when I was in grad school studying for my doctorate in Colonial history. My thesis professor would try to stump me with obscure historical names whenever I went to talk to him."

"That seems rather extreme."

"He was eccentric, but one of the best professors in the university. And it didn't help my case any that he knew my parents."

"He did? Was he from Nantucket too?"

"Sort of. His cousin used to live here and that's how he met my folks." Elizabeth had taught history in a college in Boston after getting her doctorate, but when the job at the historical society opened up, she'd jumped at the chance so she could be near her family. "You didn't bring Evelyn with you today?" she asked.

"No, she doesn't get as excited as I do around antiques. And what I need to look at today would bore her to tears."

"I've been hoping you'd come back in after we discovered those newspaper clippings about the Montagues." Elizabeth's dark eyes shone. "I'm always continually fascinated by what I learn about Nantucket history, even though I've studied it for so many years."

"You won't believe what we discovered the other day. A woman named Doris Waverly is staying at the inn right now, and her parents worked for the people who owned the Misty Harbor in the 1930s, when it was called Montague House. She told us about a secret passage into the basement that she and her mother discovered."

Elizabeth's her mouth fell open. "Seriously? Did it just lead into the basement?"

"It led into a secret room just behind the basement wall. Doris says that she thinks Jedediah Montague stored his valuables there."

"Did you find anything?"

"We found some papers that had dropped into the secret room from the room above, and they're dated around the time of the Montagues."

"Wait—there's another secret room? That's totally awesome." Even though she had a doctorate, right now Elizabeth looked like a little girl in a candy shop. "Did you bring the papers with you?"

"I brought one of them. The other one is encoded and Caroline is making copies so we can try to decode it."

"That's so James Bond."

Gracie laughed. "I guess it does seem that way. Sam says we don't have the key to unlock the cipher so we have to figure it out some other way."

"What's the other paper?"

Gracie pulled the ticket out of the envelope in her hand and gave it to Elizabeth, who handled it gingerly.

The young woman's face suddenly became intense as she scrutinized the ticket. "I recognize the name of the ticket agent. He was on a list of shipping employees from 1875."

"A list of shipping employees? That seems like such a random document to stand the test of time."

"You wouldn't believe the strange things people kept. Someone donated a box full of papers her grandmother had kept, and it included electrical bills from 1910."

"Do you recognize the name of the passenger?"

Elizabeth squinted at the scrawled name and then shook her head. "It's hard to know if Emmaline was a visitor to Nantucket or if she was a resident."

"Is there a chance she was somehow connected to Hannah Montague? The ticket date is two weeks after she disappeared, which is rather suspect, don't you think? We wondered if this Emmaline might be Hannah traveling under a false name."

"Maybe that's why it looks like this ticket was never used. She might have disappeared before she could take that ship."

"It also would mean she was intending to leave Nantucket under a false name. That doesn't look very good considering she was suspected of stealing the money from the lighthouse."

"You don't look very happy about that prospect."

"Until we found this ticket and started thinking about the possibilities of what it means, I hadn't realized how much I wanted Hannah to be innocent of all that."

"Well, this doesn't prove she stole the money. And even if it is Hannah, it just means she wanted to get away from her stepchildren secretly."

"Is there a way to find out more about Emmaline?"

"Of course. Let's head up to the document rooms."

Elizabeth led the way up the stairs to the second floor of the colonial home. Most of the rooms were temperature and humidity controlled because they housed Nantucket antiques and served as a historical museum. A few small rooms under the eaves had been filled with file cabinets of old documents pertaining to Nantucket history. Elizabeth unlocked one of the rooms and led the way inside.

"If we find anything about Emmaline, it would be in these file cabinets." Elizabeth gestured to a set of cabinets against the far wall. "These are general documents dealing with the town during the late 1800s. We also have other things like tax documents and shipping records in another room, but we'll only look through those if we can't find anything here."

"Where should we start?"

"These two cabinets are full of documents relating to the major families in Nantucket from 1800 to 1899," Elizabeth said. "They're in alphabetical order by family name."

"I'll take this one." Gracie opened a drawer marked "Meyer" and saw that it was filled with hanging file folders.

"I wish these were better organized," Elizabeth said as she pulled out a folder and began scanning the contents, which looked like some old letters. "Families in Nantucket will donate their old family papers, but there's no good place to put things like old Mrs. Hartfield's certificate for best cranberry sauce at the 1891 autumn fair, or Great-Uncle Albert's bill of sale for a Ford Model T in 1912."

"What an eclectic collection." Gracie opened the first folder, marked "Meyer, Virginia, 1810–1879" and found an old handwritten recipe for blueberry pie, an article Virginia had written on a knitted baby's cap pattern that had been cut out of a newspaper, and six overdue modiste's bills.

"No obituaries?" Gracie asked.

"Unfortunately, they're only in the copies of the old newspapers we have in the filing cabinets. One project I've been slowly working on is going through all the papers and copying down all the births and deaths into an electronic database so we can search for names, but I haven't had as much time as I wanted to lately. I'm only to 1805 right now."

"That's a huge project. Even if you had all day, every day, that would take weeks to do, maybe even months."

"Eventually I'd like to digitize all the documents in this collection. That way we wouldn't have to worry about the papers deteriorating and it would be easier to search. We could have done a search for Emmaline's name and seen if any documents mentioned her. But as it is…" Elizabeth shrugged.

Gracie glanced at the rest of the drawer and saw that it ended with "Norland." She looked for "Nickerson" but couldn't find the name.

They searched for over an hour, painstakingly going through documents, until suddenly Elizabeth said, "This doesn't have to do with Emmaline, but this is interesting."

Gracie went over to where Elizabeth had opened an old, fragile journal. The cover had originally been covered in silk, but it had holes where moths had eaten through, and the cardboard interior was clearly seen. Some of the pages were wavy from water damage, and it looked like the writing in almost the first third of the book had been washed away, but the pages in the last two-thirds of the book were less wavy and had less damage.

Elizabeth had opened it to a page that was relatively undamaged. A woman's elegant handwriting scrawled over the page, and Gracie could see she was rather heedless about the spelling of her words.

"This is a journal of Mrs. Margaret Parshall, the wife of a once-wealthy whaler," Elizabeth told Gracie. "Her husband died around the time that Nantucket Island fell into economic decline in the 1850s. She couldn't afford to move because she couldn't sell her home, so she remained on the island despite the fact that so many families left. She was actually one of the social leaders among the families still on Nantucket in the 1870s."

"Like a society matron?"

"Exactly. They didn't have many parties and balls since the economy wasn't so great, but she writes about one Christmas party she threw in 1877."

"That's not too long before Hannah disappeared."

"This is really interesting." Elizabeth pointed to a paragraph down the page in the journal. "It's mostly things like this girl was flirting with that boy, that husband making eyes at the maid while this wife had too much to drink. Reminds me of a gossip magazine. But then Mrs. Parshall writes about Jedediah and Hannah Montague. Hannah apparently showed up with some rather flashy jewelry. According to Mrs. Parshall, Jedediah seemed rather pleased about that, as if he was proud to show her off, but Hannah seemed unhappy. Mrs. Parshall gets a little catty when she mentions that most of the other women at the party would have given their eyeteeth for diamonds like that."

"Well, we know Jedediah had a great deal of money at least earlier in his marriage to Hannah, although he died with a lot of debts."

"It gets even better," Elizabeth went on. "Mrs. Parshall overheard Hannah and Jedediah arguing later that night. Apparently Hannah didn't like being on display with all those jewels. That doesn't seem to match with what we read in that newspaper clipping about Jedediah's children accusing their stepmother of spending their father's money freely."

"Do you think they might have lied to the newspaper about Hannah? But why would they do that?"

"Maybe they didn't like her, or maybe they wanted to blacken her reputation since she was suspected of stealing the money from the lighthouse. You know how people will sometimes do that. 'I always knew she was rotten.' That sort of thing."

"It makes me feel sorry for poor Hannah."

Elizabeth's eyes twinkled. "I think you were already feeling sorry for poor Hannah."

"True." Gracie smiled. "Does the journal have anything else about Hannah?"

"No. Just more gossip—Jedediah's son Fitzwalter was very properly chatting with the police chief while Lachlan was trying to steal a kiss from the maids."

"That certainly says something about Jedediah's sons. I wonder what Jedediah was really like? Do you think this account is accurate?"

"Mrs. Parshall thought it was accurate. Now, if it was true is something no one can tell us."

CHAPTER
Eight

Caroline and Evelyn lounged in chairs on the back porch, the sun filtering through the pergola slats overhead and the ocean roaring in the distance. Caroline figured that if she had been intending to do a crossword puzzle, she'd want to sit out here, so why not enjoy the sun and the surf while trying to figure out this encoded page?

Caroline had never been good at number or logic puzzles, but she'd always enjoyed word games and had been rather good at them at one point. She had a strong feeling of confidence that she could figure out this code, which she knew would help her as she guessed at the different possibilities of how the page was encoded. At the library, she had made lots of photocopies so she and her sisters would have plenty of "disposable" copies. While she was photocopying, Evelyn had picked up a couple of books to read.

Evelyn sat beside Caroline now. She had started on a book for a little while, but now she was doodling on one of the photocopied pages with Caroline's own colored pencil set, which she used to mark her favorite passages in her Bible. The sea breeze, the scent of roses from the garden, and the warm sun seemed to have made her sleepy, since her eyes were half-lidded as she drew on her sheet of paper.

Doris had also joined them outside. Caroline had explained the page was coded, but Doris had declined trying to break it. Instead, she dozed in the mild weather.

Caroline stared at the paper. She had already tried a simple cipher where every letter was shifted over a certain number of letters, but it only resulted in gobbledygook no matter what number of shifts she tried.

She'd loved word search puzzles as a child before she progressed to more complex word games, and she was good at spotting patterns among letters and words, so she tried to see if there were repetitions in the letters.

There! The letters WYKZJ were repeated once near the beginning and once near the end.

Several minutes later, she spotted the letters ZOD repeated. And then she finally found LFV repeated. She searched but couldn't find any other letters repeated.

Then something occurred to her. If this was a letter from William to Hannah—and there was a good possibility that it was, considering how he'd encrypted those postcards to her—then wouldn't the note start off as "Dear Hannah" or "Hannah" and end with "William"?

She took a pen and tried both "Dear Hannah" and "Hannah."

The first ten letters were: S, U, X, R, F, J, P, L, G, C. If that translated into "Dear Hannah," then D had become S, E had become U, and so on.

If that translated into just "Hannah," then H became S, A became U, N became X, and so on.

The "William" at the end of the letter was easier, since no matter if he signed it just "William" or "Love, William," the last seven letters had to be his name. The last seven letters on the page were: *B, K, S, W, C, K,* and *Q.* So *W* had become *B, I* had become *K,* and so on.

Caroline stared but couldn't find a pattern in how the letters were shifted. In a simple cipher, the letters were all shifted the same amount. For example, if the letters were all shifted 3 spots, then *A* became *C, B* became *D,* and so on, and it was easy to decode because you only had to figure out how many spots the letters were shifted.

But here, each letter was shifted a different number of spots. *W* was shifted six spots, *I* was shifted three spots, the first *L* was shifted eight spots and the second *L* was shifted twelve spots. How in the world had Hannah known how many spots each letter was shifted?

Evelyn had fallen asleep in her chair, but she woke up when Caroline rose to her feet.

"How about some lemonade?" Caroline asked her.

Evelyn shrugged and then said, "I guess." She got to her feet and headed back inside.

"Doris?" Caroline asked.

Doris opened her eyes, blinking them slowly a few times, and then said quite clearly, "Yes?"

"We're going in for a snack. Would you like anything?"

"I'll join you." Doris slowly rose to her feet and followed Caroline inside.

Sam had just finished a batch of blackberry cobbler that made the kitchen smell fruity and buttery at the same time. Caroline sniffed appreciatively. "Any chance we can taste test those for you?"

Sam grinned. "I figured that's why you came inside."

They had just sat at the dining room table when Gracie returned home. Her eyes lighted on the plates of cobbler. "*Oooh*, can I have some?"

"Of course." Sam rose to get her a plate.

Caroline said, "Sorry, but we're not going to wait for you." She took a bite of gooey blackberry filling and gave an ecstatic *mmm*.

"Hi, Grandma." Evelyn blew on her forkful of blackberry to cool it. "Did you have fun at the historical society?"

"Probably more than any of you would have," Gracie said, but not unkindly. "Looking through all those historical documents was a little tedious but fascinating."

"Did you find anything?" Doris looked as interested as any of them.

"Nothing about Emmaline Nickerson, but we did find something about Jedediah and Hannah Montague."

"Wait, I want to hear this," Sam said as she entered the dining room with a plate of cobbler and a cup of tea for Gracie.

After Sam had seated herself and they'd all started digging into the cobbler, Gracie said, "We found this journal of some society matron who lived in Nantucket during the same time as the Montagues. She wrote about a Christmas party she threw a couple of years before Hannah disappeared. Her journal entry was mostly gossip about the people at her party, but she mentioned about how Hannah showed up dripping in diamonds."

"Diamonds?" Caroline paused before taking another bite of cobbler. "They couldn't afford diamonds. Jedediah died deeply in debt."

"Exactly. And according to this society matron, Jedediah seemed very proud of Hannah's diamonds, but she seemed very uncomfortable wearing them. And the journal writer later overheard them arguing. Apparently Hannah hadn't wanted to be on display like that."

Sam abruptly sat back in her chair, her face grim. "That sounds eerily familiar to me."

Caroline knew immediately what she was talking about. "You mean Gerald?" she said, naming Sam's ex-husband.

"Yes."

Evelyn's eyes had grown round, but she didn't say anything. Gracie reached out to touch Sam's hand.

"Gerald wanted me to be on display for him at social events. I had to look perfect and be dressed in the most expensive dress or the flashiest jewelry. How I looked and compared to other women was a matter of social status for him."

Caroline knew Gerald had been incredibly controlling, oppressing Sam with his demands and his need to control her every move, practically her every thought.

"I was a trophy to him," Sam said. "And it sounds like Hannah might have been a trophy for Jedediah Montague too."

"Then the argument about the diamonds makes sense," Gracie said. "Hannah didn't appreciate being on display."

"But Jedediah couldn't afford those diamonds," Caroline said. "He must have wanted the islanders to think he was wealthier than he actually was."

"And the fact Hannah didn't like wearing those diamonds doesn't make sense if she was really a spendthrift, like Jedediah's children said she was in those newspaper clippings we found," Gracie said.

"Perhaps they lied," Doris said.

"Maybe," Gracie said.

"But why?" Caroline said. "Why would they want people to think Hannah was a spendthrift?"

"Maybe because it was Jedediah who was the spendthrift, not Hannah," Sam said. "And Jedediah's children didn't want people to know that, but he'd died in a ton of debt. So they decided to blame the debt on Hannah."

"That's not very nice," Evelyn said, frowning.

"I completely agree," Caroline said.

"How'd you do on the encoded page?" Gracie asked her.

"I didn't get very far," Caroline said. "I did find some repetitions." She pointed out the three clusters of letters that were repeated in the page.

"Caroline, you're amazing," Sam said, staring at the page. "How in the world did you find those? Two of them are only three letters long."

Caroline shrugged. "I've always liked word puzzles," she said, although her cheeks warmed with the praise. "And I'm good with words and letters—that's why I became a writer."

"I would never have spotted those repetitions, not in a million years." Gracie was also staring at Caroline's sheet. "What are those?"

"I figured that if this was from William to Hannah, then he must have started the letter with 'Dear Hannah' or 'Hannah' and ended with 'William.' So I tried to translate all three of those into the coded letters on the page."

"Is it 'Dear Hannah' or 'Hannah,' do you think?" Gracie said.

"It's hard to tell."

"I still think there's a key that we're missing," Sam said. "If you count how each of the letters are shifted, they're all shifted different amounts. Look at the word 'dear.' From *D* to *S* is …fifteen letters.

From *E* to *U* is sixteen letters. From *A* to *X* is twenty-four letters. From *R* to *R* is zero letters shifted."

"I don't understand," Evelyn said.

"Think of it this way," Caroline said. "Say we're going to encode your name. *E-V-E-L-Y-N*. Let's shift all the letters eight spaces. So the *E* would become…*M*. *V* would become…*D*, and so on. Your name would be…" She did a quick coding. "*MDMTGV*."

Evelyn giggled, and Caroline grinned with delight at Gracie, who suddenly looked relieved. It seemed like Evelyn hadn't laughed once since she'd come to Nantucket.

"But in this page," Sam went on, holding up a copy of the coded letter, "rather than each letter being shifted the same number, like nine, instead each letter is shifted a different amount. That means there was a key to tell Hannah how many times to shift each letter."

"For the whole page?" Evelyn asked.

"It was probably a word," Gracie said, "and it repeated itself throughout the letter."

Sam suddenly gasped. "Gracie, that's brilliant."

"It is?"

"That means these repeated letters are probably the same words, encoded using the same pattern as the key. Which means that the number of letters that they're apart will be a multiple of how many letters there are in the key."

Caroline wasn't entirely sure she understood what Sam had just said, but Sam was busy counting letters, and she thought it would be a good idea not to distract her.

After a few minutes, Sam said, "I got it. The key is seven letters long."

"Really?" Gracie said.

"This *WYKZJ* repetition is 259 letters apart from each other. The only way to get 259 is to multiply 37 by 7."

"Um…okay?" Caroline said. Numbers had a tendency to give her the heebie-jeebies.

"The *LFV* repetition is also 259 letters apart, and *ZOD* is 357 letters apart. 357 is 51 times 7."

"I think I get it," Gracie said. "Since those numbers are multiples of seven, then the key must be seven letters long."

"Grandma, you're making my head spin," Evelyn said.

"Me too," Doris said.

"That means it can't be 'Dear Hannah,'" Sam said. "That's ten letters long, and each letter is shifted a different amount of times. It must begin, 'Hannah.'"

"But 'Hannah' is only six letters long," Caroline said, "and 'William' is seven letters long."

They looked at the paper, and Sam counted how many times the letters in "Hannah" were shifted. *H* was shifted twelve letters, *A* was shifted twenty-one letters, the first *N* was eleven, the second *N* was five, *A* was six, and *H* was three.

"Twelve, twenty-one, eleven, five, six, three," Sam said.

Caroline stared at it and then said, "Those correspond to letters. Look. The twelfth letter of the alphabet is *L*. The twenty-first letter of the alphabet is *U*. Eleven is *K*, and five is *E*. 'Luke.'"

Gracie's eyes widened. "It's probably another Bible verse reference."

"So six and three aren't letters, they're the numbers six and three," Sam said. "But we don't know what the last number is."

Caroline went to the parlor and returned with their mother's worn leather Bible, which they had placed lovingly on a bookshelf. She flipped to Luke.

"Luke doesn't have sixty-three chapters," Caroline said, "so the reference is to Luke chapter six, which has"—she flipped a page—"forty-nine verses."

"It could refer to one of the verses between thirty and thirty-nine," Gracie said, "or it could mean chapter six verses three through...?" She raised her eyebrows.

"I know how we can find out," Sam said. "Let's look at 'William.'"

W was shifted six letters, I was three, the first L was eight, the second L was twelve, I was twenty-one, A was eleven, and M was five. Caroline saw the pattern immediately.

"It's cut in half," she said, "probably because it's at the end. We know the key starts with twelve, twenty-one, eleven, and five, but those are the L-I-A-M in his name. So the six, three, and eight are the last three spots of the key."

"Luke six, three through eight?" Gracie guessed.

"I think it's Luke chapter six, verse thirty-eight," Caroline said, and read from the Bible. "'Give, and it shall be given unto you; good measure, pressed down, and shaken together, and running over, men give into your bosom. For with the same measure that ye mete withal it shall be measured to you again.'" The verse in their mother's King James Bible had been lovingly highlighted with red colored pencil.

Gracie said, "I remember now. That was one of Mom's favorite verses."

"Maybe it was Hannah's favorite verse," Sam said. "William would know that."

"So the key is Luke 6:38. Now we've got to translate that," Caroline said.

"I'll do it." Sam began painstakingly translating each letter according to the key.

Gracie chatted with Caroline and Doris while Sam worked, and they opted for a second helping of cobbler while they were waiting.

"I've got it," Sam finally said and read the page.

Hannah,

I am sorry I could not meet you tonight after all. A child is dying and I could not leave the babe's bedside. Jacob insisted on taking this letter for me even though it will be dangerous for him to do so, but I think you will not mind seeing your old friend. Everything is set for you to escape. Jacob will buy your ticket under a false name. I will come to get you. Get all your possessions together to leave quickly. You will not be returning to Nantucket. Do not worry about me. Despite my calling I have no regrets about helping you escape. You will be safe soon.

Love, William

"So William was helping her to escape Nantucket," Caroline said.

"You know, that explains the secret room," Sam said. "She had gathered all her things there because William was going to help her escape."

"But she never did," Doris pointed out softly. "She never used that ticket."

A chill ran down Caroline's spine.

"Maybe William came early to take her away," Sam said weakly.

"But then, why didn't she take her things with her?" Gracie said.

"Maybe she left suddenly and didn't have time to take her things. Or"—Caroline swallowed—"maybe something happened to her before she could get away."

CHAPTER
Nine

Sam went all out for dinner that night since she had invited Pastor Stan Wildes. She was in the parlor chatting with the guests at the inn, Trish and Doris, when Pastor Stan entered the front door.

"I hope I'm not too late," he called to the room at large.

"Not at all." Trish waved him in and then held out her hand. "Trish Montgomery."

"Stan Wildes."

Trish regarded him with slightly narrowed eyes. "You don't look like a pastor."

He grinned, making his dark eyes sparkle. "What's a pastor supposed to look like?"

"Old, bald, and fat," Trish fired back.

Stan laughed and ran a hand through his rumpled salt-and-pepper curls. "I'm definitely old, but certainly not bald or fat yet."

"Certainly not. You're skinny as a rail. You need Sam's cooking to fatten you up." Doris held out her hand. "Doris Waverly."

"Nice to meet you."

"What church do you pastor?"

"Harvest Chapel."

Doris' face lit up. "I went there years ago with my parents. I'm afraid I don't remember the pastor's name, but I remember Mrs. Jones-Smith was my Sunday school teacher."

"That must be Gloria Harper's mother," Pastor Stan said. "Gloria's maiden name was Jones-Smith, and she told me her family had been going to Harvest Chapel since before she was born."

"I remember Mrs. Jones-Smith had an infant daughter, but I don't remember her baby's name," Doris said.

"It could have been Gloria or her older sister, Gladys. They both still attend Harvest Chapel."

Stan turned to Sam, who had been entertained watching the exchanges. "Hello there, Sam." His smile seemed to warm, and Sam felt the color creep up her cheeks.

"I hope you brought your appetite," she said. "I made wild rice cream soup, roast chicken, green beans, and blackberry cobbler for dessert."

"Sounds delicious." He glanced around the parlor. "Are your sisters coming too?"

"We're here," Caroline called as she, Gracie, and Evelyn walked into the parlor.

"Pastor Stan, this is my granddaughter Evelyn," Gracie said.

"How do you do?" He shook her tiny hand.

She took it with a small smile. "We were cleaning up because we were playing with Max outside."

"And where is he?" Pastor Stan asked.

"Curled up in our bedroom," Caroline said. "We had to give him a bath too, and that seemed to tucker him out."

"Everyone ready to eat?" Sam asked.

With a hearty affirmative, everyone moved into the dining room. Gracie had polished the long antique cherry table until it glowed auburn in the light from the brass chandelier above.

Sam went to get the soup tureen from the kitchen and placed it on the warming pad she'd left on the tiger oak buffet in the corner of the dining room. She got out their charmingly mismatched china soup bowls and ladled out the creamy soup, laden with aromatic vegetables, wild rice, and slivered almonds. It was one of her favorite recipes. Caroline helped her pass out the soup bowls.

"Pastor Stan, will you say the blessing?" Sam asked him, without thinking. She suddenly realized how much her faith had grown— that she would automatically ask Pastor Stan something like that. A year ago, she had felt far away from God and wary of religion, but now she felt comfort in a simple blessing over the food. Trish seemed a little startled at first, but she folded her hands and bowed her head with the rest of them.

"Lord, thank You for this delicious-smelling meal. Thank You for providing it and for the hands that prepared it."

Sam thought his voice might have deepened as he said that last phrase.

He went on, "Please bless this food to our bodies, and bless the conversation tonight. Thank You for this opportunity to fellowship with each other and make new friends. Amen."

"Amen," everyone murmured.

Sam tentatively tasted the soup. She'd tasted it twenty minutes ago when it had finished simmering, but for some reason she always worried it might somehow radically change between the stovetop and people's bowls. However, it was just as creamy and deliciously nutty as it had been twenty minutes ago.

"*Mmm*," Gracie said. "Great soup, Sam. I always love when you make this one."

"This wasn't one of Mom's recipes, is it?" Caroline asked.

"No, it's from my friend Sharon."

"She's from Minnesota?" Trish guessed.

"How did you know?" Sam said in surprise.

"I grew up in Minnesota, and this is a variation on Minnesota Wild Rice Soup." Trish smacked her lips in appreciation. "I love the almonds in it. Nice touch."

"You grew up in Minnesota?" Sam asked. "Somehow with all your exotic book locales, I thought you grew up someplace like Bombay or Greece."

"Books?" Pastor Stan's eyebrows rose as he glanced at Trish.

"I'm a romance novelist," Trish said. "Don't worry, I'm not offended you haven't heard of me, considering you're a pastor."

"Wait a moment, I remember your name, now," Pastor Stan said look of astonishment. "I don't read romance books, but I see your books sometimes on the best-seller shelves at our local bookstore."

"No way! You really aren't like any pastor I've ever met," Trish said.

Sam exchanged chagrined looks with Caroline and Gracie. They hadn't known about Trish at all, and the one person who remembered her best-selling books was their pastor.

"Do you still live in Minnesota?" Pastor Stan asked Trish.

"Yes. Well, I have a house there." The disdain in Trish's voice contrasted with the hint of pain in her eyes. "My family still lives there, though, and we don't really get along."

"I'm sorry to hear that," Pastor Stan said.

"Oh, I've gotten used to it." Trish's tone was light, but Sam somehow knew she didn't feel as casually about it as she said. "My parents are both retired university English professors. They won't ever approve of me because they think romance novels are trashy, useless entertainment."

Gracie reached over and touched Trish's hand. "I'm really enjoying your books."

Trish smiled. "Thank you. It makes me feel good to know so many people have read my stories."

The following silence could have been awkward, but Pastor Stan said with a twinkle in his eye, "Gracie, I ran into Elizabeth Adams today. She said you two were digging up buried treasure in the historical society's archives."

Trish's eyes widened. "Buried treasure?"

Gracie said, "It's not what you think. We were looking for more information about Hannah Montague."

"She used to live in this house," Caroline told Trish. "She disappeared in 1880 and no one knows what happened to her, but we found some of her old clothes and things upstairs."

"We found an encoded letter that we thought might be to Hannah from her brother, William," Gracie said. "He liked to use word puzzles and codes."

"Sam figured it out," Caroline said.

"No, Caroline did," Sam said quickly. "She found repeated sections of code that none of us would have been able to see in a million years."

"And then Sam figured out the key to decode it," Caroline said firmly.

"What did it say?" Trish asked.

"William was going to help Hannah escape Nantucket. We also found a ticket on a ship to Massachusetts, dated two weeks after Hannah disappeared, but it was never used."

"Then what happened to her?"

"We're not sure."

"So there's no way of knowing if she simply left early on a different ship, or if she was a victim of foul play," Doris said.

"What's foul play?" Evelyn asked.

"Something bad," Sam said to her.

Gracie gave a little shiver. "I don't really want to think something happened to her. I went back to the historical society today, and Elizabeth and I looked through the old ship records on the night Hannah disappeared."

"What did you find?" Sam asked.

"If Hannah did leave Nantucket, as opposed to...something else happening to her, she probably took one of the ships leaving the island that night. There were three—the *Brigadoon,* the *Lady Wingate,* and the *Copeland Crest.* They all sailed around the same time because of the tides, I think. The *Brigadoon* went to New York, the *Lady Wingate* went to Connecticut, and the *Copeland Crest* went to Massachusetts. I thought that she might want to try to go to Massachusetts since her brother had bought that original ticket for her to go there. But she wasn't on the passenger list for the *Copeland Crest.*"

"Maybe she stowed away?" Sam said.

"What time did it leave the harbor?" Caroline asked.

"A little after midnight."

"When was Hannah Montague last seen that night?" Trish asked.

"She went to the evening service at her church," Caroline said. "But no one saw her after that. Her stepchildren said she never returned home."

"What time was the evening service?"

"According to the newspaper clipping we found, it ended at nine o'clock," Gracie said. "And the *Copeland Crest* left three hours later."

"Not much time to stow away," Trish said, "but possible."

"Why would she stow away when she had a ticket for another ship in two weeks?" Doris said.

"Something must have happened to force her to leave early and unexpectedly," Trish said.

"That might be why she left all her things in the house," Gracie said. "She didn't have time to go back and get them."

"She probably hadn't planned on leaving that night at all, or she would have taken some of her things—like the money—with her to church," Caroline said.

Privately Sam thought it was probable that something terrible had happened to Hannah—instead of her just running away suddenly. But she didn't want to mention it with Evelyn at the table.

She went to retrieve the chicken, which had been resting after she took it out of the oven just before Pastor Stan had arrived. She carved it at the table, asking people which parts they wanted.

"This is delicious," Doris said. "It reminds me of the chicken my mother used to make, with that sweet glaze on it."

"It's our mom's recipe," Sam said. "It's an apricot glaze, but I also added a little orange to brighten it."

"I like it," Caroline said.

"Doris, you used to live in Nantucket?" Pastor Stan asked her.

"Oh yes. I even still have a few cousins in the area whom I'm visiting."

"Not just in Nantucket," Caroline added. "Doris used to live in this house. Isn't that amazing?"

"At the inn?" Trish asked.

"It was a private home belonging to the Fortescues when my family lived here," Doris said. "They were wealthy artists from Philadelphia, and this was their summer home. My mother was the maid first, then she became the cook, and my father was the gardener and chauffeur and general handyman."

"Doris told us about a secret passage down to the basement," Gracie said.

"It was full of cobwebs," Evelyn said.

Trish gave a shudder. "Why was there a secret passage down to the basement?"

"It went to a secret storage room," Gracie said. "Doris thinks the Montagues might have stored their valuables there, but there wasn't any treasure there when we found it."

"That's where we found the encrypted page and the ticket," Gracie said. "It had fallen from the room above."

"The passage was full of cobwebs when my mother and I found it too." Doris chuckled. "My mother went hysterical and wouldn't let me inside until she'd cleaned it all away with a broom."

"We used a broom too," Evelyn said. "And we put handkerchiefs over our heads."

"I would have wrapped my entire head in a sheet." Sam grimaced.

"If I could have and still been able to see, I would have," Gracie said to Sam in an aside.

"You two are regular Indiana Joneses." Caroline beamed.

"I love Harrison Ford," Trish said dreamily. "I modeled two of my heroes after him. One hero found a treasure chest of gold coins in a cave on the coast of France, and another hero found a jeweled crown in the mountains of Bangladesh."

Evelyn's eyebrows knit together. "Where's Bangle… Bang…"

"Bangladesh is in South Asia, next to India," Trish said.

"Beautiful country," Caroline added.

"You've been there?" Trish asked in surprise.

Caroline nodded. "I wrote several articles about it."

Caroline talked about her travels until dessert, when Doris asked Pastor Stan if certain sites in Nantucket were still the same as when she last visited.

"In some ways, Nantucket is like its own little Neverland," Pastor Stan said. "There isn't much change here, and the place is rich in history."

"I'd like to visit the Whaling Museum while I'm here." Doris chuckled. "I remember being a little bored when I was a child, but I hope I have more appreciation now. We got scolded for playing hide-and-seek among the exhibits."

Caroline's eyes were wide. "You and your parents?"

"Oh no." Doris's smile was wide. "Mother would never do anything like that. I meant me and my cousin. She stayed with us for a couple of years."

"Was she from Nantucket?"

"No, but I don't remember now where she was from. I have pictures of her, so that might jog my memory."

Gracie leaned toward Doris. "Did you bring pictures of the inn with you?"

"Why, yes. Would you like to see them tomorrow?"

"I'd love to." Gracie was practically hopping in her seat.

Sam's heart fell. "I'm sorry, I already committed to helping at the library tomorrow at their monthly children's craft day, and I promised Evelyn I'd take her."

"And Trish and I are going to a wedding consultant she knows in town," Caroline said.

Sam, knowing her sister as she did, thought that Caroline looked like she'd much rather stay with Doris and Gracie, but Caroline gave Trish a quick smile as Gracie spoke.

"Then it'll be just the two of us," Gracie told Doris.

Pastor Stan held out his plate. "Is there any more blackberry cobbler?"

"Of course." Sam had to stop herself from apologizing about it. She'd tweaked the recipe and the fruit was a little too runny now, which had made the crust soggy. But people seemed to enjoy it.

Sam rose to her feet to get more cobbler for him, but Pastor Stan waved her back down. "I can get it."

However, a couple of minutes later, he reappeared in the dining room doorway. "Do you happen to have more ice cream?"

Sam went to the kitchen with him to fetch the container of homemade ice cream from the freezer.

"That's why I couldn't find it," he said. "I was looking for a store-bought carton. The meal was fantastic, Sam, better than any other dinner I've had with all of you. Especially the cobbler."

The mention of the cobbler made Sam remember what she'd heard at the farmers market and what Shirley had told her, and she realized Pastor Stan knew the people in town fairly well. "Pastor Stan, do you know Betsy Carlisle?"

He looked surprised. "I know her, although she doesn't come to Harvest Chapel anymore."

"Why not?"

"She and her husband used to come to church regularly, and she would help with the nursery Sunday school, but after he died several years ago, she stopped attending. Why do you ask?"

"I heard some women at the farmers market talking about Betsy's winning the Summerfest baking contest."

"Yes, Betsy's won the last four years."

"They, uh…suspect that it's rigged so that a Meyer always wins. Apparently Betsy's mother won five times, and some of her aunts or cousins won a few times each."

She half expected Pastor Stan to frown at her for listening to gossip, but he only looked sad. "I think some people are jealous of Betsy for her wins."

"Shirley Addison said that her friend Lorna caught Betsy 'snooping' last year, and thinks Betsy was trying to steal Lorna's recipe."

Pastor Stan winced. "Betsy is very competitive. Maybe she was only trying to scope out the competition."

"Is Betsy friends with Lorna?"

"No, actually they're not."

So there was no reason for Betsy to be sneaking around Lorna's house in the first place, although Sam kept that thought to herself.

Pastor Stan went on, "The Meyers are a very proud, very wealthy family on the island. They don't have many friends on the island, despite the fact they've been here for generations."

Betsy wouldn't have many friends if she was indeed stealing people's recipes, but it made Sam feel sad for her that she really didn't have friends. Maybe she was close to her family the way Sam was close to Caroline and Gracie. "Now I feel guilty for listening to the gossip."

"Don't be. Betsy knows that people talk about her behind her back, especially after she won the baking contest last year. It's worse now that her husband is gone. Unlike other members of her mother's family, she used to socialize quite a bit with church members, but now she has cut herself off from other people and only socializes with her family. I've tried inviting her to church again, but she never comes, and she hasn't told me why."

"It's like Betsy has deliberately isolated herself from her former friends. I wonder why."

"If you figure that out, let me know." Pastor Stan picked up his plate of cobbler and melting ice cream and then turned to Sam with a thoughtful expression. "You know, you and Betsy might get along fairly well since you both love to cook. If you get a chance to chat with her, get to know her a little, you might even become good friends."

Sam remained in the kitchen a few seconds longer, thinking about Pastor Stan's words. That might be a good idea, instead of just listening to the gossip about Betsy. And, as perhaps Betsy had done with Lorna, maybe it would be a good idea to scope out the competition.

CHAPTER

Ten

*L*ast night at dinner, Caroline hadn't been feeling all that excited about visiting a wedding planner with Trish, but she'd promised and didn't think it would be very polite to cancel on Trish or her friend the planner at the last minute.

But now, as she sat in Linda Goodnight's office and began to describe her ideas for the wedding, she began to get more and more excited about it, and was glad Trish had taken her to see a planner.

The wedding planner wasn't glamorous or snooty like the ones Caroline had seen in the movies and on television. Linda had a wide, open smile and graying red hair cut into a simple bob. Wedding paraphernalia filled every nook of her tiny office, but everything was meticulously organized.

Linda nodded as she listened to Caroline and took notes. "Your wedding dress idea is great, but it's also the most tricky. The special fabric you want would have to be shipped in, but I know a wonderful dressmaker in town who could sew it for you if you just show her a picture of what you want. She's not a New York designer, but she's very good at replicating anything you show to her."

"I half expected you to tell me I'm crazy," Caroline said.

"You're not crazy. I think a brightly colored wedding dress rather than a white or pale one is a beautiful idea."

"I do too," said Trish. "Have you thought about how many people you're going to invite?"

"I hadn't wanted too many—"

"But if you do an exotic-themed wedding with the rose petals and the hall draped in silk and the special wedding menu, like you've been describing, don't you want to show it off to more people?"

This was the second time Trish had mentioned that, and Caroline had a nagging sense of being pushed. Her natural tendency was to immediately push back a little, but Trish had a good point, and her enthusiasm was infectious. Caroline had so many ideas for a wonderful, unique wedding atmosphere, and she wanted to invite people so they would get caught up in the romance and fantasy of it all and leave feeling like they'd had a wonderful day in a dream world.

"What's your budget?" Linda asked.

Caroline hesitated. She actually had some money saved up because she had lived very simply. Her trips had been work-related except for the times she visited her family, and those hadn't been expensive since she usually stayed with her sisters. But did she want to tap into her rainy-day fund? She turned the tables. "How much do you think all this is going to cost?"

Linda looked over her notes. "I'll give a conservative estimate of twenty thousand dollars."

Caroline couldn't breathe for a moment. "Really?"

"There are plenty of ways to cut costs," Linda said matter-of-factly, not at all dismayed by Caroline's reaction. "We can simplify the dinner menu, for instance. Go for cheaper dishes like plain chicken or fish."

But Caroline had spent a couple of hours thinking about her wedding dinner. The menu was charmingly eclectic because it included all the things she loved most and wanted to share with people—a couple of her mother's favorites, some dishes she had discovered on her travels that she'd especially loved, other foods that represented her most beloved trips.

"We can also have a smaller wedding cake for display and then plain sheet cakes to cut up for the guests," Linda said.

But the special cake Caroline had wanted was a fruit, syrup, sponge cake with cream confection she'd had in Italy. She wanted to share its delectable flavors with her friends and family. To replace it with a plain sheet cake would be disappointing.

But...twenty thousand dollars!

"Why don't you think about what elements of the wedding you want to keep, and what you can do without, and also how much you're willing to spend," Linda said kindly. "I'm very flexible. What's important to me is that your day is exactly what you want."

"Thanks," Caroline said, but inside she cringed at the thought of needing to trim some of the most creative elements of her wedding just because of something so mundane as cost.

But she couldn't possibly afford twenty thousand dollars for a wedding. She'd just bought an inn, which cut back on her travel writing—almost completely, in fact. And with getting married, what other sources of income would she have?

However, she also knew about how much money she had left in her bank account, and she had to admit that she could probably afford the twenty thousand dollars. She and George had very simple tastes, and their living expenses together would be minimal. It just scared the living daylights out of her to think of spending so much money all at once on a single event as opposed to an investment like the inn or a house.

"Another way to decrease costs is to make your own invitations." Linda found a large binder on one of her shelves. "Take this home with you and look through it. These are some of the more interesting wedding invitations my clients have made themselves. For someone who has an artistic eye like you do, I think you'll enjoy just looking through them." She had a twinkle in her eye as she handed the binder to Caroline.

Caroline flipped to the first page and gasped at the lovely invitation that had been printed on card stock, but then embellished with hand-knitted lace and clusters of twisted organdy rosettes.

"I think you're right," she breathed as she stared at the invitation. She couldn't knit, but she could already see that other brides had let loose on their creativity in making these invitations, and she couldn't wait to look through them with her sisters. Sam and Gracie would be delighted to see these.

"You mentioned your sister bakes, right?" Linda handed her another binder. "These cakes were made by professional cake designers and bakers, but I'm sure there are some designs your sister would love to try to do herself, and she could bake your wedding cake."

"Oh, and look at these." Trish had been looking through Linda's shelves, but she now grabbed a binder and flipped it open to show to Caroline. The flower arrangements were wonderfully varied, showing some that were elaborate and formal and others that were almost bohemian. "I'm sure you could get great ideas from this book too."

"Go ahead and take that," Linda said. "There's even a section of arrangements of local summer flowers that a few Nantucket brides had done for their weddings."

"Thank you," Caroline told Linda as she stood to leave. "I appreciate all the options you're giving to me."

Linda placed a hand on Caroline's arm. "I'm not here to push you to do a huge lavish wedding," she said with an understanding look on her gentle face. "You do the wedding you want to do. If it's exotic like the ideas you were describing to me, I can help you do that. Or if you want something a little simpler, I can do that too."

"But your wedding sounds amazing," Trish interjected. "I haven't ever heard of some of the things you want to do, like the part about serving tea to your sisters and their families. That's wonderful."

"It's actually a Chinese custom, to show respect to the family, but I wanted to tweak it to show my love for my sisters and their families."

They said good-bye to Linda and left her tiny office, a sweet little cottage on the edge of the town that looked like it might have once been a gardening shack, but had been renovated. They walked under the climbing roses framing the doorway and as they passed the roses clustered over the windows on their way to Trish's rental car, they walked through a cloud of spicy, delicate scent.

"Didn't I tell you how Linda was wonderful?" Trish got into her car and Caroline got in the passenger side.

"She's really nice."

"She's been a friend for a few years. She used to write romance novels too, but for the Christian market. When her business took off, she stopped writing as many books a year."

"I'm amazed she would have time to write and run her business."

"She loves both. And since her business isn't as busy here on Nantucket as it was in New York, she has more time for her writing and her family."

"That's wonderful. When I was at the peak of my travel writing, I often wished I had more time to spend with my family. I should have listened to my gut and slowed down so I could take more trips to see my mom. I'm glad my sisters and I are running the Misty Harbor Inn now. We're becoming even closer than before."

Trish hesitated and then said, "I really like how almost all the things in your wedding have some special meaning for you or your family."

"I think that as I've gotten older, I'm realizing how much my family means to me."

They drove in silence for a few minutes, but as the roads grew more open and they were on their way back to the inn, Trish began gushing more about the different ideas Caroline had had for the wedding.

Caroline joined in the conversation, and while a part of her was excited about the things she wanted to do, another part of her quailed at the expense.

Could she really spend twenty thousand dollars on her wedding? Was she crazy?

But then she thought about each element, and how she didn't want to eliminate a single one of them. They all had meaning for her, symbolism, and happy memories that she wanted to share with people.

Maybe it would be worth the cost to share some of that happiness and beauty with the people she cared about, and with the island she now called home.

Sam and Evelyn were both having a great time at the library's children's craft day. Sam flitted from child to child, helping out where she was needed, chatting with the parents who had come. One particularly difficult little boy was throwing a tantrum because his turn with the sparkly glue stick was up, and he didn't want to relinquish it to the dark-haired little girl who had been waiting patiently for it.

The little boy's mother, a thin woman with her son's curly blond hair, tried to soothe little Davy, but her nervous words only made him wail and howl louder.

Finally Sam squatted in front of Davy and addressed him in a low, soothing voice. Her calm demeanor started to affect him, because his cries slowly grew softer and softer until he was whimpering and sniffling as opposed to yelling at the top of his lungs.

"Davy, do you know what gets to happen when you share your things?"

"N-no."

The mention of the S word threatened to send him into another full-blown crying session, but Sam quickly said, "When we share what we've been using, then that means we get to use what someone else has been using. Something even cooler."

Davy didn't answer, but his eyes roved over the other items on the table, which he hadn't bothered to notice since he'd been obsessed with the sparkly glue stick. He immediately lighted on a stamp in the form of a train and Sam quickly got him a blue ink pad so he could stamp trains to his heart's content.

"I don't know how you did that, but you're amazing," Davy's mother told Sam in a low voice.

"It comes with lots of practice. It's hard not to get upset when kids are upset, and I have to make sure I stay calm and collected so that they start to calm down."

"Where's your child?"

"Oh, my daughter's all grown up. I brought my grandniece." Sam pointed to Evelyn.

"She must love you, you're so good with kids."

"I used to teach first and second grade, but I retired early."

"Really? Oh, I wish you were Davy's teacher at school. You know just how to handle him."

"It just comes with practice."

"No," the woman said fervently, "you have a gift. There are some things where either you're good at it or you're not. You have a natural instinct with children."

"Thank you."

The woman went back to watching over Davy, who was starting to eye the sparkly glue stick again, and Sam went on to see if any other child needed help.

"Thanks for helping out today, Sam." Timothy, the librarian, came up to her with a wide grin. "I'm so glad I happened to mention the craft day to Caroline last week at church so she could tell you about it. I don't think I could have handled this many people on my own. I heard what Mrs. Russell said to you. Why did you retire early?" His light brown eyes were curious.

Sam hesitated. "Well, I thought I was ready to get on with other things."

"Like what?"

"Like running the inn with my sisters, and doing more baking."

"Caroline said you were going to enter the Summerfest baking contest." He gave her his boyish grin, making him look like a college student instead of in his early thirties. "What are you entering?"

The thought of the contest made her more depressed instead of excited. "I was going to enter my blackberry cobbler."

Timothy raised his sand-colored eyebrows. "I sense a 'but.'"

"Well, I made a change to the recipe last night, and while it finally tasted the way I wanted it to, the change made the filling too watery, which made the pastry soggy."

"Was it pretty bad?"

"Not really, I don't think anyone except my sisters noticed, and that's only because they've been tasting my cobbler for the past week or two. But I was disappointed because I'm not sure what to do now. If I change it back, it won't taste the way I want it to, and I'm not sure how to tweak it." Explaining her frustration to Timothy only seemed to make her more upset. "Maybe I shouldn't enter the contest."

He gave her an encouraging pat. "Don't think that way. The way to guarantee losing is not to enter."

Sam thought about what Mrs. Russell had said about some things not being able to be learned. What if baking was something she just didn't have a natural talent for? Was she doing all this work for nothing?

"Baking has become so much more difficult than teaching ever was," Sam said. "Teaching came so easily to me, but the baking contest has made me realize that this baking stuff just doesn't come naturally to me."

"Well, maybe—" But at that moment, a crying child caught both of their attentions, and Sam never found out what Timothy had been about to say.

Sam had thought the far table the most under control. It was occupied by a dark-haired mother with her four children, the youngest only a toddler, and a woman about Sam's age with a narrow chin and long, sharp nose who had accompanied a young girl with flaxen waves, probably her granddaughter. The children seemed very quiet, with the exception of the toddler who was making quite a mess. The woman with the long nose was helping one of the dark-haired children while the dark-haired mother tried to pry something from the toddler's tight fist.

At that moment, when both adults were occupied, Sam heard the flaxen-haired girl say disdainfully to the dark-haired girl sitting next to her, "That's a terrible turtle. You can't draw at all."

The dark-haired girl went pale, but she didn't reply. She simply bent her head closer to her page and seemed to curl in on herself.

Before Sam could stoop down next to the flaxen-haired girl, she said to the other child at the table, "Don't you know that trees aren't orange? And you colored outside the lines too."

Sam had heard enough by then. She crouched down next to the flaxen-haired girl and read her name tag—"Angelica Meyer."

"Angelica, what you said to these two children was very unkind."

The child looked at Sam as if she were speaking Dutch.

"It's not nice to criticize other people's work. I think you should apologize."

The girl was old enough to understand what Sam was saying, but she was also cunning. "I don't know what 'criticize' means."

"The things you said about Dorothy's and Tommy's pictures were not nice."

"I was only telling the truth," Angelica said primly.

"Angelica," her grandmother said sharply. "Were you being rude again?"

Angelica thrust her lower lip out.

"I'm sorry," the woman said to Sam. "Angelica has been having a problem in school of being rude to the other children."

"I am not being rude," Angelica protested.

"What did you say to these children?" the woman said.

Angelica pouted a moment and then mumbled something, but all Sam caught was "ugly turtle" and "coloring outside the lines."

"That's not nice at all. You need to apologize," the woman said sternly.

"You're not my mother," the child shot back.

Even though Sam had been a teacher for so many years, the girl's rudeness to her grandmother surprised her.

But the woman took it in stride. "No, I'm not. I'm your great-aunt, which means I can tell both your mother and your grandmother what you just said to me."

Angelica looked mutinous, but she didn't reply.

"I'd like you to apologize, please."

Angelica gave a halfhearted apology to the two children, who glanced at her and seemed to inch their bodies away from her.

Sam appreciated how the woman was so firm with her grand-niece, but something about the woman's demeanor was cold and distant. She nodded to the woman and then went to the next table to see if anyone needed help.

At the table was Eugenie Briggs, whose son Michael was in Sam's Sunday preschool class. She'd chatted briefly with Eugenie the couple of times she'd done the Sunday school class in the past few weeks, and now the redhead greeted her warmly. "How's the baking going?"

"Oh…okay." Last week, she had told Eugenie about entering the baking contest, but after talking to Timothy she didn't feel like going on anymore about it.

"I know I said this before, but if you ever need a tester for your blackberry cobbler, I'm a very willing guinea pig." Eugenie winked at her.

"How do you know it'll be any good?"

"Because if it's even half as good as those chocolate chip cookies you brought the other week, and those apricot bars you brought the week before, you'll have to beat me off with a stick."

Eugenie's enthusiasm cheered Sam up. Maybe she was being too hard on herself. Just because the baking contest was a new thing for her didn't mean she had absolutely no chance of winning. She knew she couldn't be completely horrible if so many people liked her baking.

"Mama"—Michael tugged at Eugenie's sleeve—"Evelyn's never ridden a pony before. Can she come over today and ride Bob?"

"Bob?" Sam asked.

Eugenie rolled her eyes and said quietly, "Don't ask. We let him name his pony, and he wanted Bob."

Evelyn came up to Sam with pleading eyes. "Please, can I go, Aunt Sam?" Sam's heart melted when she saw Evelyn acting more like her normal cheerful self rather than being as quiet as she'd been the past week.

Sam turned to Eugenie. "Is it okay with you?"

"Of course. We'd be happy to have her for lunch, and I can bring her back to the inn at five o'clock."

"Aunt Sam?" Evelyn said.

"We'll have to ask your grandma." Sam took out her cell phone and dialed Gracie. "Hi, Gracie. It's Sam."

"How are things going at the library?"

"Great. We'll be done in about half an hour. Michael Briggs invited Evelyn over to have lunch and ride his pony afterward. Is that okay?"

"Is she dressed for it?"

Sam asked Eugenie the question, who nodded and said, "She's fine."

"Gracie, Eugenie says that the way Evelyn is dressed is fine. She can also bring Evelyn back to the inn around five."

"It's fine with me if that's what Evelyn wants."

Sam glanced at Evelyn, who was hopping from one foot to the other. "It's most definitely what Evelyn wants."

Gracie laughed. "Permission granted, then. And thank Eugenie for me."

Sam hung up and said, "You can go." It sparked off a chorus of *whoops* from both Michael and Evelyn.

"I hope this isn't too much trouble for you," Sam said to Eugenie.

"No trouble at all. Our house is pretty near the inn, and having Evelyn there will be incentive for Michael to eat all his vegetables at lunch."

Sam grinned. "You're devious."

"I do what I can."

The rest of the craft time went quickly, and Sam was cleaning up when she heard someone come up behind her. She turned to see the sharp-nosed woman from earlier. The woman seemed cooler and even more distant than before, although Sam couldn't pinpoint anything in her manner or voice to give her that impression.

She smiled at Sam. "I wanted to thank you for helping me with Angelica."

"I didn't do much. You were the one who got her to apologize."

"I never introduced myself. I'm Betsy Carlisle."

Sam suddenly made the connection. Angelica's last name had been Meyer. "I'm Sam Carter."

She shook Betsy's hand, which was slim and cool but had a firm grip.

"I'd like to invite you over for lunch to thank you for your help today," Betsy said.

The invite was worded graciously, but somehow it made Sam feel uncomfortable.

"I overheard you talking to Eugenie Briggs," Betsy went on, "so when I heard that your grandniece was going to the Briggs's house, I thought I'd ask in case you were free."

Sam could have refused politely if she wanted to, but a part of her wanted to know if this was the real reason Betsy was seeking her out. Was it just because of Angelica or had she also overheard Eugenie talking about the baking contest?

Sam didn't want to be paranoid, but she couldn't help but remember Shirley's story about her friend and Betsy's competitive drive. Was she trying to size up the competition, or was Sam just being silly to think that Betsy cared at all about Sam's recipe?

She also remembered Pastor Stan's suggestion that she get to know Betsy better. There was something about the woman's manner that Sam didn't care for, but she also didn't want to be churlish. "I'd love to come to lunch. Thank you for asking. But I'll be a little late because I have to help clean up here."

"That's not a problem. I have to take Angelica back to her mom, so it works out perfectly. Why don't you come to my house?" Betsy wrote directions on a scrap piece of paper from one of the tables and gave it to Sam. "I'll see you there in forty-five minutes? Or whenever you're done here."

"Sure. Thanks again."

"No, thank you for helping out today." Betsy gave a quick, tight smile, and then went to collect Angelica, who was sneering at a child's bouquet of tissue flowers.

Sam and Timothy finished cleaning up, and, after a quick phone call to Gracie to let her know about Betsy's invitation, Sam easily found Betsy's house on the outskirts of the town. It was a large, modern house rather than a remodeled historical building like many of the others on Nantucket Island. However, it wasn't pretentious. Rather, it was large as if made to accommodate a large number of people. Sam remembered what she'd heard about the Meyers and figured they must be a rather large clan, which might explain why Betsy had such a large home.

There was plenty of paved space in front of the house for her minivan, although Sam felt out of place parking it next to the large Cadillac SUV already parked there.

However, the large front double doors showed some signs of wear—scratches and dents, most of them lower to the ground. Sam recognized that kind of wear, because she'd seen it on the doors at her elementary school.

She rang the doorbell and Betsy answered, swinging the door wide open. "Come in."

The inside of the house was simply furnished. Betsy didn't flaunt her wealth. Instead, the furnishings were sturdy and serviceable, and they gave Sam the impression that they were well-used by large numbers of guests. There were no delicate ornaments atop the surfaces of the tables or on the wide mantel over the fireplace in the living room, nor were there a lot of glass panes in the massive china cabinet that Sam glimpsed through the open doorway into the dining room. Everything was solid oak and as childproof as possible.

Betsy led her into the kitchen. "I thought we could have lunch at the breakfast table." She gestured for Sam to take a seat at a cute oak table in a nook in the kitchen, with windows overlooking a side garden full of vegetables.

The kitchen was a chef's dream, with a huge six-burner stove, two convection ovens, a stainless steel refrigerator and a separate upright freezer right next to it. Marble countertops gleamed spotlessly and there was marble atop the large island in the center of the kitchen. Cooking pots and pans were organized on a rack of stainless steel shelving in the corner, and there seemed to be dozens of oak cabinets.

Betsy seemed to notice Sam's awestruck gaze. "I'm almost ashamed to admit how proud I am of my kitchen. I designed it myself when my husband and I were building the house."

"It's wonderful," Sam said.

"I hope you don't mind a few reheated leftovers." Betsy nodded at some pots simmering on the stove.

"Of course not. It smells delicious."

"Let's start with the salad."

She served some baby field greens, but she offered a homemade dressing made with some type of citrus that Sam couldn't figure out.

"It's *yuzu*, an Asian citrus," Betsy said. "It's one of my favorite dressings to make. It won a blue ribbon at the county fair a few years ago," she added offhandedly.

Sam could see why. The dressing was unique but not too exotic, and it was a bright flavor over the delicate greens. "I love this, although I couldn't see my grandniece appreciating it. She'd probably ask for ranch dressing instead."

Betsy made a face. "My cousins' children are the same way." Her gray eyes softened. "I really am very grateful to you for how you helped with Angelica today. If you hadn't spoken to her about what she said, I would never have known she was being so rude to those children. She's gotten better about doing that sort of thing when the adults aren't watching her."

"You handled her very well."

"But I'm still just her great-aunt, not her mother." Betsy picked at her salad. "I sometimes hesitate because of that. And it's hard since my husband and I never had children, so I'm not always sure how to handle her."

"I think you handled it well. And you should tell her mother about what you saw."

"Angelica's mother doesn't often see her being rude to others, so she doesn't reprimand her. I don't think she even really believes Angelica can be that way."

"Sometimes, a child's peers can let her know her behavior isn't acceptable."

"I hope that happens."

Sam was beginning to warm to Betsy. She seemed insecure about Angelica, or children in general, and that was an area Sam had a great deal of experience in, so she could give advice and suggestions. But then they finished their salads, and Betsy seemed to become distant again.

"Are you ready for soup?" she asked Sam.

The soup, which Betsy had reheated on the stove, was an amazing carrot soup with miso and sesame oil to give it an exotic tinge, and garnished with lightly pickled scallions. Betsy mentioned some other cooking contest where the soup had won first place and chatted about the complicated process in making the soup and the scallions, which made Sam feel almost guilty to eat the soup itself. She could never make something so elaborate, but then again, she didn't think she would want to make something like this for herself or her family either. She tended to prefer to make comforting dishes, made with fresh ingredients and tweaked so that they melted in the mouth and were just right—not too sweet or too salty or too fatty.

"Do you enter a lot of contests?" Sam asked Betsy.

"Tons," she said airily.

"How did you get into baking and contests?"

"My family has always entered baking contests. My mother won the Summerfest baking contest five times in a row until she gracefully bowed out." There was a strange metallic tone to Betsy's voice as she said those last few words, but it was so subtle, Sam wondered if she only imagined it.

"So you come from a family of good cooks?"

"Yes, on my mother's side. All of them are good in the kitchen." She paused. "How about you?"

"I learned to cook from helping my mother when I was young. None of my other sisters really enjoyed cooking and baking the way Mom and I did."

"Was she good?"

"She never entered any baking contests, but I think she was very good."

"Oh," she said, "I see."

Something about Betsy's expression and the tone of her voice made Sam feel that the woman was skeptical about how good a baker Sam's mother had been. Sam searched Betsy's face but couldn't pinpoint what it was that gave her that impression.

Still, when coupled with the rather intimidating soup and salad dressing, it made Sam feel angry. Why did someone have to enter a contest to prove they were good? Sam knew in her gut that her mother's cooking had been outstanding, and Sam had learned from her and was using her recipes.

It was rude to imply that Sam's mother hadn't been a good cook just because she hadn't won a blue ribbon, and it made Sam want to prove Betsy wrong.

"Actually, I'm tweaking one of Mom's recipes to enter into the Summerfest baking contest," Sam said with a hint of defiance.

"Oh. Are you done? Ready for the main course?" Betsy removed Sam's soup bowl and returned with a marinated chicken breast smothered in a vegetable ragout over festive orange-colored noodles.

"The pasta tastes homemade," Sam said. "I thought at first it would be tomato, but it's bell pepper puree in the pasta dough? With a hint of red pepper, right?"

Betsy's face betrayed a slightly startled expression before she answered, "Why, yes."

The chicken had been cooked perfectly—not dry and yet not undercooked. The marinade flavors melded well with the bright vegetable ragout, which tasted like it had been made with fresh ingredients.

"This is delicious." That catty side of Sam made her add, "It probably tasted even better yesterday."

Something in the depths of Betsy's eyes faltered, and Sam was immediately ashamed of what she'd said. Even though Betsy hadn't been very kind about Sam's mother, it was no call for Sam to be so snide.

But it was only a fleeting expression. Quickly Betsy's eyes became a little harder as she said, "Oh yes, my family enjoyed it very much for lunch yesterday."

"Your family?"

"My mother came over with a couple of cousins. We were discussing the Summerfest baking contest too. Mom won't enter, but she wanted to know what I'd do."

"Do you know yet?"

"No. I'll probably be inspired with something later." She said it as if it weren't important to her. Maybe it wasn't since she'd already won the last four years. Or maybe it was an act because she had won the last four years and was defending her title, so to speak.

"You're entering blackberry cobbler, you said?" Betsy asked.

Actually, Sam hadn't said. But she had mentioned the blackberry cobbler to Eugenie at the library. So Betsy had overheard Sam talking about the baking contest. Was it unreasonable of Sam to think that Betsy had invited her to lunch specifically to try to intimidate her with these elaborate dishes? Those were the actions of the type of a woman who would snoop around Shirley's friend's house in order to steal a look at her recipe.

"I'm adjusting Mom's recipe. Blackberries tend to be acidic and I wanted to mellow the flavor of the filling so that it won't be so harsh on the tongue, but will still have that brightness of summer."

"That sounds delicious." Betsy's voice was a little strangled, but she cleared her throat. "Good luck on the contest."

Her tone seemed to imply that Sam wasn't really any competition. Sam could almost hear the words she hadn't said: Don't even bother.

It made the determination harden in her chest. She was going to win this contest with her mother's recipe, and show Miss Four-Times-a-Winner that a person didn't need to enter a million contests to be a good cook.

"Have you entered many contests?" Betsy asked Sam.

"No, this will be my first. I didn't get into baking or cooking until after I retired."

"What did you do?"

"I was a first- and second-grade teacher." Sam reflected that she'd been a great deal better at teaching than this baking stuff, and she missed working with children, despite the fact she'd begun helping out in the church preschool Sunday school a couple of days a month. "I've been wondering if I retired too early."

"You're still young. There's no reason you can't go back to work for a few years if you want to. And with your experience, you could pick and choose where you wanted to teach."

Betsy's words were reasonable, but Sam bristled inwardly. Was Betsy implying that Sam ought to go back to teaching and leave this baking stuff to the "professionals"?

As Betsy went to get dessert, Sam was torn. She wanted to win this contest with her mother's recipe, but she also had some doubts about her abilities as a baker. She sometimes felt she didn't have much to do at the inn since Gracie was so good at playing hostess to the guests and Caroline had been busy lately with her wedding. All Sam did was bake some breakfast goodies for the guests and then a smaller lunch and dinner for the sisters, with an occasional larger dinner like she did the other day. What was her role at the inn?

As a teacher, she knew her role and her work hours, and she had always had a confidence in her abilities. She'd never experienced so much self-doubt as she had in the past couple of weeks since she started working on the recipe for the baking contest. Maybe she really wasn't cut out for this.

But Betsy's smug look as she placed the plates of dessert in front of them fired up Sam's rebellious side again. It was a raspberry turnover, with a crust sparkling with sugar that had been laid out in lines in a crisscross pattern rather than just sprinkled on top.

"I warmed it in the toaster oven to crisp up the crust." Betsy sank her fork into the flaky top.

Sam stared at the sugar lines in disbelief. Betsy really could give Martha Stewart a run for her money.

But she also suspected it was all for show, and that Betsy knew how perfect this dessert was and was only too happy to show Sam what she was capable of making. And that only made Sam mad.

"This is good." Actually, it was amazing, but Sam schooled her expression into thoughtfulness. "My mom had a good turnover recipe too."

Betsy gave a condescending smile, and that sealed the deal for Sam. She was definitely going to show this woman that she wasn't the only person on Nantucket Island who could bake.

CHAPTER
Eleven

After the wonderful dinner the night before, Doris slept in late and Gracie didn't see her until almost eleven o'clock. She didn't mind because it was a beautiful day again, and she had a chance to work on the garden.

Gracie was elbow-deep in soft earth when Doris walked out onto the back porch and waved hello. She sat in one of the chairs and stared out toward the ocean, delight in her eyes.

Gracie finished patting the soil around a transplanted rose cutting and dusted herself off before walking up to the porch. "Did you sleep well?"

"Too much. I seem to need more sleep these days than I used to."

"I do too. Did you want something to eat? Sam left more of that soup we had last night in the fridge for lunch."

"You're not supposed to feed your guests all the time," Doris protested.

"I keep forgetting you're a guest." Gracie laughed. "You're almost a part of this place because of the wonderful stories you've been telling us." The previous night, Doris had told a few tales about her childhood years in Nantucket, which had been so different back then. It was before the tourist boom in the fifties, so island life had been simple and relaxed.

"Now that I'm rested I'll be able to tell you even more stories." Doris walked back into the house with Gracie.

Gracie scrubbed her hands and arms at the kitchen sink. "I can't wait to see your photos. I love old photographs."

"They're not as clear as modern photos. They're kind of fuzzy." She smiled at Gracie. "Just like my memory."

"That's what gives them character. I feel almost transported back in time to see old buildings and people." Gracie gathered some muffins for Doris to snack on.

"I feel that way when I chat with my cousins."

"You've been visiting them here on the island, right? How many do you have?"

"I have five distant cousins here, all on my father's side of the family. Johnnie was too old for us, but four of them would play with me. We were such rascals."

"They never left Nantucket?"

"The three boys went to war, but they all came back mostly whole. Johnnie's missing two fingers on his left hand, and Bobby's hearing is atrocious even with his fancy hearing aids."

Doris moved to the parlor and pointed to an old photo album she had apparently placed on a table. They sat at two comfy chairs around it, and Gracie set the basket of muffins on the table. She then leaned over the photographs.

"There's Johnnie." Doris pointed to a handsome teenaged boy. "He's actually my father's cousin. They were fifteen years apart, and my father treated him like a younger brother. He came with my parents to Nantucket."

"How old was he?"

"Only fourteen, but his parents knew my father would help watch over him. He stayed at a boarding house while he worked odd jobs for plumbers and carpenters. It was the start of the Great Depression, but he always said it saved his family for him to move to Nantucket."

"Why?"

"Nantucket's fishing and the summer season were both strong throughout the thirties, so he relieved his parents of the burden of feeding him, and he was always able to get some work and send money home to them."

"What a good son." Gracie traced the confident, independent face in the photo.

Doris showed an old building. "This was the movie theater. My cousins and I would sneak in. I did tell you we were rascals."

"Did you take these photographs?"

"Actually, my father did. He always liked photography, and he sold some photos to the tourists during the summer months."

"Were there many tourists during the Depression?"

"Oh yes. Not as many as there would be later, but there was a whole colony of artists who rented cheap cabins along the wharf for the season, and they had art festivals that brought tourists from the mainland." Doris flipped through a few pages and showed a photo of a thin woman with long dark hair, looking very seventies-ish even though this was from the thirties. "This is Cleopatra."

Gracie choked. "Who?"

"I don't remember her real name, but she called herself Cleopatra. She rented one of the cottages and she was a painter. She would always give us lemon drops she had made herself."

Doris flipped back to the first pages. "Here's Bobby. His brother is Stephen." She pointed to two boys posing on bicycles. "This was the only picture my father took of them because they were always running here and there."

"Bobby is the one who lost his hearing in the war?"

"Yes. He was sixteen, and Stephen was fifteen when the war started, so they both lied about their ages and joined the navy." Doris laughed. "Some days I can't remember if I had breakfast or not, but looking at these photos helps me remember the old days so clearly."

She turned a page to a photo of four young girls. "This is us girls. Mary was Bobby and Stephen's younger sister. Their father was my father's cousin Joe, who came to Nantucket with us in 1932 to look for work. He worked at the fishery." She pointed to another girl. "That's Jane. Her mother was also my father's cousin, and they came to Nantucket a year after we moved here. Jane's father was an architect, and he managed to get work when the historical society began saving some of the Nantucket historical buildings during the Depression in order to create jobs."

"It seems like Nantucket took care of itself during those difficult times."

"People tried to. The island was very tightly knit." Doris pointed to a skinny girl with dark hair who looked very much like Jane. "That's me."

"You look very happy." Gracie was struck by the blinding smile on Doris's face in the photo.

"Oh, I had forgotten." Doris smiled almost as brightly as her younger self in the photo. "Father took this photo right after telling us we were going to go to New York for his sister's wedding. I was so excited to go see the Empire State Building. At the time it had just been built and it was the world's tallest building."

She pointed to a blonde-haired girl who looked strangely familiar to Gracie. "And this was my cousin Rosalie. She stayed with us here in the house for a couple of years, and Father took this picture just before she left to go back home."

"Rosalie? That was my mother's name." A strange, urgent pressure began to build in Gracie's chest. "Could I see that photo?"

Doris passed the album to her, and Gracie peered closely at the blonde girl. Her face looked a great deal like Caroline's, but her straight blonde hair was cut shoulder length like Gracie's. "Doris, you said Rosalie was a cousin also?"

"Like the others, she was a distant cousin. I was closer to her than to any of my other cousins because she lived with us here in Montague House. The house's owners, the Fortescues, weren't here very often because Mrs. Fortescue became sick only a few months after they bought this place from the Montague brothers. So Rosalie and I would pretend we owned the house ourselves. Or we would go down to the secret room in the basement and pretend we were prisoners in the Bastille or princesses trapped in a stone cellar."

"How old was she?"

"Our birthdays were exactly a month apart. I was born April twelfth, 1926, and she was born May twelfth."

The bottom dropped out of Gracie's stomach. "May twelfth, 1926? You're sure?"

"Yes. What's wrong, dear?"

"My mother, Rosalie, was born on May twelfth 1926. And in this photo, she looks a lot like my sister Caroline. Do you remember what her last name was?"

Doris frowned as she stared at the photo. "I… I'm not sure. Maybe… Kingsman? No, Kingsburg?"

"Kingsbury?" Gracie held her breath.

"Oh yes. Yes, that was it. She joked once that her ancestors had secretly buried a king they had assassinated."

"Doris," Gracie breathed. "You played with my mother."

"Why, that's wonderful. What a coincidence. She was a distant cousin of mine too, so that means we're related."

Doris looked absolutely thrilled, but Gracie's heart was beating fast as unease unfurled in her stomach.

"That must be why your family came here for vacations," Doris said. "Rosalie loved Nantucket. When it came time for her to leave, she almost didn't want to go."

But Gracie shook her head. The news about her mother loving Nantucket as a child only troubled her more. "Doris, I…" She couldn't finish her sentence.

"What is it? What's wrong?"

Gracie took Doris's finely veined hand in her own. "It's true, we loved vacationing here in Nantucket when we were children. But my mother"—she swallowed—"Mom told us several times that she'd never been to Nantucket before her honeymoon."

Doris's blue eyes widened.

"I don't understand." Gracie's hands trembled as they clasped Doris's. "If Mom spent two years here in Nantucket with you as a child, why would she lie to us?"

CHAPTER
Twelve

Caroline became alarmed when Gracie ran out of the inn toward them just as she and Trish pulled up. Max was at her sister's heels, barking madly.

However, Gracie didn't have a panicked "bad news" face. Rather, Caroline thought, it was her excited "you won't believe this" face.

"Hello," she greeted Trish heartily as the writer got out of her rental car.

Trish, however, flinched away from her because Max chose that moment to rise up on his hind legs to try to jump on her.

"Max!" Caroline scolded him, and he backed down, although his tail still wiggled furiously. "Trish, I'm so sorry. He didn't get mud on you, did he?"

"No. At least he stopped barking," she said with exasperation. "His barking kept me from writing yesterday."

"That's my fault," Gracie said apologetically. "Evelyn and I were out in the backyard playing with him. We'll stop doing that while you're here."

Trish flushed slightly. "No, don't stop playing with your dog and your granddaughter just because of me."

"Oh, don't worry, we'll just head down to the beach to play instead so the noise won't bother you." Gracie's smile was sweet and gentle. Trish's answering smile seemed a little abashed at her complaining.

Caroline again marveled at how Gracie could connect so easily with the guests, making them feel at home, being a perfect hostess. In contrast, Caroline sometimes felt like she was blundering around when it came to running the inn and serving the guests. She was so grateful that Gracie had decided to come live here in Nantucket and sell her house. Caroline wondered how that was going. Gracie hadn't mentioned it recently.

"Well, I need to get back to work," Trish said.

"Thanks for taking me to see Linda," Caroline said as they walked into the house.

"Isn't she fabulous? I know she'll help you with your dream wedding." Trish headed upstairs to her room.

Gracie waited until they heard Trish's door close when she grabbed Caroline's arms in a tight grip. "You won't believe what I found out today. I've been dying waiting for you and Sam to come home."

"I'm sorry I'm late. Trish and I were starving after spending all morning with the wedding planner, and I knew Sam wouldn't be making lunch because of the library craft day, so Trish and I stopped off at a restaurant in town for soup and a sandwich." She and Trish had had a surprisingly enjoyable lunch looking through the binders while they munched on their turkey cranberry sandwiches and homemade chicken noodle soup at the tiny café on the edge of the wharf. Trish had

an amazing imagination—not surprising considering her profession—
and she and Caroline had had an entertaining brainstorm about
possible invitation designs, cakes, and flowers. Caroline still wasn't
anywhere close to a decision, and the cost was still causing an ache in
her belly, but the lunchtime hour had been lots of fun.

"Wait a minute, did you say Sam wasn't home yet?" Caroline
asked. "Where's Evelyn?"

"Evelyn went to play at a friend's house—Eugenie Briggs from
church, you know her, right? Her son Michael invited Evelyn to come
ride his pony this afternoon, and since she's never ridden one, she
asked to go."

"So where did Sam go?"

"She said she got invited to Betsy Carlisle's house for lunch."

"The woman Sam was telling us about, who won the baking
contest for the last four years? She invited Sam to lunch?" Caroline
didn't have a good feeling about that. "Did Sam say why?"

Gracie shook her head. "I'm wondering if it has to do with the
contest. But what would they have to talk about?"

"I guess we'll find out when she gets home. How was the time
with Doris? I hated to miss that."

"That's what I wanted to talk to you two about. But I guess I'll
wait until Sam gets home—"

At that moment, they heard the minivan rolling up the driveway
and heading toward the carriage house. Caroline quickly stopped by
the parlor to drop off the wedding binders and then joined Gracie.
They both headed out the back toward the carriage house and were
there even before Sam had turned off the engine. Max had again
started barking in response to their haste.

"I've been waiting for you to get home," Gracie said.

"Is everything all right?"

"Everything's fine. Even better, really. You won't believe what I found out today."

"Max, hush," Caroline said to him, and he subsided.

"Let's take him for a walk," Gracie suggested. "That way he won't bother Trish."

"Was she complaining about the noise again?" Sam said as they headed toward the beach. "Yesterday she complained about how she could hear me and Evelyn talking in the kitchen. I felt bad, since she's our guest and she's here to work, but at the same time, the walls aren't soundproof and this is an inn. There's going to be some noise."

"Well, I'll be sure to have Evelyn play with Max on the beach away from the inn." Gracie took off her shoes, same as Caroline and Sam. "The problem is that Evelyn seems moody and sad, and playing with Max is one thing that makes her perk up. I don't want her to feel she has to curb her playing with Max."

"I've noticed her quietness too," Caroline said. "Is everything okay at home?"

"As far as I know," Gracie said. "Brandon thinks she might just be homesick, but something about the way she's acting makes me wonder if there's something else going on."

"Have you talked to her about it more?" Sam asked.

"Yes, but she won't tell me what's wrong. She insists she's fine."

"Maybe Caroline and I can talk to her," Sam said. "She might mention something to one of us."

"Yes, would you? I'd appreciate it." Gracie gave a long sigh.

"So what were you so excited to tell us?" Caroline didn't want to be insensitive about Evelyn, but she was dying to know what Gracie had to tell them.

"I was flipping through Doris's photo album and she was telling me about how she'd play with her cousins. Her five cousins are still here on the island, and she's been visiting them."

"When was this, again?" Caroline asked.

"Back in the early thirties. Right after the stock market crash and before the war. She had a distant cousin come stay with her and her parents here at Montague House." Gracie turned to look at her sisters. "Doris's cousin's name was Rosalie Kingsbury."

"What?" Sam burst out.

"That was Mom's maiden name," Caroline said.

"Doris is napping right now, but when you get a chance, look at the photo of Rosalie in Doris's photo album," Gracie said. "She looks exactly like Caroline. It can't be just a coincidence."

"We're related to Doris?" Caroline said.

"Distant cousins." But Gracie's face was grave. "Do you remember Mom talking about the first time she came to Nantucket?"

"I remember she talked about her first view of the beach, how wide it was, how loud the waves were, and how fresh it smelled," Caroline said.

But Sam had slowed her step. "But she said it was when she came here on her honeymoon."

The truth suddenly hit Caroline. "I remember Dad saying that too. He and Mom came to Nantucket for their honeymoon because she'd never been here before. But if Doris has a photo of her—"

"She was here as a little girl," Sam added.

"And she lied to all of us about it," Gracie finished.

The three of them fell silent for a long moment as they strolled along the beach, the sand warm under their bare feet. Max trotted back to Caroline from his wanderings, but she didn't stoop to pet him or give him attention. She was too shell-shocked to do more than stare at him as he looked up at her.

"Why would Mom lie?" Caroline finally said.

"I don't understand." Sam turned to Gracie. "Are you sure it was Mom?"

"Doris knew Rosalie's birthday because it was one month from hers."

"Don't tell me," Sam said. "May twelfth, 1926?"

Gracie nodded.

"That's too coincidental, with Mom's maiden name," Caroline said.

"And the picture, don't forget that," Gracie said. "She not only stayed here in Nantucket, she was actually here at the Misty Harbor Inn."

"Do you think that's why Mom always dreamed about buying it and running it herself?" Sam asked.

For Caroline, it was like a puzzle piece fitting into place. Like her sisters, she knew her mother loved the place but never understood exactly why it had meant so much to her. "That's why it was this inn she wanted and not some other one on Nantucket. It wasn't just that she liked this building or this spot. She loved it because she'd been here as a child."

"According to Doris, she lived here for two years," Gracie said. "She and Doris were the same age, about seven or eight. They would explore the secret passage to the basement, help her father with the garden, help her mother in the kitchen and learn to cook—"

"Last night, she said my chicken was just like her mother's," Sam said. "That recipe was from Mom. What if Mom learned it from Doris's mother?"

The connections were weaving in tighter and stronger now.

"Doris said that Rosalie loved it here," Gracie said. "She wanted to stay in Nantucket forever, but she left after two years and never came back. Doris and her family moved from Nantucket a year later, and she never saw Rosalie again."

"Why did Mom come to Nantucket?" Sam asked.

Gracie shrugged. "That's the frustrating part. Doris doesn't know why, or if her parents told her, she doesn't remember. She does remember that Rosalie never talked about her family at all, which struck her as odd at the time, but since they were friends, Doris never pushed Rosalie about it."

They walked in silence a few minutes more and then Caroline said, "I feel a little...betrayed." She felt guilty just voicing the thought.

"Me too," Sam said softly.

"There has to be a reason," Gracie reminded them. "Mom wouldn't lie about something as inconsequential as staying here in Nantucket as a child unless she had a really good reason to do it."

"Did she get into some sort of trouble while she was here?" Caroline asked. "Maybe that's why she didn't say anything."

"I don't know. Doris didn't say anything about that."

"If Mom had a reason, she took it to her grave," Sam said.

With one accord, they headed back toward the inn, but the sisters didn't speak. Caroline had mixed feelings about it all. Why had their mother lied? What was so awful or mysterious about Nantucket and the Montague House that she had deliberately misled them all, including her husband? And why did it hurt her so much to find this out after their mother was gone?

"How are things going with selling your house?" Sam asked Gracie.

Her brow clouded for a moment. "I think I need to take out a loan to make some improvements to the house before it'll sell."

"What improvements? I thought your house was in great shape," Sam said.

"I thought so too, but the Realtor says it needs upgraded toilets and things like that. I had a horrible lowball offer on the house that I refused. That's what makes me think I'll need to do something to make the house sell at a better price."

"That seems so unfair," Caroline said. It felt wrong that her sister needed to do so much to sell that house, and it would be hard because she wouldn't be there to oversee the work.

Gracie sighed. "It's what the Realtor suggested. I'll pick up a loan application from the bank the next time I'm in town, I guess."

Caroline supposed if the Realtor had determined it needed to be done, who was Caroline to say otherwise? "You might be able to get Paige to help supervise the renovations on the house. Isn't she moving to Portland soon?"

"Yes, she's looking for a new apartment because she's been interviewing for some government jobs in the city."

"Couldn't Paige buy your house?"

For a moment, there was a look of joy that glowed on Gracie's face. But then it faded. "No, Paige can't possibly afford it."

They sat at the dining room table and had tea and more cobbler. Caroline hated to admit it, but she was starting to get tired of cobbler. However, she didn't tell Sam because she seemed to be working so hard on the recipe.

"So what happened at Betsy Carlisle's house?" Gracie asked Sam.

Caroline was surprised to see Sam's face harden.

"I'm pretty sure Betsy invited me because she overheard me telling Eugenie Briggs that I was going to enter the Summerfest baking contest."

"Oh, did she want to compare notes?" Gracie asked.

Sam gave a snort. "I kind of think she wanted to intimidate me. Everything she served me was something fancy that could have been made on *Iron Chef*."

"Sounds like you weren't intimidated." Caroline smiled.

Sam blinked. There was uncertainty there for a brief moment, and then she smiled back at Caroline. "No way. She was so condescending and implied that only people who win a baking contest can be considered a good baker."

"Mom was fantastic," Caroline said hotly.

"That's why I'm going to prove Betsy wrong," Sam said. "I'm going to use Mom's recipe and see how she likes losing."

It was kind of fun to see Sam fired up this way, but a part of Caroline wondered if the competition was getting to her. She'd been already spending a ton of time on this recipe. It was becoming just a little obsessive, in Caroline's opinion.

However, Gracie seemed supportive of it, so Caroline held her tongue. But she'd watch Sam a little closer from now on.

At that moment, her cell phone rang and she saw it was George. She went into the parlor to take the call. "Hi, George."

"Are you free to look at another house?"

There was a *thump! thump!* in the pit of her stomach at the words, but she mustered up an enthusiastic, "Sure. I'm here at the inn."

"I'll pick you up in about ten minutes. Is that okay?"

"Great."

Caroline's eye fell on the three binders she'd brought back with her from the wedding planner's office, and remembering the fun brainstorming she and Trish had done at lunch, her mood lifted. She needed the right attitude for this house outing with George. Like with the wedding planning, a new house was a blank canvas, an opportunity for her to stretch her creativity muscles in making a cozy home for George and herself. And house-hunting was shopping for the right blank canvas to start on.

George arrived on time, and Caroline hopped into his car, determined to enjoy this time with him and this opportunity to look at homes. Her negative attitude about the wedding and their new home would only taint their marriage if she let herself wallow in it, so she was determined to bring only joy and hope into this new stage of her life, not regrets and misgivings.

"You're cheerful today," George commented as they drove out toward 'Sconset.

"It's a nice day, I'm spending it with you, and my sisters and I discovered something surprising today." She told him about what Gracie had found out about their mother and Doris.

She had never seen his eyebrows rise that high before. "You're related to Doris? And your mother lived in your house when she was a child?"

"Isn't it amazing? It explains why Mom loved this inn so much and wanted to buy it someday."

"She never told you about this?"

Caroline hesitated. "Well, that part does concern me. In fact, Mom told us she never visited Nantucket before her honeymoon."

"Are you sure? Why would she tell you that?"

"We don't know. But I knew my mother. She wouldn't lie about something like that if she didn't have a good reason for it, so I'm going to just give her the benefit of the doubt and focus on the wonderful aspects of what we've found out—this place, and that inn, is supposed to be ours. We belong here on Nantucket."

"I'm starting to feel like I belong here too. I can't wait for us to have our own place to call home."

"Me too," Caroline said determinedly.

Once in 'Sconset, they drove toward the ocean along a street lined with charming little bungalows. Unlike the last house they'd seen, these homes had side yards separating the houses from each other, but the homes seemed tiny. Perhaps it was just the angle and they opened up more inside.

"I want you to see two houses today," George said. "One's in our budget and one is…well, it's not impossible."

"But George, you know I don't have as much that I can contribute to the house because of the inn. I don't want you to pay too much for it."

George parked the car outside a white cottage surrounded by tall hedges flanking a white gate. There was a narrow driveway on the side, but trash cans from the neighbors blocked it. A gold Mercedes was parked on the street.

He turned and looked at her. "Caroline, you know I'd live in a shack if I could be with you. But I also want a nice home for the two of us. Someplace where we can be alone, where we can chat and sit and dream, someplace where we can be ourselves."

He didn't often use lyrical language like this, emphasizing the fact that their own space meant a great deal to him. They couldn't have that kind of privacy, that kind of intimate space of their own at the inn.

George went on, "Here on Nantucket, it's hard to find someplace like that that isn't a little pricey. But I'm willing to pay it and I don't want you to worry about how much you're contributing versus how much I'm contributing."

"I don't want you to hide our finances from me."

"I know that, and I will give you all the figures, even though I know they'll make your head spin."

The dimples stood out on his cheeks as he smiled at her, and she couldn't help but smile back. He really was a wonderful, dear man, and he knew her so well.

"Then I'll trust you in this," Caroline said.

He leaned over to give her a brief kiss. "Thank you. I won't fail your trust in me."

They got out of the car and opened the white gate, which squeaked a little as it swung open.

The real estate agent, Deborah Greenleaf, was standing in the open doorway to the tiny home and greeted them. "Welcome."

Inside, Caroline was surprised by a wide open area. The house was narrow but the living room was long and open, with a high ceiling and lots of windows to let in the light. There were large glass French doors open to a brick patio area surrounded by the tall hedge.

"A patio table and chairs would look perfect out there," Deborah said.

The living room and kitchen were all one open space, which Caroline wasn't sure she liked. The kitchen was small but adequate for herself and George—after all, she wasn't like Sam in the kitchen.

A small door off the kitchen led into a small bedroom with a bathroom.

And that was it.

"Only one bedroom?" Caroline asked.

"It's…cozy, but it's right on the ocean." Deborah led out to the patio where another gate stood in a break in the hedge. She opened the gate, and they were only a few feet from a bike path, and beyond that was the beach. This house was even closer to the beach than the inn.

"Houses next to the beach in 'Sconset are naturally a bit more expensive, which is why this one-bedroom home is only just within your budget. But it's in good shape, structurally, and this is a quiet neighborhood."

Caroline looked up and down the beach at the small clusters of families out in the sun. "How many of these houses are leased for the season?"

Deborah looked a little chagrined. "Probably more than half of them. So the neighborhood will be quiet in wintertime, but it gets busier in summer."

Caroline and her family had been one of those tourist families leasing a cottage on Nantucket, so she had nothing against vacationers, but it did mean they'd need to deal with various people who may or may not be considerate neighbors for the short time they were in their leased homes.

"I like how airy the house is with that one large room for the living room and kitchen area," Caroline said, "but it is a little small for the two of us. And I think I'd prefer a neighborhood that had more owners living there as opposed to lots of renters."

"Then you'll probably like the other home we're seeing today," Deborah said cheerfully. "Was there anything else you wanted to see here?"

"No, let's head to the other house," George said.

When they were in the car, Caroline said, "I'm sorry if I'm being picky. But it was hard to believe that house is so expensive. Still, I suppose being right on the beach—"

"Would you rather have a quieter neighborhood farther from the beach, then?"

Caroline sighed. "I'd like both a quiet neighborhood and a home right on the beach, but I doubt we'd find anything that we could afford."

She deliberately thrust from her mind the thought that the inn was in a quiet neighborhood, surrounded by houses with large lots lived in by their owners rather than rented or leased, and it was directly on the beach she loved so much.

The second house wasn't directly on the beach, but the road they drove on only climbed a few minutes away from the ocean before they turned onto a small side street lined with tall leafy trees. The houses again seemed small, but a little larger than the cottages on the seashore, and each had large side yards separating the homes.

They had been following Deborah, who parked in front of a single-story home with a tree shading the emerald green front lawn and the front of the house. She stuck a hand out her car window and waved them into the small driveway along the side of the house that led to a separate garage.

They met her outside the front door, which she'd already opened. The front stoop was rather spare, but the two windows on either side were large and inviting.

The door opened to a narrow but bright hallway with white wainscoting. A doorway on the left opened into a cozy living room with a wide brick fireplace and windows on two walls. Farther down the hallway, a doorway on the right opened into a dining room with robin's egg blue wainscoting, while a doorway on the left opened into a kitchen with sprigged wallpaper. The kitchen also had a charming inset nook that would be perfect for a breakfast table. The backyard was spacious, with trees and bushes blocking out the neighbors.

The house was lovely, and had great potential. Caroline knew she liked the neighborhood just by looking at it—the houses were all well tended with front lawns that ranged from manicured to eclectic, pointing to owners who cared about their own gardening. The ocean was close enough for her to walk to it, and yet the enclosed backyard made a nice haven just for the two of them to sit and enjoy the sunshine. She could see them sitting in two Adirondack chairs, glasses of iced tea in their hands, chatting about a book they'd read or a magazine article that fascinated them.

It was a lovely home, and yet…it wasn't the Misty Harbor Inn. They could find a house that exactly fit what Caroline envisioned for the two of them, but it still wouldn't be where she longed to be.

But George wouldn't be happy at the inn, and Caroline was determined to think of him rather than herself. He had good reasons for wanting their own house, and she loved him enough to want what was important to him.

"What do you think?" Deborah asked.

"It's beautiful," Caroline said. "But how much is it?"

"It's a little outside our original budget," George said, "but we could make it work."

Caroline bit her lip, but didn't want to repeat her concerns. She had told George she'd trust him.

She wandered through the rooms, admiring the large numbers of windows letting in the sunlight, the rustic wooden beams on the ceilings that lent charm to the atmosphere in the place. Caroline began to envision how she'd make the place their own, her mind beginning to draw strokes of color to this blank canvas. Perhaps antique wingback chairs in the living room, just like at the inn. This room could be the library, and she could find a brass chandelier to throw light on the fireplace. She could find another antique buffet for the dining room—it wouldn't have a gryphon like at the inn, but she was sure she could find something beautiful with lots of character.

"How much time do we have before we have to make a decision?" Caroline asked Deborah.

"The housing market is slow right now because it's nearing the tail end of summer. Most people buy houses at the beginning of the year, and it drastically slows down in the fall—maybe because most people who buy houses here want a vacation home, and they're not quite ready to buy it right as they return home from a summer at the beach with the kids going back to school. At the same time, you don't want to wait too long in case someone else snatches it up."

"Would you know if someone else was seriously looking at it?" George asked.

"Sure, in a small place like Nantucket," Deborah said, "I can let you two know right away."

"That would be wonderful," Caroline said. "I'd like to take some time to think about it."

"No problem."

Deborah locked up the house after them, and Caroline and George went to the car out in the garage.

"The house is awfully expensive," Caroline said to George.

He stopped in the act of starting the car and turned to her with eyes that seemed to see right into her soul. "I don't want you to have to worry about the cost."

"I know you told me that, but I just went to a wedding planner this morning and with everything I want for the wedding, it could cost a lot. I can cover it—I have plenty in savings—but that means it's money I can't contribute to the house, so it's making me feel a little guilty about the wedding plans."

He took her hands in his and rubbed his thumbs over her knuckles. "I want you to have the wedding you've always wanted. Don't let the house affect your plans. What's important to me is that you get what you want."

She gave a rueful laugh. "But I want you to get what you want."

He gave a hearty chuckle. "Look at the pair of us. There's got to be a way for both of us to get what we want for this wedding and this new stage of our lives."

He started the car and they started the drive back to the inn, but Caroline's mind was far from easy about things. Had she made the right decision in getting married? She loved George, but the financial decisions they had to make were causing her so much stress.

It would have been cheaper, she thought wryly, *for us just to have stayed friends.*

CHAPTER
Thirteen

The blackberry cobbler recipe still wasn't right. Sam frowned at it where it sat on the counter.

She didn't realize the bottle of vanilla extract had tipped over at the edge of the sink and was emptying its contents down the drain until it was almost empty. She saw the dark bottle and snatched it up, but only a few drops remained at the bottom.

She needed vanilla extract just in general, although she didn't think she needed it for the pecan ginger muffin recipe she had seen on the Food Network and had wanted to try and serve to the guests the next morning. But the day was nice outside, not too hot thanks to a gentle breeze, and she decided to walk to town to buy more extract as well as baking powder, since she was running low. It would also help clear her head after this frustrating morning of baking.

On her way to the store, she passed Jedediah's, the café on Main Street, and after buying the vanilla and baking powder, she headed back there to splurge on a mocha. As she approached the front doors, two young women exited the café, and Sam recognized one of them as the mother of curly-haired little Davy from the library craft day.

She recognized Sam also. "Hello, I don't think I introduced myself yesterday. I'm Alicia Russell, Davy's mom."

"Hi, I'm Sam Carter."

"I'm so glad I ran into you. Were your ears burning? I was just talking about you to my friend. This is Lenora Worth. She's the sixth-grade teacher at Davy's school."

Sam shook hands with the thin young woman who had a wide smile and thick, ash-blonde waves cut chin-length to frame her heart-shaped face.

"Why were you talking about me?" Sam asked Alicia.

"Lenora and I are in the same book club that meets here at Jedediah's. After our meeting, she and I were chatting, and she mentioned that her school has an opening for a second-grade teacher."

"I work for a small private Christian school, Daley Academy," Lenora said. "It's a little ways outside of town."

"When Lenora told me about the opening, I remembered you had said you used to teach first and second grade. I was telling Lenora about how well you handled Davy yesterday."

"I'm flattered, but really, it was nothing," Sam said. "Davy is a naturally good-natured boy."

"He was putty in your hands," Alicia insisted. "Do you think you'd ever consider coming out of retirement to teach for a few years?"

Sam was still determined to do her best for the Summerfest baking contest to try to prove herself and show up that condescending Betsy Carlisle, but what about after the contest? She didn't want to be a serial baking contestant like Betsy and her family.

Volunteering at the preschool Sunday school at church had made her realize that she still loved working with children, plus it seemed to come naturally to her. And she was only in her fifties. Going back to work now would be rather less stressful than her last position, since she would be working because she enjoyed it and not because she needed to pay her rent. Plus she could happily retire again when she felt like it.

She had always taught in public schools. A part of her hesitated because it was a Christian school. Did she really want to work there, and would they even want her? She had drifted away for a time, but her faith in God had once again become important to her, and she couldn't imagine a better place to teach again. And she was sure she could both teach and help run the inn.

"That might be something I'm interested in," she said.

Alicia beamed. "I would love it if they hired you. Then you would be Davy's teacher in a couple of years."

"How could I get an application form?"

"The job just opened, so they haven't distributed the forms yet," Lenora said. "But the school isn't far from here. Did you want to head there now to pick up an application, and I can give you a tour too?"

"Do you have time? I don't want to interrupt you."

"I'm free for the next couple of hours."

"And book club is over, so I need to pick up Davy from his cousin's house," Alicia said.

"That's fine. I'd love to see the school."

Sam rode in Lenora's car to Daley Academy, which was a cluster of yellow buildings on a wide tract of land outside of town. The landscaping was professionally done, but the school also boasted well-used playgrounds, a track field, and a baseball field.

Lenora used her key to let them into the main building. The school was closed for the summer, so the air smelled faintly musty, but the hallways and rooms were neat and clean. The office was a small square room with desks that had been packed away for the summer with computers shut down and file cabinets locked up.

Lenora went to one of the desks and picked up a paper from a stack on the center of it. "Here you go. I helped the school secretary with these only yesterday, which is why I knew about the job opening so early."

"What happened to the previous second-grade teacher?"

"She decided to retire. She's almost sixty-nine and she's been at this school since it opened in 1974."

That said a lot about the school, that a teacher would love working there for so long, well past regular retirement age. Sam glanced at the application form, which wasn't very extensive.

"With your experience as a teacher, you won't have any problems getting an interview," Lenora said. "Want to see the campus?"

"I'd love to."

They explored the classrooms, which included a computer lab, a science lab, and a brightly decorated kindergarten room that was larger than the other classrooms. The classrooms in general were well stocked with books and supplies, which surprised Sam.

"In my last school, we had a hard time getting enough supplies for the kids."

"Since this is a private school, our funding comes from trust funds and private donors. We've been very blessed. It really helps us as teachers to be able to concentrate on the kids and not be limited by resources."

The school had a spacious gym where Lenora said she coached the girls' volleyball team. There were various sport teams at the school, but Lenora admitted the school wasn't very competitive in athletics since it was so small.

"And this is the chapel." She led Sam toward a large building with a large pointed roof that framed a triangular painted glass panel. She unlocked the front double doors and they entered.

The plush carpet muffled their footsteps as they walked down the center aisle. Wooden pews on either side had probably been here since the school opened and had the appearance of being well-worn but also lovingly taken care of. Another stained-glass panel was at the front behind the altar, but the raised stage had a surprisingly modern musical setup, with a drum set, a piano, and cords flowing over the stage floor like waves.

"What are the cords for?" Sam asked.

"They're for the electrical and sound hookups for the worship band. We have a student worship band for Friday morning service here at school." She gave Sam an impish grin. "The kids love it, although the founding pastor would probably be turning in his grave to hear the drum set."

"A pastor founded this school?"

"This was originally a church. It opened in the sixties and expanded to a school in 1974. It's not used as a church anymore, but we still hold chapel every Friday morning. The pastor from Harvest Chapel comes to lead the service for us."

Suddenly Sam realized something she hadn't thought of before. She knew that some churches did expand into private schools—what if William Elliott's church had done the same? After they'd discovered old Mr. Elliott's journal, she and Gracie had gone online to see if they could find William Elliott's church, but they hadn't known in which state to look, and a Google search for his name had given them so many results, they had only been able to wade through a few dozen pages of links, none of them useful.

But now, thanks to the ticket, they suspected his church had been in Massachusetts. What if Daley Academy had access to databases for private Massachusetts schools that had originally been churches? Would she find William Elliott's church?

"Lenora, I know you just met me, but I wonder if you might be able to do me a favor."

Lenora raised her eyebrows expectantly.

"My sisters and I run the Misty Harbor Inn, which used to be owned by an old whaler, Jedediah Montague. Jedediah's second wife was Hannah Montague, and her brother William Elliott had a church in Massachusetts, we think, in the late 1800s. We've been trying to find it and had no luck, but it just occurred to me that his church might have become a school, just like Daley Academy."

"Oh. That makes sense. Daley is part of a much larger association of church-based schools like ours. Did you want to use our databases to search for it? I believe it lists present-day schools as well as historical records."

"Would you mind helping me do that?"

"Of course not. I grew up in Nantucket so I remember reading about Montague House and Hannah Montague's disappearance in the late nineteenth century." Lenora locked the chapel back up and led the way back to the office. "We can use the secretary's computer. I can log in with my password."

"Thank you so much."

Sam had occasionally done searches for other schools using the databases at her previous school. The databases often had a short description of the schools' statistics, and each entry also had a short paragraph about the school's history, which often included the name of the founders. If William Elliott's church had become a school, it would be in the databases, and they'd be able to search for his name to find it.

Lenora fired up the desktop computer and logged in. She opened up an advanced search window and limited it to schools in Massachusetts. She then put the name "William Elliott" in the search box and hit the "Search" button.

The school databases were extensive, so Sam wasn't surprised it took a couple of minutes for the search to complete. There were forty-two results, and they went through each school.

For many of the schools, the name "William Elliott" referred to a school staff member like the principal, vice-principal, or a teacher. Sam thought they'd found it when they saw William Elliott mentioned in the short historical blurb of one school, but it turned out that this William Elliott wasn't a minister but a banker who had funded the school when it first opened in 1982.

Then, near the end of the list, they found it.

Trinity Cross Academy in Adams, Massachusetts, had originally been Trinity Cross Church, founded in 1872 by William Elliott.

Sam's heart beat faster as Lenora printed out the information on the printer next to the computer. "I wonder if this is it," Sam said. "The date seems about right, late nineteenth century."

"Do you think William had something to do with Hannah's disappearance?"

"We're pretty sure he was Hannah's brother. We have the information that we found in the newspapers, and we found a set of cards written in a sort of code that William had sent to Hannah. But we also found old Mr. Elliott's journal where he mentions that William used to visit with his sister here on Nantucket after she married. William founded a church, but his father didn't know where because they had lost touch. There's no mention about what happened to Hannah, but if she ran away, it makes sense that she might have gone to her brother's church."

"If you do find out what happened to her, will you let me know? It's such an intriguing mystery."

"I'll be sure to do that. It's been exciting to discover things about the people who lived in our very own house over a century ago."

"That's one of the things I love about Nantucket. There's so much history here, and it's all been very well preserved."

They continued searching the last few entries, but there was nothing about a reverend William Elliott from the late nineteenth century founding the church that the school grew out of.

"Well, this has been fun." Lenora shut down the computer. "I feel a little like Miss Marple."

Lenora drove Sam all the way back to the inn, insisting that she'd like to see the house again since they'd just been doing some research related to it. She gazed up at it as Sam climbed out of her SUV.

"You guys have done a beautiful job of restoring it," Lenora said. "I remember it being a nice old house when I was a child, but it began to deteriorate with the last owners."

"It still creaks and leaks and feels its age, but we've come to love it."

"It shows. I hope you'll eventually work at Daley Academy."

"I'll turn in the application in a couple of days. Thanks for the ride."

Sam entered the inn. She was about to call out to her sisters when she remembered that Trish was upstairs working, so she instead headed to their bedrooms near the back of the first floor, but didn't find them. She didn't see Max around anywhere either.

Then she suddenly heard a huge crash from the carriage house.

CHAPTER
Fourteen

*I*t all happened because Evelyn had been in a particularly strange mood. After a long walk along the beach with Max, Gracie and Evelyn had headed back to the inn. During the walk, Evelyn had been oddly pensive, staring out at the ocean and ignoring Max so that it ended up being Gracie who played with him as they walked.

As they approached the back of the inn, however, Max caught sight of a cat that Gracie had never seen before. He started barking and took off after the cat, which scurried up the stairs to the back porch and slithered through the door into the house, which someone had left ajar.

Alarmed, Gracie ran toward the house. Evelyn saw the cat also and ran past her grandmother, pounding up the stairs to the back porch and into the house.

Gracie followed. "Evelyn, *shh!* Don't make too much noise."

She entered the kitchen in time to see the cat streaking past her legs and back out of the house. She snatched up a barking Max before he could follow the cat.

Heavy steps sounded heading down the stairs, and Trish Montgomery appeared in the doorway to the kitchen. Her face was almost as pink as her loose dress, and her fuchsia-colored lips had drawn down into a deep frown.

"I'm so sorry, Trish," Gracie said before Trish could speak. "I'll keep Max quiet. We just got back from a walk."

"I need to finish this manuscript," Trish said in a grating voice. "My publisher has a very tight printing schedule, and they'll charge me if my manuscript is late and causes them to get off schedule."

"I'm very sorry. We'll be quiet." Max squirmed, and she had a hard time keeping him from wiggling out of her arms.

"Had I known there would be a child *and* a dog, I don't know that I would have made the reservation," Trish snapped, and she marched back upstairs.

"I'm sorry for making so much noise, Grandma." Evelyn's face crumpled. "I promise to be quieter from now on."

Gracie had to squelch a flare of irritation at Trish for hurting her granddaughter's feelings. "Oh, sweetheart, there's nothing to be sorry for. You were only trying to help with Max and the cat." She let Max down so she could put her arms around Evelyn, but the dog quickly began barking again and jumping at the closed back door.

"Max!" Gracie had to grab at him again.

"I'll take him to the bedroom." Evelyn took the dog from Gracie's arms and buried her face in Max's silky fur.

Gracie wanted to talk to Evelyn, but the girl turned away and headed back to the bedrooms before she could speak.

Gracie made herself a cup of tea and collapsed at the dining room table. What was wrong with her granddaughter? She remembered

Paige being moody and quiet at times when she hit her teenage years, but Evelyn was only eight, and she certainly hadn't had the violent mood swings of a teenager.

Maybe Brandon would be able to talk to her again? Gracie glanced at the clock. He'd be at work, but he might have a few minutes where she could speak to him.

She pulled out her cell phone and called, and he answered on the second ring.

"Hi, Mom."

"Is this a good time to talk? I don't want to interrupt you."

"I have a couple of minutes before my next meeting. What's up?"

"Well, it's Evelyn."

"Is she still being quiet?"

"Yes. Did she say anything to you when you talked to her yesterday?"

"I asked her how she was doing more than once, and she always insisted she was fine," Brandon said. "But I did notice she seemed kind of quiet. Do you think maybe she's homesick?"

"I thought of that, but she doesn't mention home at all."

"I'm not sure if I should be relieved or insulted," Brandon joked.

Gracie then heard muffled voices in the background, and Brandon said, "Sorry, Mom, I've got to go. I'll call you tonight."

Gracie said good-bye and hung up.

A knock at the front door made Gracie rise to her feet. Bill Dekker entered the inn, and his eyes lit up when he saw her. Gracie couldn't stop her heart from lifting at the sight of him. "Hi, Bill," she said, trying to sound casual. "What brings you here?"

"Hi, Gracie." His presence filled the small foyer, and he ran a hand through his long hair. "I ran into Sam yesterday at the grocery store and she mentioned she was pretty concerned about the storm that's supposed to hit in a couple of days."

"Yes, we were up late last night talking about it," Gracie said. "Do we need to board the windows?"

"I've been keeping track of the weather reports, and now they're saying the storm might pass us. We'll have rain and strong winds, but it won't be too bad."

"Oh, that's good." Gracie hadn't wanted to frighten their guests by boarding up the windows and telling them to head into the basement. "The house will be okay?"

"It should be fine." There was a slightly awkward pause, then Bill asked, "How was the House and Garden tour?"

In all the goings-on at the inn, Gracie had nearly forgotten about her outing with David Starbuck. But she also had a feeling Bill still wasn't entirely happy she'd gone on the tour with David. His faint jealousy made her feel somehow guilty as she answered. "Oh, it was fun. There were lots of beautiful gardens. I got some ideas for our own backyard."

Bill looked like he wanted to say something, but he seemed to change his mind and instead nodded a little curtly. Perhaps he wanted to know more about the company she kept rather than the plants. David had been pleasant as a companion because they both loved gardening, but Gracie didn't have this slightly uncomfortable shortness of breath with David like she did now, with Bill standing a little too close to her.

A slower, more cautious step came down the stairs now, and soon Doris appeared in the dining room doorway. "Oh, hello," she said to Bill.

He smiled and nodded at her and then said to Gracie, "I had better go. If you have any questions about the storm, just let me know."

"Thank you, Bill."

"Anytime." He gave her a look and a smile that made her stomach give a slight blip, and then he was gone.

"I hope I didn't scare that nice young man away," Doris said to Gracie.

"Not at all. Bill has been a wonderful help around the inn. He's done most of the repair work that we couldn't do ourselves."

"He seems very capable. He's also quite handsome, isn't he?" Doris' expression was innocent, but Gracie could have sworn there was a mischievous twinkle in her eye.

"Did you want some tea?" Gracie asked her.

"Oh, that sounds lovely."

Gracie made a steaming mug and brought it to where Doris had sat in the dining room. "Would you rather sit in the parlor?"

"Oh no. I like looking at your clock." Doris pointed to the carved Black Forest clock on the wall, which had an eagle and stag on it. "My mother had a clock with a deer's head in bas relief carved into the base. I don't know what happened to it, because it was missing from her house when she died and none of the cousins knew where it had gone."

"That's sad."

"When we lived here, Mother had a tiny brass clock she kept on the dresser. It gave a little *tick, tick* that sounded throughout the room."

"I don't think I've ever been up to the second floor of the carriage house. We cleaned out the bottom floor, but the top floor was so full of stuff that we just left it for another day, since we didn't need the storage space."

"Mother kept the apartment very neat and clean, and back then, we didn't have many things. I once drew a flying horse on the wall under the window, but I felt so guilty about it that I moved my bedside table to hide it, and I don't think Mother ever found out. I wonder if it's still there."

Suddenly Gracie knew what might keep Evelyn busy and out of earshot of Trish's room. "Would you like to find out today? We can go up to look."

"I would love that. It would make me feel like my mother was close to me again, to be up in that apartment once more."

"I have to warn you, it's very dirty. It's packed with things from the previous owners of the inn, and I don't know if anyone has even lived there since your family left."

"I don't mind the dirt. And it might be fun to look through other people's things—I'm afraid I'm terribly nosy at heart."

Gracie had been keeping an eye on the time, and she went to collect Evelyn. "Put on some play clothes."

"Grandma, I'm too old for 'play clothes.'" Her eyes were wide and earnest. "I have school clothes, and lounging clothes, and soccer clothes, and party clothes, and—"

"How about the clothes you wore when we explored the secret passageway?"

"Oh. Sure, I can wear those."

Gracie helped Doris slowly make her way to the carriage house, supporting her elbow on one side while Evelyn walked slowly on her other side, giving her plenty of space for her cane. They'd done a good job clearing the carriage house for the Packard and Sam's minivan, so there was plenty of room to maneuver toward the back of the carriage house and out another door.

Alongside the back of the carriage house rose a flight of sturdy wooden steps to a landing and a door that had once been painted green and white. As Gracie helped Doris up the stairs, Evelyn asked, "Why did we have to go into the carriage house just to go outside again?"

"Why don't you go around the side of the carriage house and see," Gracie said.

Evelyn darted around the corner. "Hey, it's full of weeds."

"Exactly. You and I can tackle them later."

"When I lived here, there was a clear path around the side of the carriage house to these stairs," Doris said. "The Fortescues had a big shiny car that my father maintained for them, and they kept it locked up inside."

At the top of the stairs, Gracie paused to dig the key out of her pocket and unlock the door. They hadn't opened this door in several months, so she hoped it would open easily.

She had to give it a sharp thrust with her shoulder, but it finally opened inward, and they were met with stacks of old cardboard boxes that had once held bananas, according to the printing on the outside.

"We looked through one or two of the boxes when we first moved in," Gracie said, "but they mostly contained junk that the previous owners had left behind, like half-used paint cans and bags of metal washers and some old home repair books."

"What are we looking for?" Evelyn asked rather dubiously.

"Anything that might be from when Mrs. Waverly lived here," Gracie said.

"We have to look through all that?" Evelyn pointed at the boxes as if they were haystacks.

"I doubt you'll find any of Mrs. Waverly's things in a box of stuff from the eighties," Gracie pointed out.

"Mrs. Waverly, when did you live here?"

"The thirties, my dear."

"Wow." Evelyn looked impressed. "That's a long time ago!"

Gracie and Mrs. Waverly shared a smile. "I suppose to you, that seems prehistoric," Gracie said to her granddaughter.

"I know you're not that old, Grandma."

Gracie entered the loft and found that there was a small cleared floor area behind the open door, so she waited until Evelyn and Doris had entered the room and then closed the door. Light streamed in from the windows high above just under the eaves. The glass panes were coated with dust but weren't obscured by boxes. Gracie also knew from when she'd seen the outside that there were large windows set in two of the walls of the loft apartment, but the boxes blocked them from view at the moment.

"Let's clear a space for us to work." Gracie pushed some boxes out of the clear space, Evelyn helping. Then Gracie began unstacking boxes and placing them on the floor. "You two search through them, and I'll restack them if they don't have anything interesting in them."

They found lots of things that probably should have been thrown out by the previous owners, such as old bills, keys without locks, random screws, sporting magazines. They also found some old towels and sheets, which Gracie wondered if they might use as rags, and she found a box of old desk accessories that included a box of markers. She managed to find one that worked and marked the boxes of towels and sheets, setting them aside.

They slowly worked their way deeper into the room, and Gracie was careful in how she restacked the boxes. She stacked them neatly against the wall, and grouped them so that the boxes of things to throw away were nearest the door and easily accessible, while the boxes of things they might be able to use were stacked together in the corner.

Suddenly Doris gave a soft cry. "I recognize this desk. It stood in the far corner."

The desk was a simple wooden desk with four drawers, two on each side. The handles were beautiful brass scrolls.

"My mother would sit at it to write letters, and my father would sit to take notes in his gardening journal."

"What's inside?" Evelyn pulled at one of the left side drawers. It didn't open easily, and she had to tug hard, but it finally slid open to reveal some old blank envelopes, a few pencils, and some very old stamps.

Evelyn picked them up. "I've never seen stamps like these before."

"They're from the thirties. A stamp collector would be drooling over them," Gracie said. "Put them in an envelope and let's be sure to take it back into the inn with us."

Evelyn did as she was asked and gave the envelope to Gracie. She bent to look through the rest of the drawer, but only came up with some blank pages of stationery, each with a delicate spray of pink roses printed in the bottom right corner.

Evelyn then grasped the handle of the drawer below it and pulled hard, expecting it to stick like the top drawer, but it slid open quickly and flew out of the desk. Evelyn landed on her backside, still holding the drawer, which thudded to the floor between her sprawled legs.

"Are you all right?" Gracie leaned over her. "Did the drawer fall on you? It's heavy."

"I'm fine. I just didn't expect it to come out so fast." She then suddenly gasped and pointed at the desk. "Look!"

Gracie and Doris looked at the gaping hole where the drawer had been. At the back of the space was a small bundle of white. Gracie reached in and removed it.

It was a bundle of old envelopes, tied with a ribbon that had once been green but had faded to a soft sage color. The top envelope was addressed to Charity Mattingly in a slanting, elegant hand, with the street address of the inn.

Doris put a shaking hand to her lips. "Those are my mother's letters."

"How wonderful." Gracie held them out to her. "They must have fallen behind the drawer. I hope she didn't miss them too much."

"How precious." Doris fingered her mother's name on the envelope and held it to her heart. "When we're done here, let's go inside and read them."

"We can go now," Gracie offered.

Doris shook her head emphatically. "Let's see what else we find first. I'm positively energized now. And I'll savor the letters all the more for the waiting."

The other drawers proved less exciting. They held a few more pencils, an old almanac, an old church tract, and a rusted pair of scissors.

"This is in the middle of the room. Let's move this to the side so we'll have more space," Gracie said. She and Evelyn pushed and shoved the desk toward the corner with the boxes they had already gone through.

"Look." Doris pointed toward the far wall. "What's that?"

At the foot of another stack of boxes was a broken footstool, but Gracie immediately saw that it was an antique. The cushion had been hand-embroidered, although the silks had faded to a muted mesh of grays and creams and there were large holes where rodents had chewed through to the cotton stuffing underneath. Two of the legs were broken, but the remaining legs were hand-carved in the shape of claws.

"What a shame. This might be over a hundred years old." Gracie dusted off the cushion.

The broken footstool lay next to two stacks of boxes, but Gracie realized that they weren't cardboard, they were wooden crates. They looked like they had been fruit or vegetable crates, but the labels were faded or torn.

"Evelyn, I might need your help to unstack these," Gracie said. Her granddaughter wasn't much help on the topmost crate, but she helped Gracie lift down the others. Gracie's arms were beginning to tire from the heavy lifting, but she was enjoying this digging into the past, even if most of their findings were destined for the trash bin.

They opened one of the wooden crates, and Gracie knew they'd hit a gold mine.

These crates must have been left when the Montague brothers sold the house in 1929 to the Fortescues. None of the items inside were particularly valuable, but their age made them fascinating and possibly collectible. They sorted through vintage pillboxes and cigar boxes, a half-used desk blotter, dried ink bottles, stacks of papers that looked like bills and receipts, some old newspapers, some empty glass jars and bottles.

"It's just more trash," Evelyn said.

"No, it's treasure," Gracie said. "These things are all from the twenties or earlier. Even these glass bottles are things that some people collect."

"People collect old empty bottles? Grandma, you're kidding me."

"One man's trash is another man's treasure." She gingerly handled a stiff wool jacket that had been stuffed into the bottom of a crate. "I wonder how these crates got here in the carriage house. Where were they when you lived here, Doris?"

"I remember the attic was stuffed with old things the Montague brothers left when they sold the house. The stock market had just crashed, so they sold the manor to the Fortescues for a song. They also left much of their things. Some the Fortescues kept, like the furniture. Other things they meant to throw out, but I guess they never got around to it, so it all just sat in the attic gathering dust. I remember Mother wanted to clean some of it out, but she didn't dare because she wasn't sure what the Fortescues would want to keep."

"I think that when Ezra Fortescue sold the house to the Grace Brothers Hotel Group in 1950, they must have taken all the stuff in the attic and just shoved it in here," Gracie said.

"Yes, my family was gone by then," Doris said. "When Ezra Fortescue took his wife overseas for her health in 1937, he shut up the house and let my parents go. Mrs. Fortescue died in the 1940s, I think. I remember my parents heard about it and told me. Ezra sold the house a few years later probably because he had never loved it the way Mabel had."

"The Grace Brothers Hotel Group renovated it into the inn." Gracie picked up an empty box that had once held fishing lures, according to the printing on the outside. "To them, all this was probably just junk, but I'm glad they kept it rather than simply throwing it away."

Gracie lifted a crate to test its weight. It wasn't too heavy. "Let's take this into the inn."

Evelyn was quick to help her, and they began to carefully carry it down the flight of stairs, and Doris followed slowly, holding on to the railing.

However, Evelyn stumbled on the second step from the bottom and Gracie lost her grip on the box. It fell to the ground with a terrible crash, the sound reverberating throughout the backyard.

"Oops." Trish was probably going to be livid about the noise.

Running footsteps sounded, and then Sam appeared around the side of the carriage house, but she couldn't approach any closer because of the tall weeds. "Are you all right?"

"We're fine, we just dropped a box." Gracie looked sadly at the broken wooden crate, but luckily it had been filled with paper and boxes and not any of the fragile glass bottles. "Sam, could you bring us a cardboard box from the house? I want to carry this stuff inside."

"Sure thing." Sam disappeared and reappeared a few minutes later, this time coming through the door from the carriage house so she could hand Gracie the box.

They stooped and sifted through the wooden pieces to find items to put in the box.

"Evelyn, would you please get a paper bag? Actually, two bags. We'll double-bag them and then put the broken wooden pieces inside."

They had cleaned up the area in a jiffy and soon were sitting at the dining room table again. Sam had gotten some newspapers to lay down so Gracie could put each of the items down without worrying about scarring the antique dining table.

"Oooh." Sam picked up a vintage chocolate box. Although it was empty, the picture on the cover was beautiful.

"You won't believe what we discovered up in that loft area," Gracie said. "Doris found an old desk that her parents had used when they lived up there."

"And I found some old letters," Evelyn added.

"Yes, Evelyn was very clever," Doris said. "She pulled out a drawer and we found a packet of letters that had fallen in the back." She produced the ribbon-tied packet. "They were my mother's."

"Really?" Sam asked. "How wonderful!

"Are you going to read them?" Evelyn asked. Letters were apparently more interesting to her than the things in the crate that Gracie had brought in.

"I'm almost afraid to read them because they belonged to her." But Doris began undoing the ribbon. "How strange to find them after all these years."

Doris began reading the letters, although she also kindly gave a couple to Evelyn to read, probably to help keep her occupied while Gracie looked through her treasure trove. Besides the boxes, she had an old wool men's jacket, a couple of ties, and even a small leather box that held an old-fashioned man's collar. There were also a few old letters addressed to Lachlan Montague, and all from young women. They were rather coy and flirtatious in their notes to him, and apparently had all dated him at one point or another.

Gracie laughed and then sniffed one of the pages. "I think I can still smell perfume."

"Let me smell that." Sam sniffed and giggled and then looked at the page. "It's from Harriet Marsh, a schoolteacher. Oh, I almost forgot. I think I found William Elliott's church in Massachusetts today."

"You forgot a juicy piece of news like that?" Gracie asked her.

"Hang on, let me get my laptop." Sam went to their rooms and returned with her laptop, which she set up on the table with a piece of printed paper. "I met a teacher today outside of Jedediah's café. Her school is Daley Academy, and it used to be a church that expanded into a school. It got me thinking that maybe William's church turned into a school, so we looked through the school databases and found this."

She typed in a website address, and she and Gracie peered at the screen. Trinity Cross Academy had once been Trinity Cross Church in Adams, Massachusetts. The church had been founded by William Elliott in 1872.

"Here are pictures of it." Sam clicked on the thumbnails.

The school was a small, smart-looking academy with children in navy blue- and gold-trimmed uniforms. The pictures showed modern schoolrooms and a beautifully manicured campus.

"And look. Here are some old pictures of the original buildings." Sam clicked on another thumbnail.

Gracie and Sam both gasped at the same time. "Is that what I think it is?" Gracie squinted at the laptop screen.

"I think so." With a few clicks of the mouse, Sam had enlarged the picture of the original chapel for the school.

The chapel had been an old building when the photo was taken, which according to the photo credit had been in 1932. The wooden structure was small and looked rather weather-beaten by the thirties. But what captured the sisters' attention was the symbol painted over the front doors—three crosses on a hill.

They'd seen that symbol before, embroidered on the handkerchief that held the money they'd found in the secret room upstairs, in Hannah Montague's chest.

"If that symbol was on the handkerchief," Sam said, "does that mean that the handkerchief belonged to William?"

"And if the handkerchief belonged to William," Gracie said, "maybe he's the one who gave the money to Hannah. So maybe it's just as we thought: she didn't steal it from the lighthouse like everyone thinks she did."

A swell of joy rose in Gracie's chest. She had never wanted to believe Hannah had stolen the money, and here was evidence that perhaps she hadn't. If she'd gotten money from her brother, she hadn't needed to steal the money from the lighthouse.

"But in the newspaper we found, Lachlan and Fitzwalter Montague implied that Hannah stole the money," Sam said.

"But William and Hannah's father said he suspected Lachlan and Fitzwalter of stealing that money. He just couldn't prove it. So maybe they said that in the paper to blame Hannah for the money that they stole."

"This almost proves that the money we found wasn't the money from the lighthouse," Sam said. "Which means the lighthouse money is still missing."

"The Montague brothers probably spent it long ago," Gracie said.

"But we still don't know what exactly happened to Hannah." Sam's hand went to her throat. "Maybe she discovered her stepchildren had stolen the money and so they"—she glanced over and saw Evelyn listening intently—"there was some *foul play?*"

Sam stared again at the picture of the old chapel. "At least we know now where William Elliott went. It's too bad his father never found out so he could make amends with his son."

"If Hannah ran away," Gracie said, not wanting to believe that Hannah had been murdered in cold blood, "she would have run to her brother's church, wouldn't she?"

"Sure."

"So I'll talk to Elizabeth Adams tomorrow. She might know how we'd be able to search if there was a Hannah Elliott or a Hannah Montague in William's town back in the 1880s."

"That's a good idea."

"Forgive me, girls," Doris said. "You had mentioned to me that your mother never told you about living here in Nantucket with my family, is that correct?"

Gracie nodded. "In fact, she told us specifically that she hadn't been here before her honeymoon." She still had a hard time with the fact their mother had lied to them.

"I think I found out why." Doris held out one of the letters to her. "These are to my mother, from Rosalie's mother. Your grandmother."

Gracie read out loud, so Sam could hear:

"Colorado Springs, 1935. Dear Charity, I hope this letter finds you well. I am beginning to feel better. I will no longer hide from you that I worried for my health for many months after arriving at Harris Sanitarium, but the doctors now say that I am on the mend. I am very relieved. I could not bear to wonder what would happen to my sweet Rosalie if I succumbed to this dread disease as her father did."

"Disease?" Sam peered at the letter. "I thought our grandfather died of pneumonia. What exactly did she have?"

Gracie read on: "'I received Rosalie's letters but I have been too ill to write back until now. She obviously loves spending time with Doris and loves Nantucket. I know you will remember what I asked from you when I said good-bye to Rosalie at the train station, and I have asked Rosalie to vow never to speak of where I have gone and why, but I am beginning to fear that she loves Nantucket so much that when I am better and she has returned home, she will accidentally speak of it to her friends. Please remind her of her promise to me never to speak of this time in her life when she and I are apart. No one must know I was in a sanitarium. It must be as if it never happened. You and I understand the consequences if people knew the truth, but she is only a child and may not realize it. So please speak to her about it, being her mother in my absence. Thank you again for being willing to take her for so long a time, and in such secrecy from our other relatives. I was at first upset to hear that you were moving to so isolated a place as Nantucket, but now I gladly repent of my words to you because that isolation enables me to protect Rosalie from what might occur if people knew she were with you and where I am. Give my love to your husband and to Doris. With affection, Margaret.'"

"What did she have?" Sam looked completely perplexed. "What was so awful that she had to keep it a secret?"

"But it must have been curable too," Gracie said. "She obviously got better."

"I barely remember Grandmother Kingsbury."

"Me too. Caroline would probably remember her better." Gracie turned to Doris. "Did you ever meet Rosalie's mother?"

"I don't know. I only remember Rosalie. But I don't think I did."

Gracie looked again at the letter. "It seems like your mother and Grandmother Kingsbury were close to each other. But you said you never saw Rosalie again?"

Doris nodded. "I missed her. We moved from Nantucket to New York a year after Rosalie went home, because the Fortescues closed the house. Then Mother became ill, and we moved to Charleston to see some doctors there. She died several years later, and when Father and I moved back to New York, he tried to contact one or two of her relatives, but they had moved away."

"So it sounds like Grandma Kingsbury and your mother were cousins, as opposed to your father," Sam said.

"Yes, it makes sense, although no one ever said so."

"And all your cousins here on Nantucket are from your father's side, you said?" Gracie asked.

Doris nodded. "I'm afraid they won't know anything about this."

Gracie could read her sister's face, even though she didn't verbally express what she was feeling. Gracie felt the same way—why so much secrecy? They now know why their mother had lied—but what exactly had she been hiding?

"I can do a search for Harris Sanitarium in Colorado Springs," Gracie said. "And maybe Elizabeth Adams from the historical society will help us, especially if the sanitarium closed at some point. She might know someone who would have access to old databases and records. I wonder what terrible disease our grandmother had."

Evelyn suddenly giggled

Gracie's granddaughter had listened with rapt attention as Gracie read the letter, but when they began discussing Doris's family connections, she had gone back to reading Doris's mother's letters. Now she sat and leaned on the table with her chin in her hand, reading a letter with a look of glee on her face.

"What exactly are you reading, young lady?" Gracie asked.

Evelyn froze and then her eyes swiveled to Gracie, wide with guilt. "Er..."

Gracie held out her hand, and Evelyn reluctantly handed the letter to her.

"What is it?" Sam asked.

Gracie scanned the lines and then felt heat creep up her neck. She swiftly handed it to Doris. "It's, uh, a letter from your father to your mother. When they were dating."

"Oh." Two spots of color appeared in Doris's cheeks, but she gave a gamine grin. "It must be very interesting reading for young girls." She winked at Evelyn.

"There wouldn't happen to be any letters from your father to your mother after they married, would there?" Gracie asked.

"I'm not sure. Why?"

"If that letter is any indication, you may need to screen those before letting Evelyn read them. Just in case any are, uh, PG-13."

CHAPTER

Fifteen

Sam stared out at the light drizzle outside the next morning. "Oh, that's too bad," she said out loud.

"What's too bad?" Gracie entered the kitchen with Evelyn.

"Breakfast is on the stovetop." Sam pointed to a frittata she'd baked that morning. "And there are scones today too." She nodded to a cloth-covered basket on the counter.

"What's too bad?" Gracie asked again as she dished up frittata for Evelyn.

"The weather. I need more eggs and when I went out the other day, I forgot to pick up baking soda and baking powder too."

"Just use the car." Caroline entered the kitchen. "*Mmm*, smells good."

"Weren't you going to go to the historical society today?" Sam asked Gracie.

"No reason we can't both go and stop off at the store on the way home."

"And Evelyn and I will hold the fort." Caroline leaned against the island in the middle of the kitchen and munched on a scone.

"Unless you want to come with us?" Gracie asked her granddaughter.

Evelyn took a moment to think about it, but a glance at the steady rain caused her to make a face. "No, I'll stay with Aunt Caroline. I don't want to get wet."

"And how do you know you won't get wet staying here with me?" Caroline made as if to tickle her, and Evelyn giggled. It lifted Sam's heart to hear Evelyn laughing, although Trish might object to the noise.

Just as Sam thought that, Gracie said, "Evelyn! Watch the noise."

Evelyn's face fell. "Sorry, Grandma!"

But then she added, "It was Aunt Caroline's fault too." Caroline had such a guilty look on her face that Sam had to laugh, and Gracie joined in. Evelyn's countenance brightened and she laughed too. Sam thought to herself that Evelyn might have her mother's coloring, but her facial features were all Marris.

So Sam and Gracie headed to town in her minivan. They drove slowly not just because of the drizzle but also because it was fun to chat. They'd told Caroline the night before about what they'd discovered about their mother from Doris's letter and also about how Sam had discovered where William Elliott's church had been.

"I'll talk to Elizabeth about looking for Hannah Elliott or Hannah Montague in Adams, Massachusetts," Gracie said. "I know we couldn't find anything online last night, but Elizabeth might know someone who has access to old records from that area."

"Could you believe how many Hannahs there were in the area in the late 1800s? So much for that bright idea of mine."

"It wasn't a bad idea. Who knew it was such a popular name during that time period?"

"We really bombed out on our Google search, huh? I was hoping we'd find more information about Harris Sanitarium. Too bad we don't know anyone who lives in Colorado Springs. We could have asked them to visit their local historical society to find out any information on old sanitariums and what diseases they treated in the thirties."

"There's still no guarantee we'd be able to find out what Grandmother Kingsbury had. The sanitarium could treat any number of diseases."

"For some reason 'sanitarium' makes me think maybe it was some type of mental illness. Maybe that's why she didn't want Mom to tell anyone she had been hospitalized."

"But Grandmother Kingsbury referred to it as a disease that killed her husband too. That wouldn't be a mental illness, not unless it was contagious."

The historian, Elizabeth, was leading a tiny and rather soggy tour group throughout the house when they stopped by the historical society, so Gracie and Sam went to the grocery store for supplies first. A short while later, they drove up to the historical society building just as the lot was emptying of cars.

"Good timing," Elizabeth said as they rushed into the house through the drizzle. "I just finished the tour."

"How have you been?" Gracie said.

"Busy, but not too busy to check the rest of those files we were going through. I still couldn't find mention of an Emmaline Nickerson, although there were a handful of Nickersons in Nantucket in the early to mid-1800s. None in the late 1800s, though."

"I appreciate your looking into that for us," Gracie said. "I certainly don't want to pull you from your regular work."

"You didn't. It's totally fun, plus it really does have to do with my work since that ticket is related to historical Nantucket. I have it for you if you want to take it home with you today."

Gracie gave Sam a slightly guilty look. "I haven't talked about it with my sisters yet, but I was thinking maybe we would donate it to the historical society in time."

"I think that's a good idea," Sam quickly said. "I don't think Caroline would have a problem with that. And there are a few other things in the house we could probably donate. It would be nice to have them examined and preserved rather than us keeping hold of them."

"Oh, but they're related to the history of your house." Elizabeth looked concerned.

"They're related to the history of Nantucket, and it might be better to have them here in case someone else needed to do exhaustive, tedious research about the 1880s." Gracie smiled at the young woman.

"I'm always up for exhaustive, tedious research when you bring me interesting historical mysteries to solve."

"We have another one for you today, and I hope you can help us," Gracie said. "We found an old letter written to a woman who used to live in Montague Manor in the thirties, and the letter writer is writing from a sanitarium in Colorado Springs. She apparently had some terrible disease that she eventually recovered from, but she didn't want anyone to know she was in the sanitarium being treated. And her husband had died from whatever disease it was." Gracie handed her a copy they'd made of the letter.

"*Hmm*." Elizabeth read the letter and then stared at the molding on the ceiling as she thought about it. "I'm not well versed in the

1930s—I studied mostly Colonial American history—but I do have a few friends who are professors at a university in Boston who might be able to help me. I don't know if they'd be able to tell you what disease she had, but they'd at least know who to ask about Harris Sanitarium in Colorado Springs and what diseases they treated."

"We'd be so grateful for anything they could tell us," Gracie said.

"I'll shoot them an e-mail today."

"We have another favor to ask," Sam said. "We discovered that Hannah Montague's brother founded a church in Adams, Massachusetts, in 1872. We were wondering if maybe Hannah ran away to her brother the night she disappeared."

"It's possible. Gracie and I searched the ship records for that night, and she wasn't on any passenger lists, but she could have stowed away on a ship headed to Massachusetts."

"We searched online for a Hannah Elliott or Hannah Montague in Adams, but we were wondering if you had access to any databases."

"I don't necessarily have access to databases, but I do know a few people who do. I can talk to Irene Stuart at the Maple Hill Historical Society—she's a well-respected expert in Massachusetts history and if she can't find Hannah in Adams, no one can."

"I hope Hannah was there," Gracie said. "I'd hate to think she never made it because something happened to her."

"Me too," Sam said. After hearing about the journal entry Gracie and Elizabeth had found that described Jedediah Montague, Sam felt a closer affinity to Hannah, because she knew what it was like to have a controlling husband.

"How's your granddaughter enjoying her stay in Nantucket?" Elizabeth asked.

"Oh." Gracie's expression fell. "I think she's enjoying it."

Sam resisted the urge to reach out and hug Gracie. While Evelyn wasn't melancholy all the time, she was still quieter than Sam was used to, and she knew Gracie was worried about her.

Gracie continued, "She's probably doing something wild and crazy with her aunt Caroline right now. She didn't want to brave the rain."

"And the historical society isn't exactly a happening place," Elizabeth said with a smile.

"I'm sorry, but we should probably go," Sam said. "I've got eggs in the car. Thanks for all your help."

"Yes, thanks so much, Elizabeth." Gracie waved good-bye and they headed out.

As they were driving home, Sam asked, "Have you talked to Brandon about Evelyn?"

Gracie sighed deeply. "He wonders if she's homesick, but she never talks about home at all."

"You know, maybe that's the key." Sam thought back to what she'd observed in Evelyn recently. "I haven't heard her talk about her parents or her brothers. That's pretty odd, don't you think?"

"I noticed that too. But what does it mean?"

"Maybe something happened at home?"

"But Brandon would have told me."

"Maybe she's angry or sad at the twins, or at her mom. It's possible she didn't tell anyone."

Gracie frowned at the road. "Do you really think it's something like that?"

"I do think it has something to do with home. You should talk to Brandon again, and Stacy too."

"I'll try. They've been so busy with the twins being sick, so they don't stay on the phone for very long."

"Well, make them stay on the phone. This is their daughter."

"You're right. Rather than calling them up out of the blue when they might not be free, I'll e-mail Brandon and set up a time when he can free himself up to talk."

"That's a good idea."

They arrived at the inn just as the sun peeked out and the drizzle abated. "It might turn out to be a nice day after all. Maybe the weather report is wrong about the tropical storm." Sam picked up the groceries from the car, and they headed into the house through the back door.

Sam froze in the doorway. She felt her grip slipping on the eggs and fumbled to get them, but they fell to the floor in a splatter of yellow yolk.

Betsy Carlisle was standing with Evelyn at the counter and looking through the kitchen cabinets.

"Oh." Betsy's cheeks turned bright pink. "We were just waiting for you to come home."

"Hi, Grandma. Hi, Aunt Sam." Evelyn's greeting sounded wary as she picked up on the tension between Sam and Betsy.

Sam struggled to control herself. "Look how clumsy I am. Evelyn, could you please get me a few towels to pick this up?" She bent to try to scoop the raw eggs into the container.

Betsy also grabbed some paper towels from the roll on the counter and bent to help, but she avoided Sam's eye. Evelyn seemed to want to be extra helpful and scrubbed rather vigorously at the eggs, but she only ground the broken shells into the floor in her enthusiasm.

"Here, Evelyn, why don't you help me put Aunt Sam's other things away?" Gracie gently pulled Evelyn away.

What had Betsy been doing? "Where's Caroline?" Sam tried to ask lightly, casually.

"Aunt Caroline had to answer the phone." Evelyn pointed toward the foyer.

"I'm sorry for barging in on you." Betsy stood with the dirty paper towels and went to throw them into the trash can. "I stopped by to chat and see how you were doing."

"That's nice of you," Sam said in a neutral voice, but inside she was burning with curiosity and suspicion. What was Betsy doing here? Was she snooping like she'd done with Shirley's friend Lorna? Or was Sam just being paranoid?

"You haven't met my other sister, have you? Gracie, this is Betsy Carlisle. We had lunch the other day, remember I told you?"

"Oh yes. Nice to meet you." Gracie's smile was as gracious as always, but Sam detected a slight misgiving in her eyes. Gracie must have remembered what Sam had told her about Betsy, and she was obviously just as suspicious as Sam after seeing Betsy with Evelyn looking inside Sam's kitchen cabinets.

Caroline then entered the kitchen, all smiles. "Sorry that took so long. That was a potential new guest asking about the inn. Oh, hi, guys." She eyed the mess on the floor and felt the slight tension in the room. "Something spill?"

"I dropped some eggs," Sam said.

"Oh no! Before I went to answer the phone, I promised Betsy a tour and then some tea. Let me put the kettle on—"

"I'll make the tea," Gracie said. "Why don't you give Betsy the tour."

Sam had never been more grateful for Gracie's smooth way of taking charge of a situation. Unaware of the true source of the tension in the kitchen, Caroline led Betsy upstairs to see the rooms, and Sam let out the breath she hadn't realized she'd been holding.

"Are you okay?" Gracie asked her.

"No. Why is she here?"

Gracie gave her a meaningful look and then glanced subtly at Evelyn, who stared up at them with big eyes. "Did I do something wrong?" Evelyn asked in a small voice.

"No, of course not." Sam knelt in front of her. "You didn't do anything wrong."

"But you could do us a favor," Gracie said in a light voice. "What do you say?"

"S-sure."

"Can you tell us what you and Mrs. Carlisle were talking about?"

"Uh…" Evelyn's eyes slid to the cabinets.

"We're only curious what you talked about."

"Well, she asked me if I helped you in the kitchen, and I said that sometimes I did."

"You're a very good helper," Sam said. "What else did you talk about?"

"She asked what I helped you with last, and I said it was the blackberry cobbler."

Sam's heartbeat stilled for a brief moment and then started back up again, faster than before. But she kept her voice casual as she asked, "Then what?"

"She asked if I remembered what ingredients you put in it, so I showed her." Evelyn's face crumpled. "I'm sorry, Grandma! Should I have not done that?"

"We would never ask you to lie to someone or be rude to them," Gracie said, "so you did the right thing. Otherwise you'd have either lied to Mrs. Carlisle or been rude to her. We're very proud of you."

Evelyn nodded, but she still looked distressed.

"And just for that, you and I can make another batch of blackberry cobbler today if you want," Sam said.

Evelyn hesitated and then said, "Could I just have some chocolate chip cookies instead? I'm getting kind of tired of cobbler."

Sam and Gracie both gave snorts of laughter. "Chocolate chip cookies it is," Sam said. "I made some yesterday."

But as she looked at Gracie, a cold fury began to build inside her. *How dare Betsy Carlisle come to my house and trick Evelyn into revealing my recipe ingredients?* she thought. *That was lower than low.*

Gracie could see the anger in her eyes, and she gave Sam a warning look. Sam could almost read her mind: *Not in front of Evelyn.*

Sam took a deep, full breath and tried to calm down.

Caroline's cheerful voice preceded her down the stairs. "You wouldn't believe how much work it was to fix the place up. I'm just so glad to have my sisters with me. This entire project has drawn us closer together, and this house has become very dear to us."

"It shows," Betsy said softly.

They entered the foyer and Betsy glanced at her watch and said, "Well, I should be going. Thank you for the tour."

"Would you like to join us for some tea?"

"No, thank you. Perhaps I can take a rain check. Please say good-bye to your sisters and Evelyn for me. Good-bye."

There was the sound of the front door opening and closing, and then Caroline entered the kitchen. "So that was Betsy Carlisle? She seemed nice. Quiet, but nice."

For Evelyn's sake, Sam had to check the angry outburst that was dying to come out of her.

At that moment, the front door opened again, and Sam had the thought that Betsy had returned. But she recognized the soft, slow tread on the floor. The sisters and Evelyn went to the foyer to greet Doris, who was walking steadily with her cane.

"Hello," she greeted them. "I was just visiting my cousin Bobby."

"Did you walk?" Evelyn asked.

"No, his daughter picked me up and dropped me off," Doris said.

"Would you like something?" Sam asked. "Tea? Maybe a scone?"

"If it's not too much trouble, I'd love some."

"Why don't you have a seat in the parlor and rest your feet?" Gracie went in to plump up a pillow at a wingback chair.

"Can I have tea with you?" Evelyn asked Doris.

"I would love for you to have tea with me."

Sam returned with a tea tray piled high with scones and also the last of the chocolate chip cookies she'd baked. She had steeped some Earl Grey for Doris, which she preferred, and also some non-caffeinated chocolate banana-flavored tea for Evelyn.

"Now, you and I will have a proper tea together," Doris said to Evelyn. To the sisters, who were hovering, she said, "You three go off and do what you need to do. I'm in good company here."

Evelyn beamed, and Sam was relieved that she seemed to no longer be distressed about the incident with Betsy.

The sisters went into the kitchen, where Sam steeped a pot of tea for themselves. She needed something soothing or she'd start banging pots and pans around in her frustration.

Keeping her voice low, Sam said to Gracie, "You heard that with your own ears. I'm not being paranoid."

"Heard what?" Caroline looked perplexed.

"While you were on the phone, that woman was pumping our grandniece for information about my blackberry cobbler recipe," Sam hissed.

"Surely not."

But Gracie nodded. "If what Evelyn says is true, and we have no reason to suspect her of not telling us exactly what happened, Betsy asked her to show her what ingredients Sam put in her blackberry cobbler."

Caroline's mouth opened, then she closed it with a snap. "And here I was upstairs regaling her with rosy stories about Mom wanting to buy this place, and us fulfilling her dream and fixing up the inn."

Sam poured the tea into three cups and handed out the milk and sugar jar. She spooned a heaping pile of sugar into her mug.

"Maybe she didn't find out much."

"I'm sure she didn't, but it just makes me so mad that she was asking Evelyn about it in the first place."

"In a way, it's rather flattering." Caroline sipped her tea.

"What?" Sam said.

"Think about it. She considers you serious enough competition that she would stoop to coming over and trying to figure out your secret."

Sam took a breath to retort, but then released it. In a strange way, Caroline's argument was true. "It still doesn't make me any less mad about what she did."

"Of course, but don't let it eat away at you." Gracie snagged a scone.

"Yeah. Instead, beat her socks off." Caroline grinned.

"Believe me, I intend to," Sam said fervently.

"How did it go with Evelyn today?" Gracie asked Caroline.

"Fun. The dusters gave me an idea. I made wire fairy wings that I put on her and I threw on that green blanket like a cloak. Then we went around the parlor and brandished the dusters like wands. We even got some dusting done."

"Caroline, only you could get an eight-year-old to dust like it was a game of pretend. You're like Tom Sawyer getting the kids to whitewash his fence."

Caroline laughed. "Well, I don't know that I'd do it again. She almost took out a lamp and a picture frame with the wire wings I put on her."

Sam couldn't help but laugh.

"George called and wants to take me to see another house." Caroline's voice tightened as she spoke, but otherwise she seemed cheerful enough. "I told him I'd call as soon as the two of you got back."

"Go ahead," Sam said. "We'll hold down the fort."

After Caroline had left with George, and Sam was washing up their three mugs in the sink, Gracie said, "Let's distract you."

"I don't need to be distracted."

"Yes, you do. You're glaring at that poor mug as if it insulted you."

Sam stared down at the sudsy mug in her hands. She supposed she might have been frowning at it.

"Rinse that, and we'll look through the Montague brothers' things."

"That's a good distraction?"

"Hannah's father suspected the Montague brothers of stealing that money, remember? Maybe we'll find something in their things that proves it."

That actually wasn't a bad idea.

Gracie went to the parlor to tell Doris and Evelyn where they were going to be while Sam finished the mugs. Then the sisters went out back to the carriage house and climbed the steps.

Gracie had remembered to bring the key and unlocked the door, and they entered the loft apartment. The outside air had warmed after the rain stopped but the air inside the apartment was still cool.

"It's so stuffy in here." Gracie wove her way between stacks of boxes to one of the windows and with some tugging managed to open it. Sam soon smelled the faint scent of the roses from the garden carried on a light breeze into the room.

"You don't think the Montague brothers would have destroyed any evidence if they'd stolen the money?" Sam began unstacking the wooden crates.

"I have a gut feeling they weren't as thorough as they like to think they were. Think about it. They never found Hannah's secret room even though they grew up right in the house. They obviously kept a lot of junk." Gracie gestured to the crates. "Which means they probably weren't very good about keeping things neat, or they'd have thrown much of this stuff out. I mean, who keeps thirty-five half-used pencils?" Gracie had counted them from the last crate she'd unpacked.

"Maybe they were frugal and didn't want to throw them away if they could still be used."

"But an organized man would know where his used pencils were so he could finish using them before sharpening a new one."

"Good point."

"I'd really like to find something to clear Hannah's name." Gracie opened the top of a crate, and they peered inside.

Even Sam had to admit that the Montague brothers were likely slobs. The crate was full of odds and ends and trash. They found pages torn out of a book, but not the book the pages belonged to; three candle stubs and an empty box of matches; a basket with a hole too large to have been made by a rodent; and an empty whiskey flask with a broken cover.

They made a pile of things to throw away, and a pile of things that might be salvageable or collectible. Among the collectibles was a pocket watch with a broken face, not engraved but very sturdily made; a pair of spectacles, in perfect condition; a full box of cigars that somehow had survived the ravages of time; and a small bottle of women's perfume, still sealed.

"Probably a gift for one of Lachlan's many girlfriends." Gracie laid the perfume on the collectibles pile with care.

They finished sorting through one of the crates, and Gracie put the collectibles pile inside it. They opened a second crate, which looked like the contents of a desk had been swept haphazardly inside: a half-used blotter, ink bottles, a few pens, an empty ledger book, blank pieces of paper, a badly tarnished silver letter opener.

Gracie examined the letter opener while Sam shook the ink bottles. They were dried up. She was about to throw them away when Gracie said, "No, don't. Some collectors might want to try to reconstitute the ink."

"They like old ink?" Sam couldn't fathom the idea when they could go buy new ink from the store.

"It's antique ink."

Sam sighed. "This is why I'm not an expert on antiques like you are."

"I'm not an expert. I just like them."

Sam picked up the blotter, which was mostly a bunch of scribbles. She aimlessly flipped through the other pages…and froze.

Hannah Montague's name was written several times on the last page in a neat hand.

"Gracie." Sam thrust the blotter at her.

They peered at it, but Gracie said, "There isn't enough light. Let's go to the window."

They made their way to the window, and now Sam could see the page clearly. "Did Hannah use this blotter?"

"I'm not sure." Gracie caressed the leather of the blotter. "It could be from 1880. It's amazingly well preserved."

To Sam the leather looked in terrible shape, but she supposed leather that was over a hundred years old would have normally deteriorated.

"The name looks odd, though." Gracie squinted at it, and Sam did too. The lines were shaky as if the hand that had written it had been quivering.

"And look, farther down the page, it says, 'I'm sorry.'" Sam frowned at it. "Sorry for what? And why is it written four times?"

"And why would Hannah write this on her husband's blotter? Wealthy women in those days had their own stationery desks and journals and blotters."

"Look, 'Hannah Montague' is written once, but just 'Hannah' is written three times."

"Do you think maybe one of her stepsons wrote this?" A faintly disgusted look crossed Gracie's face. "Could one of them have been in love with her? She couldn't have been much older than they were at the time."

"It might explain the 'I'm sorries,' but the idea is kind of…icky, to borrow Evelyn's word."

"The 'I'm sorry' could mean something else too," Gracie said slowly.

"What do you mean?"

"Maybe one of her stepsons did something to Hannah." Gracie pointed to the four "I'm sorries" down the page. "This could be the scribblings of a guilty conscience."

CHAPTER
Sixteen

Caroline could only stare in wonder at the antique whaling cottage as they drove up to it. "This is the house?" she asked in wonder.

"Bill Dekker is actually the one who told me about this." George parked the car on the street. "He's been hired by the owners to fix it up, and in talking to him, they mentioned that they intended to sell it, but it hasn't gone on the market officially yet. They also said they'd be willing to sell it for a much lower price if the buyers paid cash."

It was Bill Dekker and not their Realtor who met them at the quaint front door. "Hi there, Caroline."

"Hello."

Bill's eyes drifted beyond her. Caroline turned to look, but no one was there.

Bill's neck began to glow a soft red. "I had sort of hoped Gracie might have come with you," he said.

Caroline bit back her smile. Even if Gracie didn't admit there was anything between them, Bill apparently wanted to be more than friends with her sister.

As Bill unlocked the front door, Caroline asked, "Are the owners here?"

"No, this is their vacation home. They live in New Hampshire." He opened the door and they entered a tiny foyer with a narrow hallway. "I've been fixing the plumbing for them—it's always caused problems because it wasn't properly done when the place was renovated back in the seventies."

They entered a room on the left, which looked like it might have once been two bedrooms, but which was now converted into a living room with a fireplace in the center. "How old is the house?" Caroline asked.

"It was built in 1834 by a whaling captain." Bill grinned, and his dimples flashed. "A bit like the Misty Harbor, but without the added intrigue of a vanishing widow."

The room across the hallway from the living room was a charming dining room with a bay window. There was another door leading from the dining room into the kitchen.

"The kitchen was completely renovated in about 1975," Bill said. "The owners at the time expanded out the back of the house so they could double the size of the kitchen area."

It was a lovely, light room with large windows. The appliances were new, but it looked like the countertops and walls could use some work. Also, the sink had been completely opened up where Bill was working on the pipes.

"If you did buy this house, you'd probably need to do some work on the kitchen. The grout's starting to crumble in some areas on the countertop, but the cabinets are sturdy. They were made with real oak and they've been kept in good condition."

There was a second door from the kitchen back into the narrow hallway, and directly across from the doorway was an open doorway that led to a tiny stairwell. It didn't spiral like the staircase at the inn, but it had a lovely carved banister that must have been custom-made for the stairs when the house was built.

They climbed to the second floor where there was a wider hallway that had a set of French doors at the far end. Caroline gravitated toward them and stepped out into a balcony that overlooked the ocean only a couple of blocks away.

"This used to be a widow's walk." The ocean breeze blew Bill's shaggy hair into a wild mane around his head as he stood next to Caroline on the balcony. "It became very unstable and dangerous, but the renovators tore it down rather than fixed it, which is a shame."

The reentered the hallway and turned into one of the two doors on the right, which was a tiny bedroom. The ceiling was slanted with the roof, but the walls had been painted a cheerful yellow recently, and there were large windows on two walls. The bedroom connected to a Jack and Jill bathroom, which connected to the second bedroom, a mirror of the first except that the walls were a soft blue.

"This is the master bedroom." Bill led them across the hall to the only door, which opened into a spacious bedroom. Two bedrooms had probably been combined into this one and a master bathroom added.

"The pipes here need replacing, as well as downstairs, but it would also mean you could renovate the bathroom. The tiles and colors are a bit outdated."

The master bedroom had a balcony of its own, facing the line of the shore as it wound its way down the island.

"But the best part is downstairs." Bill led the way back down and, at the base of the stairwell, took them through a small door just under the stairs and out into the backyard.

There Caroline saw a darling little guesthouse with roses climbing over the doorway and windows. They entered to find a spacious room with a half bath and a kitchenette.

"I thought this might be good for an office for you," George said.

"Oh, George, it's beautiful." The room had lots of windows and a high ceiling that made it seem even brighter. She whispered to him, "Can we really afford this?"

Bill cheerfully said, "I'll be in the kitchen if you need me."

"Thanks, Bill." George closed the door behind him and faced Caroline. "It's pretty pricey, even with the discount if we paid cash, but I think it would be worth it."

Caroline gave him a steady look at his vague answer.

He gave a good-natured sigh. "Yes, we'll have to have a few frugal years, but only a handful of them. And we wouldn't have a mortgage because we'll be paying for the house in its entirety."

He had a point. She remembered her friends complaining about their mortgages, which had only fired her more to want to own a house outright.

The house was lovely. It had all the charm of an antique home, it was near the ocean, the rooms were beautiful...

But it wasn't Misty Harbor Inn. It wasn't the house her mother had lived in and loved, the inn she had dreamed of owning, the inn she'd woven her plans around. This house was at least forty-five minutes away from her sisters, and it seemed like a million years to Caroline after the closeness they'd shared in the past year.

George read her thoughts in her face. "What's wrong?"

She couldn't speak, she just shook her head.

"What is it? You can tell me."

"No, I can't." Caroline felt tears well up in her eyes, and she tried to get hold of herself.

"Yes, you can." He placed his hands on her shoulders.

"Oh, George, I want to live in the inn after we get married."

There, she'd said it. And just as she had feared, a veil of sadness fell over his features.

"I'm sorry, Caroline. I understand, but I just don't feel comfortable living under the same roof as your sisters. I don't want to live in one of the rooms in the inn, even if we live in one of the second floor rooms, and definitely not one of the two bedrooms on the first floor. There would be no privacy, and I'm not used to that."

He reached out to cup her cheek. "I know how much you love the house, but I think it would be a better thing for our marriage if we had our own space. Marriage is going to change your relationship with your sisters. You know that—you went through it when Sam and Gracie first married."

Caroline nodded. She remembered how surprised she'd been when their relationships had become so different in such subtle ways. And they hadn't even been living together at the time. Now that she had living in such close quarters with her family for the past year, it would take time to get accustomed to married life. She knew that she and George would need their own space and privacy as they figured out how to be married to each other.

She wiped her tears with the back of her hand. "I understand why we can't live at the inn. I know the reasons and I agree with them completely. But right now, my heart is still in the Misty Harbor Inn. It's the place where my sisters and I bonded as we fixed it up, living our mother's dream for her. Now we know that it's where Mom's heart was from her childhood years spent there." She sniffled. "But I love you, and I want what's best for the two of us. I just need some time to shift my way of thinking. Go ahead and put in the bid for this house. I know it'll be a beautiful little bungalow for the two of us. I would be happy living in a garbage can, as long as I'm with you."

George enveloped her in a strong embrace. "I won't do anything until we've both had a chance to think and pray about it. If we're meant to have this house, God will enable us to have this house, and He'll tell us clearly that we're supposed to live here."

George looked deeply in Caroline's eyes. "I want you to be happy, but even more than that, I want our marriage to be built on our love for God and for each other. Love doesn't run roughshod over the other person."

"Oh, George." Caroline was going to cry again if he kept this up.

"We'll figure it out." George held on to her tightly. "I love you, and nothing is going to change that."

Thank goodness Sam had thought to check the expiration dates. She had discovered that the bottle of yeast she'd just picked up had expired several months earlier.

Sam headed back to the shelf and found that while some bottles were fresh, about six other bottles were out of date.

Sam put a fresh bottle of yeast in her basket and then taking one of the expired bottles, she went in search of a store employee.

She saw two of them speaking to each other. One employee, a freckle-faced young man, had a cart full of grocery items, while the other looked and acted like a more senior employee. Sam approached them and stood silently by, waiting for them to finish their conversation.

The senior employee looked straight at her... then deliberately ignored her as he continued speaking to the freckled boy.

Sam was a little annoyed. Not even a "We'll be with you in a moment, ma'am." Well, maybe they were discussing something extremely important.

Actually, the senior employee seemed to be micromanaging the freckled boy about a delivery order he was getting together for a customer.

"Now, did you remember to pick the small young lettuces, like it says in her order?" He looked in the shopping cart behind the freckled boy. "Yes, looks like you did. She likes them smaller. Did you get the oranges yet? No? Well, make sure they're not bruised."

That seemed rather obvious to Sam.

"And the order says specifically pastry flour. This is all-purpose."

Sam's annoyance grew. This senior employee seemed to be speaking to the boy as if he were a problem employee or completely stupid. What was so important that he had to go through this entire customer's grocery list?

"And see, the list says the vine tomatoes, not the separate tomatoes, so make sure you choose the vine tomatoes. And that's two bags of flour. You need to go back and get a bag of pastry flour and a bag of bread flour—not this all-purpose stuff."

Why was he repeating himself? The freckled boy looked as frustrated as Sam felt.

She gently cleared her throat. The senior employee looked at her for a second, then turned away from her and kept speaking to the boy.

"It gets back to me if this order is messed up, so don't mess it up. Remember not to pick bruised oranges for Mrs. Carlisle."

Carlisle? Sam sidled closer to the cart. The two employees had their backs to her so they didn't notice when she peeked at the printed grocery list lying in the upper basket.

The store had a delivery service in which a customer could go online and fill out a grocery list, and then the store would deliver the items the next day and charge the credit card on file. The printed list had the customer's name clearly at the top: "Betsy Carlisle."

Just seeing her name reignited the burning in Sam's gut. How dare she invade Sam's home and take advantage of her grandniece? And all for a baking competition? How underhanded could someone get?

The more Sam remembered the events from the day before, the angrier she got. She also became more and more annoyed as the senior employee kept deliberately ignoring her. *What happened to customer service around here?* she thought.

The idea came into Sam's brain in a flash, and in a split second, it was done. She saw the jar of yeast in the cart, apparently from Betsy's grocery list. Sam snatched it up and replaced it with the expired bottle.

There! With a glare at the senior employee, Sam stalked away.

She'd gotten only a few steps when she deeply regretted what she'd done. Betsy would probably not check the expiration date of the yeast when she first used it, and if she wasn't paying close enough attention, she'd use the expired yeast, and it would ruin whatever she was baking.

Sam shouldn't have switched the yeast. It was petty and mean and… She turned around to go back and undo what she'd done, but a voice stopped her.

"Ma'am? I saw you waiting to speak to those two employees, but they seem to be busy. Can I help you?" The manager of the store stood in front of her, his face friendly and helpful.

Sam eyed the two employees. The senior employee had finally stopped speaking to the freckled boy, and the boy had swiftly moved away to complete his order.

"Ma'am?" the manager prompted again.

Sam swallowed. "I noticed that there are expired bottles of yeast on the shelf." She eyed the boy as he disappeared around the end of a row of shelves. "And there's an expired bag of cornmeal too."

The manager looked genuinely distressed. "I'm so sorry, we'll get right on it."

"Ma'am, you were waiting to speak to me?" It was the senior employee who had finally approached Sam, now that she was speaking to his manager. Whereas before he had been insolent, now he had an unctuous expression that turned Sam's stomach and fired her anger.

"You looked straight at me twice and deliberately kept speaking to that boy," Sam said sternly to him as if he were a recalcitrant student.

The manager's brows drew together, and his face grew thunderous. He turned to the senior employee. "I want to see you in my office right now." He turned back to Sam with a grim but apologetic look. "I'm very sorry for how you were treated, ma'am. I assure you I will take care of it."

Sam suddenly caught sight of the freckled boy over the manager's shoulder. He was heading out the door of the store. She quickly said to the manager, "Thank you very much."

Sam hurried toward the doors to the store, dropping her basket of unpaid groceries on top of a display of oranges. But even as the doors opened, she saw the freckled boy backing a van out of a parking space. In the space of another second, he had thrown the van in gear and driven off.

She was too late.

CHAPTER
Seventeen

Gracie had barely entered the historical society building when Elizabeth came running lightly down the stairs. "Hi, Gracie, Caroline. I'm so glad you could make it."

"We're glad you thought to invite us for your video chat," Gracie said.

"Considering it's your little mystery, it seemed only right," Elizabeth led the way to her tiny office in back on the first floor, tucked away behind the large meeting room where the historical society and the preservation society had their monthly meetings. "Is Evelyn at home with Sam?"

"No, she's spending the day with her new friend Michael and his fascinating pony."

"Ah." Elizabeth's office was packed with file cabinets and bookshelves. It wasn't messy, but it did look like she had a lot of projects going on at once, for there were stray file folders and open books and stacks of papers on every flat surface. Her desk stood at one end of the long room while a small round table and four chairs stood at the other end.

"Have a seat." Elizabeth gestured to the chairs around the table while she scooped up some stacks of papers on the table and transferred them to her desk. She then grabbed her laptop and took it to the table, opening it so that all three of them could see the screen.

With a few clicks on her trackpad, she had opened the video chat application. She checked the time. "We're a few minutes early, but let me buzz Irene just in case she's already at her desk."

In seconds, the face of a fortyish woman with brown hair pulled back in a twist and brown eyes appeared in the laptop screen. Everything about her looked very smart and efficient, and the impression was solidified when Irene smiled and said, "Hello, ladies. I'm glad I decided to get to my desk early to organize some of the obituaries."

"Hi, Irene. Ladies, this is Irene Stuart, historian at the Maple Hill Historical Society. Irene, this is Gracie Gold and Caroline Marris. They're the Nantucket residents who asked me to look into Hannah Montague."

"I hope we didn't take you away from your other work," Gracie said.

"I was ready for a break." Irene gave a grimace. "I've been arguing with Josiah Bradford for days."

Gracie gave a start of surprise, but Elizabeth seemed to take it in stride. "Who's Josiah? Related to General Bradford?"

"Yes, he's Nathaniel Bradford's nephew, and we recently discovered a journal he wrote. But some of the battles he's describing are completely wrong, and so I've been telling him."

To Gracie and Caroline, Elizabeth explained, with a twinkle in her eye, "Nathaniel Bradford was a revolutionary war general."

"Oh." So this Josiah Bradford whom Irene was talking about had actually been dead for a couple of centuries. "I thought at first that this Josiah was still alive, and you were fighting with him."

Irene looked startled for a moment and then she laughed. "Sorry, it's a quirk of mine I picked up when I worked at the John F. Kennedy Presidential Library. No, I've been trying to match Josiah's journal entries with actual revolutionary war battles, but it seems like Josiah made things up, left and right. So when you called me about Hannah Montague, I needed a break from Josiah's fibbing."

Irene seemed to be rooting for something on her desk, the charm bracelet on her wrist jangling, and finally she came up with some pieces of paper. "I went to the Adams Historical Society— it was a good chance to catch up with John, a friend of mine who works there. We did a pretty thorough search for Hannah Montague and Hannah Elliott, but I'm afraid we didn't come up with anything."

Why had Irene wanted to video chat just to tell them that?

"So naturally," Irene continued, "I suspected she remarried."

Gracie blinked. For some reason she hadn't even thought about that

Irene said, "In those days, it wasn't unheard of for a widow to marry soon after her husband died, and for a widow who had just run away, she'd probably want a husband's protection right quick. So John and I went searching through the parish marriage records and we ran into a problem. There are gaping holes in the records."

"Did someone take the records? Was there a fire?" Elizabeth asked.

"There was a fire, in a sense. During the worst winter of the Depression, apparently many of the churches in the town of Adams started burning the oldest records for fuel."

Elizabeth winced. "I can understand, but that makes me cringe."

"I know. Can you imagine? Anyway, that's why there are gaps in the records. They started with the oldest records first since they figured fewer people would be likely to care about older marriages and deaths and births."

"But Hannah still could have run away to Adams and gotten married, right?" Caroline said. "Even if there isn't a record of it."

"True. The problem is that we don't know her married name. I might have been able to trace her through any children but since I don't know her new surname, assuming she remarried, I wouldn't know where to start." But—Irene then pulled out a new paper—"since Hannah was a dead end, I went searching through her brother's family."

Wow, Irene was incredibly thorough. Gracie was highly impressed.

"The problem is that William Elliott's wife had several miscarriages—I found that out because the Adams Historical Society has the old journal of the local doctor at the time, who took notes on his patients, and so I searched through it and found William's wife's name—Deborah—and each of her miscarriages. She had exactly one child, Ruth, who was apparently very sickly—there are lots of entries in the journal about the doctor being called for often because the child seemed to catch every flu and cold bug in the county. When I searched the marriage records, I didn't find a record of Ruth marrying, however that might be because the church records were burned during the Depression."

"How sad," Caroline said. "To try so hard to have a child and to keep having miscarriages."

Gracie felt a quiet drop of sadness drip in her heart. She'd had a miscarriage four weeks into her marriage—she hadn't even realized she'd been pregnant. She always wondered about that baby, who it would have grown up to be. But she'd had Brandon a year later, and he had filled her with such joy that her sadness had melted away.

"Now, before the three of you accuse me of wasting your time," Irene said while rooting for yet another paper on her desk, "I dug a little deeper and I found something that might interest you. Elizabeth had mentioned to me about the ticket and the name on it, so I searched for Emmaline Nickerson and I found her."

"You did?" Gracie leaned forward in her seat.

"It was in a newspaper obituary. Elizabeth, I'll scan this and e-mail it to you, but it doesn't say much. Emmaline Nickerson died at seventy years of age in 1960. The obituary says she's survived by her great-nieces, Jordan Ramsgate and Elinor Burgess."

"Great-nieces," Gracie said. "So her sibling's children's children."

"I'm afraid it doesn't say much else, but I can dig deeper," Irene said. "The problem is that we don't know if Emmaline married or not, and if Nickerson is her maiden name or her married name. Same for Jordan's and Elinor's surnames."

"We don't even know if she's connected to Hannah," Caroline said. "She would have been born several years after Hannah disappeared."

"It's not a common name, though," Irene said. "She might be somehow related to Hannah. She might even have been her daughter. I did a search for Hannah Nickerson, but didn't find anything—again, because the records were destroyed. But I haven't searched all the newspaper obituaries yet, and the Historical Society has almost all the newspaper editions from about 1915. If she died before that, we're out of luck, but if she died after 1915, we might find her."

"How are you going to search?" Elizabeth asked. "Are you going to look through each newspaper one by one?"

Irene looked faintly guilty. "Is there any other way to search? You know as well as I do that 'tedious research' is a historian's middle name."

Caroline blanched, and Gracie felt the same. "Irene, we don't want you to spend so much time searching for us if you have other work to do."

Irene waved her hand, and her charm bracelet jangled. "It's not a problem. If I have other work that comes up, I'll take care of it first, but this is an interesting little mystery. And I always love a good challenge."

Suddenly a box came up on Elizabeth's screen that obscured Irene's face.

"What's that?" Caroline said in surprise.

"What's what?" Irene asked. "What happened? Did you lose picture? I can still see you."

"Sorry." Elizabeth clicked on the box, which read, "Message from Jerry Burke, re: Harris Sanitarium, Colorado Springs." "I had set my computer to alert me when I get e-mails, and it creates a bubble in the middle of my screen that's right over your nose, Irene."

Irene chuckled.

"Is that e-mail about the sanitarium we asked you to look at?" Gracie said.

"Sanitarium?" Irene said.

As Elizabeth clicked to clear the box on the screen, Gracie explained, "This doesn't have anything to do with Hannah. We found an old letter that was sent to a woman who used to live in our house in the thirties. The letter writer, Margaret, had been sent to Harris Sanitarium in Colorado Springs for some disease, but she was insistent that no one know she went away to be treated. She was afraid of what people would say."

"Mental illness?" Irene asked.

"We don't think so, because Margaret's husband died of it. All we had was the name of the sanitarium."

"Irene, I asked Jerry Burkes about it," Elizabeth said.

Irene looked thoughtful. "You know, Jerry is great with data and records, but from what you described, this disease your letter-writer had seemed to have social implications that made her want to be secretive about it. The person you should talk to is Geraldine Purse at King's University in Boston. She specializes in historical social trends and cultural changes, and she's done some work on the Depression years lately. I met her a year ago at a convention after reading a couple of her articles in some of my historical journals. I have her e-mail address somewhere." Irene looked through some of her desk drawers. "No, I have her office phone number. Here it is."

Elizabeth wrote down the information as Irene spoke. "Thanks, Irene. That sounds like it's exactly who we need to talk to."

"You know so many people," Caroline said.

"When you've been in the business for as long as I have, and taught at so many different conventions and events, you get to know people's faces and names," Irene said. "It's actually a very small community, we historians. Was there anything else you needed?"

"You've given us tons," Elizabeth said.

"I'll keep looking into Emmaline Nickerson for you," Irene said. "Elizabeth, I'll send you an e-mail if I find something."

"Don't let us take you from more important work," Gracie said to her.

"Don't worry, it's more interesting than that pompous Josiah Bradford. Okay, then. Have a good day. Bye!" And Irene signed out of the video chat.

"I'm pretty sure I read one of Geraldine Purse's articles for my thesis," Elizabeth said. "She wrote about cultural shifts during the Revolutionary War in the state of Massachusetts, and the article gave me some information for my project." She glanced at the time. "I'm not sure what her summer hours are, but she might be in her office. I'll give her a call right now."

"Does that mean we can listen in?" Caroline asked.

"Of course. It'll save me having to relate the info to you later." Elizabeth put her phone on speaker and dialed while Gracie and Caroline drew their chairs closer to the desk so they could hear.

The phone rang, and then a deep woman's voice said wearily, "Geraldine Purse."

"Professor Purse, this is Elizabeth Adams from the Nantucket Historical Society."

The woman's voice perked up noticeably. "Oh, hello. For a second there, I thought you might be another of my students asking for an extension."

"Are you teaching this summer?"

"Two classes, plus I'm supervising two doctoral students teaching and trying to help a third one graduate." She had an edge of frustration to her voice, but it disappeared as she asked, "How can I help you?"

"I'm on speakerphone with Gracie Gold and Caroline Marris, sisters who have bought a colonial home here in Nantucket."

"Hello," Gracie and Caroline both said.

Elizabeth continued, "In the house, they found a letter that was written to someone who lived there in the thirties. It's certainly raised some questions because the letter writer apparently has an unnamed disease that she won't mention, and we're curious as to what it might be. Let me read you the letter."

Elizabeth read Grandmother Kingsbury's letter and when she finished, Geraldine immediately said, "She had TB."

The three of them stared at each other. That was fast.

"You're sure?" Elizabeth said.

"Positive. Last year I did a series of articles on the Depression years for *American Social History Journal*." There was the sound of desk drawers opening and closing and then the sound of papers being flipped through. "Back then, there was a stigma attached to tuberculosis because it was so contagious, and so many people died from it. People who contracted the disease were considered 'unclean' and were shunned."

"Like lepers in the Bible?" Caroline asked.

"Worse, because TB was contracted more easily. Socially, it created huge rifts in families because if one family member had it or died from it, the community would shun the entire family of the victim for fear of the disease. Many people went to extreme lengths to hide the fact that a family member had died from TB. If this Margaret had it, it would explain why she didn't want her daughter to speak of the fact that her mother was in a sanitarium. Sanitariums treated a variety of diseases, but the ones in Colorado Springs were noted for their work with TB, which used to be called consumption. The science of the time was very inexact, but people thought that Colorado's thin, dry air would help cure different ailments. So if the daughter ever mentioned Colorado Springs, people might know Margaret had been institutionalized for TB."

"Margaret wanted to make sure her daughter—our mother— didn't tell anyone about even being in Nantucket, because then people would ask why she'd gone and where her mother had been during that time," Gracie said.

"If people found out Margaret had had TB, they would guess that her husband died of TB," Professor Purse added. "She'd be isolated from all her friends, the community might shun the entire family—extended cousins and all—because the disease was so contagious."

"That's horrible," Caroline said.

"People were ignorant," Professor Purse said. "They didn't understand the disease or how to prevent contracting it."

"Poor Margaret," Gracie said. "She only wanted to protect her daughter and her family."

They suddenly heard some muffled sounds in the background and another voice speaking. Professor Purse answered someone and then said in the phone, "Was there anything else?"

"No. Thank you so much for your time," Elizabeth said.

"Not at all." She hung up.

Caroline sat in her chair, looking sad. "So Margaret was embarrassed at having contracted TB."

"And probably equally embarrassed that her husband died from it," Elizabeth said. "At least we solved one of your mysteries today. I was feeling I had a pretty poor track record."

"Don't be silly. You've been a wonderful help," Gracie said. "You've helped us discover so many things about the people who lived in our house."

"And our own family," Caroline added.

"It's amazing, isn't it, the many stories associated with these old buildings?" Elizabeth said.

"For us, it makes the building feel more like home," Caroline said fervently.

"Yes," Gracie said.

After they took their leave of Elizabeth and were driving home, Gracie said, "So Grandmother Kingsbury asked Mom to never tell anyone about being sick, or being at that sanitarium."

"Or being institutionalized at all," Caroline said. "People probably thought the two of them had moved away for the two years our mom was here in Nantucket."

"Mom could never mention Nantucket for fear someone would ask about it and discover her mom wasn't with her while she was here."

"That's a horrible burden to carry."

They drove in silence for a while, and then Caroline said, "One thing about Mom, when she made a promise, she kept it."

"She definitely kept it. She didn't tell us. She didn't tell Dad. She probably never told anyone."

Caroline glanced at her sister. "Mom took Grandma's secret with her to her grave."

CHAPTER
Eighteen

Sam was ready to cry. Or scream. Or throw something. Instead, she dumped her last batch of cobbler into the trash.

This was her second batch of the day and both of them had turned out horribly. The worst part was that she didn't have the faintest idea what she had done wrong.

She'd been baffled when the first batch of cobbler had had a strange consistency and tasted bitter. She thought she must have done something wrong, so she made it again, being doubly careful about how much of each ingredient she put in it.

But it had turned out almost the same, with that odd bitter taste that left a metallic residue on her tongue. Yuck.

What in the world had she done wrong?

Sam went to the counter and looked through her notes. She had tweaked the recipe slightly from the last time she'd made it. What had she done that caused this to happen?

She threw her pen down on the counter in disgust. What was wrong with her? Why couldn't she do this?

And a voice whispered in her head, *You're not cut out for this.*

Sam had doubted herself lots of times before, but somehow, this time it was different. The doubt was more insidious, dug deeper, burrowed down inside her. Maybe because this was more important to her than other things she'd done. She had to defend her mother's memory; she had to prove that horrible Betsy Carlisle wrong.

The guilt of what she'd done gnawed at her. She shouldn't have switched the bottles of yeast.

Why had she done it? It had been such a petty thing to do. And surely her remorse must count for something, right?

Well, it was done. She had to focus here on the problem with her cobbler. She had to fix this because she didn't have much time before the Summerfest baking competition.

A part of her wondered if this was some sort of divine retribution for what she'd done to Betsy, but she knew it was only coincidence. Still, the timing seemed pretty suspicious. Was God trying to tell her something?

She hadn't been very close to God for the past few years, and she had been fine. But when she jumped into buying this inn and spent more time with her sisters, she had started occasionally attending church because they were both very faithful.

Then she'd been asked to help in the preschool Sunday school at Harvest Chapel because one of the Sunday school teachers had broken her leg and Caroline had blithely suggested Sam since she'd been a teacher. Sam had discovered she loved the children and her fellow workers and the children's parents too. She had slowly started to feel like she was becoming a part of Harvest Chapel. People would chat with her, ask her how she was, invite her for coffee. They seemed to enjoy just getting to know her.

And slowly, through getting to know these people, she had somehow started getting to know God more.

So was He trying to get her attention for some reason? Sam couldn't figure out what He was trying to say to her.

True, she'd been really wrong in switching Betsy's bottle of yeast, but the woman had been sneaky and underhanded. She had disparaged Sam's mother, or so it felt to Sam, and wasn't that good enough reason to try to show her up?

Thinking about her mother suddenly made tears well up in her eyes. She was silently weeping while standing and leaning against the counter, Max whining and pawing at her leg, when Caroline and Gracie came home.

"Sam!" Gracie rushed to her side.

"What's wrong?" Caroline put an arm around Sam.

"It's…it's nothing." Sam wiped at her face with a dish towel.

"It is not nothing," Gracie said.

"You can tell us." Caroline rubbed her shoulder. "We're your sisters. We love you."

That made Sam cry harder, and it was a few minutes before she said in a choked voice, "I'm just…I feel like such a failure."

"Why in the world would you think that?" Caroline asked.

"Did Betsy Carlisle say something else to you?" demanded Gracie.

"No. It's just that my last two batches of cobbler have been absolutely horrible, and I don't know why."

"I'm sure they're not that bad—" Gracie began, but Sam shoved toward her the plate that had a sample of the last batch.

Gracie and Caroline both took bites with expressions on their faces of doing it only to humor her, but they both made horrible grimaces as they tasted it, and Caroline actually spit it out into the sink.

"See?" Sam's voice had risen until she sounded a little hysterical.

"And you don't know what you did wrong?"

"I have no clue. I'm so new to all this. What was I thinking to try to enter a baking contest?"

At her words, Gracie became still, and then her eyes softened. "Maybe that's the problem. Sam, when you first started baking for the inn, I'd see you in here singing and having so much fun. You had this light in your eyes—"

"Like you were in love again," Caroline said.

"But then I've seen you slaving away in here for the past few weeks," Gracie said. "And you're stressed, unhappy, frustrated—"

"A regular Oscar the Grouch," Caroline said, but with a wink.

"Caroline," Gracie admonished, not amused. "Anyway, Sam, you've become such a different person from the way you used to be before this contest."

"It's because I wasn't trying to perfect a recipe. I was just trying different ones."

"You perfected that muffin recipe," Caroline said. "You made it four different days until you had it the way you wanted it. But you weren't crying into your dish towels over that."

"But this is important," Sam said. "This is for Mom, to prove Betsy Carlisle isn't all that—"

"I think your competitiveness and indignation at Betsy have stolen your joy in baking," Gracie said.

The word she used, "joy," seemed to sink in Sam like a stone that slowly moved through her until it hit bottom. She remembered feeling joy in her baking—only a few weeks ago. She hadn't felt it recently.

"It doesn't matter if you're an award-winning baker or not," Gracie said.

"And it doesn't matter that Mom never won a baking contest," Caroline added.

"The important thing is that baking has made you happier than you've been in a long time," Gracie said. "You should learn to trust this new creative side of you and be thankful for what God has given to you."

Caroline nodded. "God has given you an amazing gift for baking."

"No, he hasn't." Sam wiped at her eyes. "I'm so clueless about it."

"Then you take time to learn," Gracie said stoutly. "Even Mozart didn't pick up a violin for the first time and play perfectly. He had to learn first."

"I feel so inadequate and insecure," Sam moaned. "Look at that cobbler."

"That's not inadequacy, that's just inexperience," Caroline said. "There's a difference."

"You'll get better at troubleshooting with the more experience you get, and the more you learn about baking," Gracie said.

"Mom wouldn't want you crying like this," Caroline said. "She wouldn't want you being so competitive and so frustrated. She would want you to just be happy baking like you used to be in the kitchen with her."

Sam remembered sunny days in their kitchen, helping her mother with tarts and cakes and cookies. She remembered sunny days in later years with her mother, helping her make dinner for the family.

In her memories, her mother was always smiling. Always relaxed. Always happy in doing what she enjoyed so much.

"This is just so different from what I used to do," Sam said. "Teaching came so easily to me. It still does."

"I think this is a great opportunity for you to stretch more creative muscles," Caroline said. "You've made some amazing dishes since you started baking for the inn. You've been full of delightful anticipation, like a painter with a blank canvas."

Had she really? Yes, that visual seemed to resonate with Sam.

"Now, no more crying." Caroline took the dish towel and wiped Sam's face for her like she used to when they were children. "You're going to leave that cobbler alone today and just relax."

"I used to relax by baking," Sam said with a shaky laugh.

"Well, today you're going to relax by walking along the beach with us." Gracie linked her arm in Sam's and Caroline took her other arm.

"But no one's staffing the phone," Sam said.

"The answering machine will pick up," Gracie said, "and we can call them back. Trish and Doris will be fine for a while."

It was such a treat to take off their shoes and walk along the warm sand, the sun in their faces and the wind running fingers through their hair. Sam was with her sisters, enjoying the closeness that made it okay for them to say nothing at all.

Finally Sam asked, "So why did Elizabeth Adams ask you to see her today? And at so specific a time?"

"Oh, Sam, we found out why Mom didn't say anything about living in Nantucket with Doris," Gracie said.

"Grandma Kingsbury had tuberculosis," Caroline said. "That's what Grandpa Kingsbury died of too."

"Grandma Kingsbury went to that sanitarium to get treatment, but there was such a social stigma attached to TB at the time that she wanted to keep it secret that she had it," Gracie said. "She didn't want Mom to mention living in Nantucket with her cousins because then people would find out she was there without her mother, and they'd ask questions. If they found out Grandma Kingsbury had TB, it would have made things really difficult for the family."

"People apparently shunned TB victims and their families back then," Caroline said. "Grandma Kingsbury didn't want Mom to have to go through that."

"So she made Mom promise never to tell anyone about Nantucket, even though Mom had enjoyed this place so much," Gracie said.

Something unfurled inside of Sam that she hadn't realized had been squeezed tight. She didn't feel the hurt that their mother had lied to them, the confusion and difficulty in trying to believe she had a good reason for it. Now she knew, and she realized she should have trusted her mother more.

"She always told us to be sure to keep our promises," Sam said. "I guess she kept hers too."

They were silent for a long moment, then Gracie asked Caroline, "How are your wedding plans going? You haven't said much about them recently."

Max nudged Gracie's hand at that moment, so she didn't see the look of panic that flashed across Caroline's face, but Sam saw it. "Caro—" Sam began.

"Things are going great," Caroline said brightly. "I wish I had that invitations binder with me so I could show you the design I think I'm going to use—with some alterations, of course. I never thought I'd have so much fun creating my own wedding invitations. People aren't going to want to throw them away."

Caroline continued chatting excitedly about her elaborate wedding plans, which now had expanded to inviting what sounded like half of Nantucket Island because she was thinking of asking one of the artists near the wharf to paint a large canvas on the day of the wedding, with guests adding their own bits, which Caroline could then have framed to put in her office.

"It'll be a more creative guest book," Caroline said.

The wedding plans sounded frenzied to Sam, but since Caroline obviously wanted them to be excited and happy for her, Sam didn't ask her sister about the panicked look she'd seen. But she decided she'd bring it up later, perhaps. Caroline had bullied Sam into sharing her own fears and worries, so Sam could do no less.

After all, what were sisters for?

CHAPTER
Nineteen

"Good morning." Caroline avoided Sam's eye as she entered the kitchen the next day. The previous night, Sam had caught her alone and asked her if things really were okay with the wedding plans. With the stress Sam had been feeling with the baking contest, and the worry Gracie had about Evelyn's strange moods, Caroline hadn't wanted to add to her sisters' burdens, so she had put Sam off, but Sam knew something was wrong.

Gracie and Evelyn entered the kitchen a scant few seconds after Caroline did, saving her from needing to make conversation with Sam.

"What's for breakfast?" Gracie asked.

"I already had some of the cinnamon raisin bread left over from yesterday, but Trish came downstairs earlier and snagged all but the last two slices. Doris said she's having breakfast with one of her cousins, and they already picked her up. So it's just us." Sam pointed to the basket. "Two slices there, and I can make you each an omelet."

"Yum," Evelyn said. "I want a cheese omelet, please."

"None for me, thanks," Caroline told her.

"What are your plans today?" Sam asked them all as she began making omelets.

"We're taking Max for another run on the beach," Gracie said. "Evelyn wants to hunt for more seashells. Then we'll be back here to do some of the laundry."

"I'm supposed to meet with the wedding planner today," Caroline said.

"Can I go with you?" Sam asked casually. "Sounds like fun."

Gracie was beaming. "Oh, that does sound like fun. What do you think, Evelyn? Did you want to go?"

Evelyn gave her grandmother a look that plainly said, *Do I have to?*

Gracie laughed. "Maybe we'll stick to the original plan and walk the beach. But Sam, you go with Caroline."

Caroline couldn't say no, so she mustered up a smile. "Sure. I need to leave in a few minutes."

"Great. I'll leave the dishes for later." Sam turned off the stove and dished up the omelets for Gracie and Evelyn.

"Have fun." Gracie waved to them as they left the kitchen.

Sam waited until they were in the car, heading into town. "You were talking in your sleep last night."

Caroline had had a nightmare, actually, about the wedding. The silk draping over the guest tables had arrived but it was a green-gray camouflage design rather than scarlet, the cake had been some child's birthday cake by mistake, the band began to play a polka, and then George had been brought in on a scooter driven by a circus monkey wearing a fez. Caroline woke up with a cry, but she had hoped Sam hadn't heard her. Wishful thinking.

"You were crying about it not being what you wanted," Sam said.

"Oh." Caroline tried to pass it off with a laugh. "It was a nightmare about the wedding. Everything was going wrong, and I was wondering what had happened to all my careful planning."

"You talked me down from the roof yesterday, so today it's my turn. What's really going on with the wedding planning? Something is bothering you if you're having nightmares about it."

"I'm fine. I'm a little frazzled because it's exciting and overwhelming to be able to be as creative as I want to be in the planning stages. But it's going to be so fantastic. Like one of those mind-boggling Cirque du Soleil shows. But without the acrobatics."

"But I thought you wanted it to be simple. That's what you said earlier last month."

"Earlier last month I wasn't sure what I really wanted. I didn't want one of those typical tulle-and-flowers weddings."

"But all this planning and work and decisions to make—are you happy with all this?"

Caroline wasn't exactly happy with all the stuff she had to do, but she hadn't been terribly excited about the wedding planning last month either. "Now that I've realized that I can make my wedding exotic and unique, I'm letting loose with all my creativity. I know I'd much rather have a unique wedding than something I've seen before in a magazine."

"Yes, I can see how you'd feel that way. I'm just worried because it's causing you a lot of stress."

She was right, it was causing Caroline quite a bit of stress. Originally she had been carried away by Trish's enthusiasm and ideas, and then later she had thrown herself into these elaborate—and expensive— plans mostly to take her mind off of the fact she was resigning herself to moving out of the inn after the ceremony. "I'll be fine. Things will get better soon." She hoped.

When they arrived at Linda Goodnight's romantic cottage office in town, Sam marveled over the beautiful roses over the doorway and window.

When Linda opened the door to them, she seemed startled to see Sam. "Hello. Come on in. I apologize; I was only expecting Caroline today." She had only set out two chairs at a small round table, so she hastened to get a third.

"This is my sister Sam."

"I hope I'm not imposing," Sam said.

"Not at all. Are you going to be involved in the planning?" Linda asked.

"I'm here to help Caroline any way I can. I want her wedding to be exactly what she wants it to be." Sam gave her sister a steady look that made Caroline uncomfortable.

Linda seemed to catch the look between them, but rather than making the mood awkward between the three of them, Linda relaxed somewhat. "You seem to have Caroline's best interests at heart."

"I do," Sam said fervently.

"Then I'm glad you're here." Linda faced Caroline squarely. "When planning a wedding, it's always great to have different people give you ideas, and for you to brainstorm about all the possibilities. That's always the best part."

"Trish and I had a great time brainstorming at lunch after we left my last appointment," Caroline said. "We came up with some great ideas."

"It's always good to have an overflow of ideas," Linda said. "But after that initial brainstorming phase, you want to sift through all the things you like and don't like about each idea and toss the ones that you aren't thrilled about, or that would be too expensive, or that would be too tedious, or that would only cause you stress." She seemed to emphasize that last word.

Caroline squirmed in her chair. A lot of her planning ideas for the wedding were exactly that: expensive, tedious—and stressful.

"Caroline." Linda reached out to clasp her hands. "I've known Trish a long time, and she has amazing creativity. But she can also be very forceful. With Trish, what should just be a brainstorming session can feel like a planning session."

Sam began to nod and smile.

"You have some wonderful ideas for your wedding, but I also want you to think about what would make you one hundred percent happy. There were a lot of terrific things you wanted to do, but weigh them against cost in money and stress in your life. Your wedding should not be stressful."

Caroline could only stare at her. It was as if Linda was throwing her a lifeline, rescuing her from the churning waves and strong undercurrent that her wedding planning had become.

"But I don't want my wedding to be boring," Caroline said. "All the simple weddings I saw were so…boring."

Linda laughed. "Simple needn't mean boring. It doesn't mean a white shift dress and white flowers and nothing else. It might be too expensive to ship in the special fabric you wanted and have the dress made up by a seamstress, but instead, you could have a dress with a colorful silk shawl as your veil."

"Really?" Somehow it had never occurred to Caroline that a simple wedding could also be exotic, or that an exotic wedding didn't have to be elaborate. "I do have a large silk shawl I bought overseas. It's printed with scarlet pimpernels."

"And I have Aunt Matilda's 1940s evening dress," Sam suddenly said. "Do you remember? It was pinkish peach with a deep red crepe trim."

It wouldn't be as flamboyantly colorful as the dress Caroline had originally envisioned, but she now saw that wearing their aunt's vintage evening gown would be so special, and the pimpernel shawl would add a vibrant touch of color.

"And a smaller wedding would allow you to have that special Italian wedding cake, since you'll have fewer guests, and you can still do the tea ceremony for your family." Linda gave Caroline's hands a squeeze. "You don't have to have a huge wedding to include all these special things."

"What Italian cake?" Sam sounded excited. "Maybe I could try making it. What's it like? Is it difficult to make?"

"It's divine," Caroline said. "You and I can try searching for a recipe online."

"Let's look at the other ideas you had," Linda said. "We'll figure out what you really want to do, and what you might be able to do without."

Caroline felt sheepish. "I'm sorry if I went a little overboard for a while there."

"You're a breeze," Linda said. "At least you hadn't reached a point where you had decided to wanted to elope."

"If you had eloped," Sam said with a stern look, "Gracie and I would have hunted you down."

As Caroline had been describing the Italian wedding cake, Sam was reminded of an incident involving another cake. Her mother had made a cake for Gracie's class to celebrate Gracie's birthday, but the afternoon before, Sam had stuck her finger into the creamy frosting and taken a gigantic chunk out of the side. Her mother had made Sam go to Gracie to apologize. Sam had also had to make a new cake for Gracie, with her mother's help.

While this wasn't exactly a finger full of frosting, Sam knew her mother would want her to make things right with Betsy. So she dropped off her sister at the inn and headed toward Betsy's home.

A good night's sleep had made her feel more centered in this entire baking thing. After hearing about their mother the day before, she also somehow felt closer to her, and wanted to honor her with the recipes she was using.

Her mother would have wanted her to confess all to Betsy Carlisle, so that's what Sam went to do.

The weather had turned ugly. This morning, the report had said there was a large storm brewing out in the Atlantic, and they'd keep an eye on it. Now, the report said the storm was growing and might be heading quickly toward Nantucket by late tonight. It was only noon, and the sky looked dark and heavy.

Sam drove up to Betsy's house and knocked on the door. When Betsy answered, her face paled at the sight of Sam. Sam wondered if she felt guilty about being at the inn the other day, or if she already knew about the yeast.

"Sam," Betsy breathed. "What are you— Is there something I can help you with?"

"May I come in?"

"Oh, of course." Betsy immediately swung the door open. "Please excuse the mess, I had several of my cousins' children over yesterday, and I was in the middle of cleaning."

Playing with her cousins' children obviously involved food, which didn't surprise Sam since so many of the Meyers seemed to cook well. A low folding table had been laid out in the living room and it was still covered with what looked like homemade play dough. Pieces were still on the floor, and it looked like some had been smashed onto the walls. Sam could imagine Gracie having a heart attack over that.

"Come into the kitchen."

Play dough sat on the island in the middle of the kitchen, but these had apparently been molded into shapes and then baked and painted. Sam peered at them, wondering if they were difficult to make. Evelyn might like something like that.

"Would you like tea? Coffee?"

"Nothing for me, thanks." Sam could have used a cup of tea, but had a feeling that once she confessed to Betsy, she'd be unceremoniously asked to leave the house pretty quickly.

"I'll make a pot, and if you change your mind, you're welcome to a cup."

Betsy's hospitality made Sam feel guilty. Betsy had tried to figure out Sam's recipe through Evelyn, she hadn't forgotten about that, but what Sam had done was completely uncalled for, and Betsy being a good hostess was only making Sam's insides churn.

Betsy sat at the breakfast table with Sam, setting down the pot of tea and two cups, as well as a plate of cookies. Sam was surprised to see that rather than being pretty and neat, they were decorated with a mash of colors and sprinkles.

"Cookie?" Betsy offered, biting into one. "We made them yesterday."

"No thank you. Betsy, I have to confess something."

Betsy froze in the act of chewing, and her face seemed to grow paler.

"I was at the grocery store yesterday," Sam said miserably, "and I was still upset that you had pumped my grandniece Evelyn about my cobbler recipe."

Betsy looked like she might faint. Sam hurried on, "I saw the grocery boy collecting your items for delivery, and I switched the yeast with a bottle that had expired. I'm really sorry, and it was very petty of me. Please forgive me." There, she'd confessed.

Betsy froze. Sam swallowed a couple of times, but didn't know what to say to break the tense silence.

"That's what I came to say." Sam rose to her feet. "I'm really sorry. I'll be going—"

"I put baking soda in your baking powder," Betsy said in a rush.

Sam stared at her. "What?"

"When I was with your niece. When she wasn't looking, I put baking soda in your baking powder."

Sam slowly sank back into her chair. "Uh…I'm not sure what that would do."

"Your pastries would be flat and have a bitter or soapy taste."

Sam remembered the horrible batches of blackberry cobbler from the day before. The consistency had been strange, and the taste had been metallic. And she'd made cinnamon bread in the morning, which didn't use baking powder, so she hadn't noticed the substitution until she tried making the cobbler.

Tears gleamed in Betsy's eyes. "I'm so sorry. It was awful of me."

Maybe because of how Sam's sisters had been so supportive the day before, but something made Sam reach over to touch Betsy's hand. "I'm sorry too. After all, I substituted your yeast. I don't know if you've used it yet."

"No." Betsy wiped her eyes with a napkin. "It's just an extra bottle because my other one is getting low."

"I'm sure you can tell the grocery store, and they'll replace it."

Betsy nodded.

Sam hesitated and then said, "I had no idea why my cobbler turned out so badly yesterday." She had been feeling like a failure, but now, after hearing what the cause of the problem was, she realized that she simply hadn't had enough experience or knowledge of baking to have been able to figure it out. It hadn't had to do with a knack for baking or things coming easily for her—it was simply a matter of learning and practice. "Gracie and Caroline were right," she said softly.

"What?"

"My sisters were trying to tell me not to lose faith in myself just because I had a bad baking day, and they were right. I love baking too much to let a setback get me down. It's something I've discovered I enjoy too much."

Betsy looked down at her cup of tea and bit her lip. "I really enjoyed talking to Caroline the other day. And Evelyn too—I love children, maybe because my husband and I never had any."

"Evelyn's a good kid."

"I was so struck by how Caroline spoke of the three of you. You're so close. So unlike my own sisters, my cousins."

"But you have such a huge family. You seem to get together a lot."

Betsy's mouth grew hard. "My mother has always been very critical of me. The only area in which she praised me has been my cooking and baking."

"That's terrible." Sam couldn't stop herself before the words flew out of her mouth. "I'm sorry, that was rude of me."

"It's true." Betsy gave a one-shoulder shrug. "I've been going to a therapist in 'Sconset for years now, and only recently have I felt like I could start to move on from her overbearing shadow."

"I can't imagine what it must have been like."

"I can believe that. The way you spoke about your mother says that she was a wonderful woman."

Sam was once again reminded of how deep the bond between her sisters was, and was grateful for it. She'd never realized how God had truly blessed her. Had blessed them all.

"I'm sorry about the entire thing in your kitchen," Betsy said. "Plying Evelyn for information about your recipe, adding baking soda to your baking powder. I've been so driven all year because my mother never lets me forget that she won the Summerfest baking contest five times until she voluntarily stopped entering. After I won it last year, my fourth win, I've been so determined to win it again, to prove I'm as good as she is. And maybe"—Betsy lowered her gaze again—"maybe to try to win her approval, in a sad sort of way."

"I don't think it's sad. I think it's natural."

"My therapist says that I need to break free. It's just so hard. My mother has always compared me to my sisters and my cousins, and made me feel inadequate in almost every aspect of my life—my schooling, my friends, my job, the fact we never had children."

Sam couldn't believe her mother had been so awful. She had had students with dysfunctional families, and now she realized that her students might have grown up to be like Betsy, beaten down by a critical mother, surrounded by competitive sisters and cousins.

Praying still felt a little foreign to her, but a sudden prayer seemed to breathe from her soul. *Thank You, Lord, for my own family. We were happy. We're happy now.*

Sam also remembered what Pastor Stan had mentioned about Betsy's isolating herself from her church family after her husband died, surrounding herself with her dysfunctional family instead. "You obviously love children. Why don't you come help me in the Sunday preschool at Harvest Chapel this Sunday?"

"Oh... Oh, I couldn't—"

"Why not? Break free. Isn't that what you said your therapist told you to do?"

Betsy looked out through the window. "Church was always something more important to my husband than to me, although I did enjoy going. But after he died, it seemed my mother needed me for this or that, and something always came up."

"I'm sure there are people at church who would love to see you again. And if you don't want to talk to anyone, that's fine—you can just stay with me in the classroom."

"But I haven't been to church in so long. I wouldn't know—"

"I was away from God for a long time too. I only recently started going back to church. It's always hard putting yourself in a new situation, but I had my sisters with me. You'll have me and my sisters."

Sam's mention of her sisters caused a glint of longing in Betsy's eyes. She had probably loved talking to Caroline because it brought her into the family circle at the inn, for that brief span of time. Sam realized how desperately Betsy needed a friend from outside her family unit.

"If you'd like to come, meet me at the inn at eight forty-five on Sunday. We can drive together." Sam stood up to take her leave.

"And if you decide not to come this Sunday, no problem. The offer always stands."

"Thank you," Betsy said quietly. "I'll think about it."

As Sam drove back home under a leaden sky, she hoped Betsy would decide to come to church with her. Pastor Stan had been surprisingly accurate in his assessment of Betsy and how she and Sam were rather alike.

Maybe he'd also be right that the two of them might become friends.

CHAPTER
Twenty

Gracie was relieved to see Sam enter the kitchen. "I'm glad you're home. I was afraid you'd be caught out in this bad weather."

Sam frowned. "I thought the latest weather report said the storm was going to pass us by?"

"It is, but the winds are still pretty strong. Evelyn"—Gracie gave a sharp look to her granddaughter, who was playing chase with Max around the island in the kitchen—"please keep it down."

"I am keeping it down."

Technically, she wasn't making any noise with her mouth, but she was chasing Max around the kitchen, and her shoes on the wooden floor were beginning to pound a little too hard.

"Try to run a little softer. Ms. Montgomery is in the parlor working."

"I saw Trish had set up on her computer at one of the small tables." Sam bent over the steaming saucepan of milk Gracie was heating on the stove.

"That's for hot chocolate. Want some?"

"Sounds cozy. Sure."

Gracie poured some hot milk into a mug and stirred in cocoa powder. "We lost our cable television connection, maybe because of the storm, and since our Internet is through the cable company too, we lost Internet too. Trish said she needs to get online, so she set up a dial-up connection through the wall jack in the parlor."

"Doesn't she have a phone jack in her room?"

"She said she tried it but it didn't work. Since she hadn't used the telephone in her room since she came, she didn't notice it wasn't working."

Sam groaned. "Just another thing we have to fix."

"Yes. Poor Trish—first the water faucet and now the phone line."

"Oh, that's right. When she first arrived, the water tap didn't work."

"The poor woman has had the worst luck when it comes to things breaking down in this house. Evelyn, what did I say about being quiet? Ms. Montgomery is in the parlor."

"It's not my fault, Max ran into my feet and I almost fell." Evelyn almost immediately went back to chasing Max. Luckily he hadn't started barking; he was panting too hard to do that.

Thunder had started rumbling in the distance, but nothing very loud until that moment, when a deep *crack* resounded throughout the house, making the walls seem to vibrate. At that moment, Caroline had just entered the kitchen, and the sound made her jump in the doorway, the kitchen door ajar.

Max started and then raced through Caroline's legs and out of the kitchen.

"Max!" Evelyn raced after him, wriggling past her great-aunt.

"Evelyn, keep your voice down." Gracie hurried after them. "Bring Max back into the kitchen."

Unfortunately, Max had bolted into the parlor. Trish had risen to her feet in frustration as Max circled her, amped up by playing with Evelyn and scared from the sound of the thunderclap. Evelyn raced after him, calling, "Max, it was only thunder, come back—"

"Gracie, there you are." Trish looked harried and highly annoyed. "Could you please get this dog and your granddaughter away? I'm trying to work—"

Suddenly, Evelyn ran into the telephone cord that ran from Trish's laptop computer into the phone jack in the wall. Her legs jerked the power cable, sending the laptop off the small side table where it was lying and hurtling it to the floor with a sickening *crunch.*

There was a deafening silence in the room for a second. Then Trish shrieked and lunged for her computer on the floor.

Evelyn stood rooted where she was, frozen in shock and guilt. Her breath came in gasps, and a sheen of tears began to form over her eyes. "I'm... I'm sorry..."

Trish didn't hear her. The laptop screen was completely black. She tapped desperately at the keys, pressed the power button, shoved the power cord more firmly into the computer. Nothing.

A sound like a strangled cat came from Trish's throat. "My... manuscript..."

"Trish..." Gracie said helplessly.

"You!" Trish rounded furiously on Evelyn. "Do you know what will happen if I can't recover my manuscript? No wonder your parents left you here if you're this awful at home!"

Gracie couldn't breathe, she was so shocked at Trish's words. A soft gasp behind her sounded like Caroline.

"Hey," Sam protested.

Evelyn had turned deathly white, she was almost transparent. Her entire body shook violently. Her eyes were wide, horrified. Then her mouth closed in a grimace of pain, and she fled the parlor.

But Trish wasn't finished. She turned to Gracie and her sisters. "I expected a professionally run inn, not a day care. I knew about your dog, but if I had known you had a child here, I would never have come. If my manuscript is lost—" She started sobbing hysterically, and she dropped heavily into the chair. "If my manuscript is lost... It can't be lost...."

Gracie wasn't sure if she should approach the woman while she was so upset, but she couldn't let her sit there crying alone. She supposed Trish losing all her work on her computer would be like the sisters watching the Misty Harbor Inn go up in flames.

Gracie approached her cautiously, then laid a tentative hand on Trish's shaking shoulder.

"I'm sorry," Trish said, choking. "I'm sorry. I shouldn't have yelled at her. I shouldn't have yelled at you. I have a terrible temper sometimes. And my manuscript—" She started crying even harder. "All that work..."

"Did you, uh, back it up?" Sam asked.

Trish's tears became louder and more forceful. "That's why I needed the Internet connection. I back everything up to a service online, and I hadn't backed it up. I'd been too busy writing to remember to back up my file. My last backup was when I was only ten percent into the manuscript. And I finished it tonight." Trish began to wail.

"I'm so sorry," Gracie said. "I should have had a firmer control over Evelyn."

"I should have been the one controlling Max," Caroline said.

"Where is Evelyn?" Sam looked around.

Gracie stood and looked around the room. "Probably in the bedroom." Max had disappeared too.

"I'll go talk to her." Sam left.

"There are places that retrieve lost data," Gracie said. "Please allow us to send your computer there and pay for it."

Trish sniffled and nodded, her shoulders slumping. "I don't have any other options. I've written so many novels, but this was… this one was special."

The pain in her voice tore at Gracie's heart. She remembered Trish's comment about her English professor parents not approving of her books. "This wasn't a romance novel?" she asked gently.

"It was a literary women's fiction novel." Trish's lip trembled. "This was supposed to make my family proud of me."

Gracie ached for Trish. She could only imagine the longing in the woman's heart for approval from her parents when it seemed like only certain achievements would earn their love. She took a deep breath and then said softly, " You might or might not make your family proud of you, but that's not something you can control. It's not something you can force them to do. You need to instead focus on doing what makes yourself proud. You need to write for yourself. Ultimately, that's the only thing that matters."

Trish dissolved into tears, and for a moment Gracie was worried she'd hurt Trish's feelings more.

Suddenly Doris appeared at Trish's side. Gracie hadn't even noticed that she had entered the parlor. Doris took the seat next to Trish and began gently caressing her hands. "It'll be all right, dear. Everything will work out." Her soothing voice and soothing presence started to make Trish's sobs slowly fade.

Caroline went to go make tea, and soon Trish had calmed down to only hiccups and an occasional sob. She turned to Gracie and Doris. "Thank you. You're absolutely right. And I'm very sorry I yelled at Evelyn."

Then Sam returned to the parlor, but the look on her face made Gracie's stomach churn.

"I found Max and locked him in the bedroom. But I can't find Evelyn," Sam said.

"Oh no. Oh no." Trish began to cry again. "It's my fault. It's all my fault."

"Let's not panic yet," Gracie said. "Sam, where did you check?"

"All over the house, although not very thoroughly. I went through all the rooms and called her name."

"She was pretty upset when she ran off, so maybe she isn't answering because she wants to be alone?" Caroline said.

She had been moody lately, but somehow Gracie couldn't see her deliberately not answering her great-aunt's calls. "Let's search the house again."

"Let me help." Trish rose unsteadily to her feet.

"No, you've had a shock. Why don't you sit here with Doris?" Caroline laid a gentle hand on Trish's shoulder.

"But it's my fault she ran off."

"She's probably feeling guilty for breaking your computer," Gracie said.

The reminder of her lost manuscript made more tears cascade down Trish's reddened cheeks, and she sank back down into the chair. Doris began stroking her hands again.

At that moment, the lights flickered and then went out. The wind around the house was growing louder, and sprays of rain machine-gunned the windows.

Trish gave a little shriek of surprise. Even Gracie felt a chill run over her arms as the room was plunged into complete darkness.

"No one move," Sam said.

Gracie heard Sam heading through the parlor toward the kitchen. In moments she returned with a birthday candle in her fingers. "Good thing I remembered where the old candles were. Give me a second to get the flashlights." She made her way to a bookshelf at the far end of the parlor and rooted around in a basket on the bottom shelf. In moments she had handed Gracie and Caroline flashlights. "We only have two."

"I have a few candles in the bedroom." Caroline darted into the kitchen and toward their bedrooms at the back of the house, and she returned with her arms loaded with three large jar candles. She set them down on tables near Trish and Doris and lit them.

"Let's look for Evelyn," Gracie said.

Sam and Caroline took the first floor while Gracie looked thoroughly around the second floor. She even braved entering Hannah's secret room, with the flimsy floorboards ominously creaking under her weight, but Evelyn wasn't there.

She returned to the first floor parlor, and Doris said that Sam and Caroline had gone to search the secret basement room. Gracie headed to the library and met them as they exited the dark passageway.

"No Evelyn," Sam said.

Caroline gave a disgusted shiver. "It's horrible to go down there in the dark."

"Where could she have gone?" A jingling of panic began in Gracie's stomach.

"I'll bet she's in the carriage house," Sam said, and the three of them headed to the back door. They all paused a moment before flinging open the door.

Rain came pelting into the house like icy bullets. Gracie winced but raced outside against the downpour, hearing Caroline and Sam slipping and sliding behind her on the wet grass.

Then darted into the carriage house and immediately began calling for Evelyn while searching with their flashlights. But she wasn't curled up in the Packard station wagon or the minivan, nor was she huddled along the walls.

They went out the back door of the carriage house and raced up the stairs to the second floor. At the top of the landing, with rain running down her back in a river, Gracie realized she'd forgotten the key. She turned to her sisters and realized only Caroline was there.

"Where's Sam?"

Caroline turned around. "She was right behind me."

"I forgot the key."

"Rats." Caroline turned to hurry down the stairs, but suddenly the back door of the carriage house opened, and Sam headed up the stairs.

"I forgot the—" Gracie started to say, but Sam held her hand up. The key was clasped between her white fingertips. "I went to get it."

Gracie stepped aside and unlocked the door, and they stumbled into the loft apartment. Gracie smelled the mustiness stronger in the dark, somehow. Caroline gave a soft, "*Oof.*"

"Are you all right?"

"I just walked into a stack of boxes."

"Evelyn?" Gracie called.

They walked the entire maze of boxes, calling Evelyn's name. The jittery feeling in Gracie's stomach began to turn into a raging tempest like the one outside. Her granddaughter wouldn't not answer when her two aunts and grandma were calling her so insistently.

"She's not here," Sam finally said.

"But she has to be here!" Gracie was startled to hear her voice rise so frantically.

"We must have missed her in the house," Caroline said weakly.

"She has to be somewhere." Gracie turned and hurried out of the loft. The rain hit her face like a slap, but she rushed down the stairs, sliding a couple of times but catching herself with a firm grip on the railing. She yanked open the back door to the carriage house and then headed inside.

She went straight through and out into the backyard, yelling, "Evelyn! Evelyn!" It seemed like the darkness screamed at her, until she realized it was the wind. She scanned the beach but couldn't see beyond the first dunes.

"Gracie, we have to call the police." Sam's firm voice was at her ear, and Caroline grabbed Gracie by the elbow, steering her toward the house.

She resisted. "She has to be out here somewhere. What if she's hurt?"

"Gracie, let's call the police. They'll know what to do."

She let her sisters lead her into the house. They had to half-support her because her legs were weak and wobbly.

When they had stumbled into the kitchen through the back door, Sam said to Caroline, "You take her into the parlor. I'll get some towels."

Caroline helped Gracie into the parlor, and she sank gratefully into a chair. Doris had straightened as they entered, her face concerned. "You didn't find her?"

Caroline shook her head.

"You're both soaked through."

Sam hurried into the parlor with her arms full of towels. Caroline draped one over Gracie, but she began to shiver instead of feeling warmer. "We have to call the police."

Sam went to get her cell phone.

Then Doris suddenly spoke. While her voice was lilting as always, there was a sharp urgency to her tone. "There was a bad storm once when I lived here, a few months before we left Nantucket and moved to New York. Miss Quincy came to get us, and we hid in her root cellar."

"Quincy?" Sam stopped punching the numbers on her cell phone. "Next door is Quincy Court."

"It used to belong to Miss Quincy. She was very old at the time, at least she seemed old to me. There's a root cellar right on the edge of the property between Montague House and Quincy Court. We hid down there during the storm."

"Do you remember where it is?" Trish asked.

"We can't let Doris go out into the storm," Caroline objected.

"It isn't hard to find if you know what to look for," Doris said. "On the edges of the two properties, near where the fence sags, there's a small rise in the ground on the Quincy Court side of the fence. If you go around to the other side of it, you'll see the trapdoor. You can't see the door from the Montague House side of the fence."

Which explained why none of the sisters had seen the trapdoor. Gracie jumped to her feet. "When Evelyn disappeared that one day, she said she was in Shirley's yard. Maybe she found the trapdoor."

"Let's put on rain jackets," Sam said.

"We're already wet." Gracie grabbed the flashlight and headed out to the back door again.

They hurried across the backyard, toward Quincy Court this time, and Gracie ran along the edge of the fence. There was where it sagged a little. She couldn't see anything on the other side of the fence because of the thicket of rose branches woven along the railing.

They found a place where they could hop the fence and scanned the ground with their flashlights, looking for a rise of earth. It was difficult to find because there were even more rosebushes on this side of the fence that obscured the ground in places.

"Here!" Gracie caught sight of a wooden slat through a thicket of weeds at the base of a large, thorny rosebush. She and her sisters pulled at the weeds, but the weeds were only hiding the trapdoor by draping over it, they weren't growing on top of it. It was a very small trapdoor, perhaps three feet by three feet, made of old wooden boards nailed together with a rusted handle. Gracie pulled open the door.

"Evelyn?" she called.

Her heart stopped as a small voice said timidly, "Grandma?"

Hot tears rushed to her eyes, mixing with the cold rain. She shone the flashlight down into the hole and saw steep wooden steps leading down.

"Evelyn, are you all right?" Gracie was already stumbling down the stairs, shining her light around the small room at the bottom.

Evelyn was getting to her feet, rising from a nest of quilts that Gracie recognized from one of the empty guest rooms at the inn. A candle in a rusted holder sat on the ground next to her.

"We found you. Thank You, dear Lord," Gracie breathed as she grabbed Evelyn and squeezed her tight.

"*Oomph,*" Evelyn said into her chest. "Grandma, I can't breathe."

Gracie released her and grabbing her by the shoulders, shook her a couple of times. "Don't you ever run away like that again, do you hear me? We were worried sick."

Evelyn's face crumpled. "I'm…I'm sorry," she said in a small voice.

Gracie immediately regretted her stern tone. "I'm sorry, sweetheart, I didn't mean to scold you. I was just so worried. We couldn't find you in the inn."

But Evelyn just kept crying. In fact, her sobs became harder and louder.

"What is it?" Gracie asked in confusion.

"Is it…is it true?" Evelyn said in a choked voice.

"Is what true?"

"Is it true that Mom and Dad don't want me back?"

"Of course that's not true! Trish didn't mean what she was saying."

"But…you said Daddy would come to take me back home, but whenever he calls, he never says when."

Gracie remembered the day Brandon had left on the ferry, and she had taken Evelyn for ice cream. Evelyn had wanted to know for certain that her parents would want her back, and while Gracie had reassured her, she had dismissed her fears as those of a child missing her parents. And Gracie supposed it might seem that way, with Brandon hustling Evelyn off so hastily and not being able to speak to her for very long each time he called because the twins had been so sick.

"Your daddy is going to bring you back home. Do you remember what I told you about the twins?"

"They have a bug."

"It's called scarlet fever. It takes two weeks or more before they're no longer contagious. Your daddy didn't want you to get sick, but he always intended for you to come back home."

Evelyn began to cry again. "He never talks to me. When he calls. He only talks to you. Or he only asks to make sure I'm being good."

"Oh, sweetheart." Gracie wrapped her in an embrace. She had forgotten about how Paige had been emotionally needy the first time she went away to summer camp. She would have to speak to Brandon about how to talk to young girls who were homesick.

The light from the candle suddenly tilted, and Gracie saw Sam pick up the candle holder and the quilt from the floor. She tilted her head toward the trapdoor opening. "Shirley's up there."

"In this rain? Oh no."

With her arm still around Evelyn, Gracie headed up the stairs. She heard Shirley saying to Caroline, "You're just lucky I happened to catch sight of you before I called the police. I thought you were a bunch of burglars coming to rob me."

"Sorry, Shirley." Caroline had a hint of amusement in her voice. "We were a little frantic at the time, or we'd have gone up to the house to let you know."

"Yes, yes, you explained about Evelyn. But next time—"

"Shirley, you should get out of this rain," Gracie said as they cleared the top of the trapdoor.

Shirley's white hair, usually drawn up in a bun, now was plastered like a cap on her head. She caught sight of Evelyn and *tsked*. "You poor thing. I made some soup tonight. I'll bring over a pot."

She hustled back into her house before Gracie could protest.

"Let's get into the house," Sam said.

They scurried through the chilling rain and made it back into the kitchen. Trish and Doris were there with extra towels.

"We were watching for you." Trish wrapped a towel around Evelyn. "I'm so sorry for what I said, honey. It was inexcusable. Will you please forgive me?"

Evelyn nodded solemnly. "I'm... I'm sorry for breaking your computer," she said in a small voice.

A pang of sorrow crossed Trish's face, but she nodded and tried to smile. "I didn't mean what I said. Of course your parents want you back home."

"Of course they do." Gracie gave Evelyn another hug.

"You're so lucky to have your family," Trish said. "They were frantic searching for you."

"Family will always love you," Gracie said to Evelyn. "Never forget that. And family will always want you back."

CHAPTER
Twenty-one

The storm was still a thick downpour the next day, although the thunder had abated and the winds had slowed. Sam had washed out Shirley's soup pot—which she'd brought over the night before, in the pouring rain—and decided to head over to return it to her.

Sam found Gracie chatting with Doris in the parlor. "Where's Evelyn? I know Michael's mom is coming to pick her up in an hour, but I'm going to return Shirley's pot to her, and I think she should come with me since she hid in Shirley's root cellar."

"She's upstairs helping Caroline straighten the room she took the quilt from. I'll get her." Gracie left the room.

"I'd like to come over too, if that's all right," Doris said. "I don't think I've met your neighbor yet."

"Of course. I'm sure Shirley would love to meet you."

Shirley indeed wanted to meet Doris. She'd been several years younger than Doris when she lived in Montague House, so they hadn't played together, but they shared memories of old places in Nantucket and people the two of them had known.

"Did you ever know Miss Quincy?" Doris sat back in her chair and sipped the strong coffee she'd made for them.

"Who's Miss Quincy?" Evelyn munched on another cookie from the platter Shirley had brought out. Originally the plate had been in the center of the coffee table, but it had slowly migrated until it was directly in front of Evelyn's chair.

"Miss Quincy used to own this house," Doris said.

"I never met her," Shirley said. "I think she sold her house to my husband's father, maybe soon after you had left. The elder Mr. Addison lived here for as long as I can remember. He died only a few years after I married his son, and my husband inherited the house. I've lived here ever since."

"Did you know about the root cellar?" Sam asked.

"Of course I did. My husband told me about it, and I made sure never to go down there." She eyed Evelyn. "How did you find it?"

Evelyn paused in the act of eating another cookie, and set it down on her plate. "I, uh...found it. A long time ago."

Sam couldn't believe Evelyn had gone into that dark hole— probably full of cobwebs when she first found it—but Gracie had mentioned that Evelyn had been unafraid when they discovered the secret passage in the library.

"Are you the reason my plants have been crushed for the past couple of weeks?" Shirley demanded.

Sam thought back to the weeds that had been growing around the trapdoor. *Plants, eh?*

"I'm sorry, Mrs. Addison," Evelyn said.

Shirley glared at her, though she had a twinkle in her eyes. "Just make sure you don't do that anymore."

"I won't."

"Whatever happened to that writer woman?" Shirley asked.

"Trish left early this morning with her computer," Sam said.

"It still doesn't turn on?"

Sam shook her head. "Trish said she'd take it to a computer repair office in New York that her publisher recommended. Apparently the computer guys said that since the computer only fell, and there wasn't water or anything like that involved, they were almost positive they could get her manuscript off of her hard drive."

"*Humph*," Shirley said.

"And Evelyn is leaving tomorrow," Gracie said. "Her father called this morning to say that the twins have gotten a clean bill of health and he's coming to get her to take her home."

Evelyn beamed. "But today I get to ride Michael's pony one last time."

Shirley *harrumphed* and shoved the plate even closer to her. "Have another cookie."

"I was surprised to see a root cellar in a house so close to the beach," Gracie said.

"From what Miss Quincy told me, the cellar had been part of the basement of the original house, which had a fire years ago," Doris said. "When Miss Quincy's father rebuilt it, he only renovated the undamaged parts of the building and tore down some of the burned bits, which left the root cellar out in the backyard the way it is."

"What was Miss Quincy like?" Sam asked.

"Oh, she was feisty and strong-minded." Doris's twinkling gaze landed on Shirley for a brief moment. "She would often invite my mother and me over for tea, or she'd come to Montague House for tea. She and my mother grew very close, which was why, when the storm blew in, she came for us and took us down into the root cellar. I was so frightened, but then Miss Quincy lit a candle, and my mother read from her Bible, and everything seemed all right."

"There's a Bible down there," Evelyn said.

Sam started in surprise and looked at her. "There is?"

"It was on the shelf."

"What shelf?" Gracie asked.

"There was a bookshelf behind where I was sitting. I'll go get it." Evelyn jumped up and ran off before anyone could say anything.

"I'm sorry, Shirley, do you want me to call her back?" Gracie had already half risen from her chair, but Shirley waved her back down.

"It'll keep her from eating more cookies, anyway." Shirley glanced down at the few left on the plate.

"I doubt it would be my mother's Bible," Doris said. "I have it. Mother gave it to me."

Evelyn returned, waving a large black leather-covered book. "Here it is." She handed it to Doris.

But Doris's face froze as she stared down at the Bible. "Oh my," she breathed. "Oh my. I had forgotten."

"What is it?" Sam leaned forward to touch her shoulder.

"This"—Doris's voice was weak—"this is my mother's Bible."

"But I thought you said—" Shirley began, but Doris shook her head. "I had forgotten all about this. This was her old Bible. I didn't even remember this one, or wonder where it had gone when she got her new one. I remember one Christmas, when we were in New York, my father gave Mother a new Bible. That's the one I have. I had completely forgotten she used to have this one."

Sam leaned closer to look at it. The black leather was very old and cracked, and a cross had been stamped or burned into the bottom left corner of the front cover. "Are you sure?"

"The book was old even when my mother used it. I remember this cross. But I should open it to check." She opened the book.

The first blank page had a hand-drawn family tree.

"Is that your family tree?" Gracie had also leaned forward, peering at the Bible over Doris' shoulder.

"There I am." Doris pointed toward the bottom of the tree. "Doris, 1926" had been written below "Charity m. John, 1925." "And there's Mother," Doris said.

Sam's eye wandered up the tree, and she nearly jumped out of her chair when she saw the name "Hannah Elliott" near the top of the tree. "Doris! Gracie!"

"Oh my," Doris said.

"Hannah m. Jedediah Montague, 1875" had been written near the top of the tree. Then another line had been written from Hannah's name to "m. Jacob Nickerson, 1881."

"Nickerson!" Gracie yelped.

"Look at her mother's name." Sam pointed to where Hannah's parents were written as "Emmaline m. Isaac Elliott, 1851."

"On that ticket, the false name took Hannah's mother's first name and Jacob Nickerson's last name," Gracie said.

"She already knew Jacob," Sam said suddenly. "In the note, a man named Jacob met her that night at the lighthouse to give her the ticket, the money, and William's note."

Sam glanced back down at the Bible and saw William's name next to Hannah's, with the name of his wife and the date of their marriage. William had a handful of children, but the dates of their deaths were listed. They must have been his wife's miscarriages.

"Grandma." Evelyn pointed to a name further down the tree.

Sam read, "Margaret m. David Kingsbury, 1925" and under it, "Rosalie Kingsbury, born 1926."

Mom.

She nearly fell off her chair. Gracie gave a visible start. They looked at each other in shock for a moment and then back at the Bible.

Sam traced the lineage back. After Hannah married Jacob Nickerson, she had had a son, Joseph, and three daughters: Alberta, Susannah, and Emmaline.

Joseph had two daughters, who married and had children.

Emmaline Nickerson never married. In the obituary, Emmaline had been survived by her two great-nieces. Sam could now see that they were apparently Joseph's granddaughters.

Alberta married and had two sons and one daughter, Charity, who had one daughter, Doris.

Alberta's sister Susannah married and had a son and one daughter, Margaret. Margaret married David Kingsbury and had a daughter, Rosalie Kingsbury.

Doris suddenly sneezed, and Sam realized she and Gracie had been crowding around her looking at the Bible. "I'm sorry," Sam said.

"Not at all." Doris looked amused. "I can understand you were properly surprised by all this. I know I am."

"I can't believe this," Gracie said in a faint voice. "We're related to Hannah." She looked at Doris. "You're related to Hannah."

"I'm related to Hannah too," Evelyn said.

"And to think you discovered this in my root cellar." Shirley grinned.

"This is proof Hannah wasn't murdered," Sam said. "She ran away that night and made it to her brother's church. Then she married Jacob Nickerson the very next year."

"Once she left Nantucket and married, no one would ever know who she really was unless they found the Bible with her name in it,"

Gracie said. "This is her only tie to the Montagues because it has her first marriage written in it."

"The woman whose mystery we've been trying to solve." Sam pointed to the Bible. "And she was right here, all along."

"Wait a minute," Caroline said. "Repeat that?"

Caroline could only listen with a fuzzy head as Sam and Gracie pointed to the Bible in Doris's lap and talked about who married whom and had so many daughters, and then ended with, "We three and Doris are related to Hannah Montague. Or rather, Hannah Nickerson."

Caroline couldn't speak for a full minute. Finally she said, "You're sure?"

"Positive. It's all in the Bible."

Doris handed Caroline the Bible, and she looked at the family tree, handwritten on the blank page and updated through the years by various family members. She saw her mother's name near the bottom, and Doris's name.

"This is fantastic!" Caroline squealed, and with a laugh, they all gathered in a group hug around Doris. "We'll have to let Elizabeth Adams know too!"

"I'm so glad to know Hannah wasn't murdered," Gracie said. "Instead, she just ran away from here."

"And to think, Doris and Mom both lived here too," Caroline said.

Sam suddenly stilled, and her eyes narrowed. "That's just a little...coincidental, isn't it?"

Caroline caught on to what she was saying. "Hey, you're right. What are the odds that Doris's mother, Charity, just happened to find work in her grandmother's old house."

"In the 1930s, Hannah Nickerson might have still been alive," Gracie said slowly. "The Bible doesn't have Hannah's death date on it."

"She would have been in her seventies when Doris's mother moved to Nantucket," Sam said.

"Do you think perhaps my mother got a job here at Montague House deliberately?" Doris said.

Caroline sighed. "It doesn't matter what we think. There's no way to know or find out."

Doris cocked her head to the side. "There might be. The cousins I've been visiting with here on Nantucket are all related on my father's side, but Johnnie is older than the rest of us. He and my father were cousins, about fifteen years apart. They were very close, and he came with us to Nantucket when we moved here for work. Johnnie might remember how my mother got the job at Montague House."

"Could we talk to him?" Sam asked.

"Let me call him to see if he'll be able to talk to us today," Doris said.

Gracie almost ran to get the cordless phone, and the three sisters looked at each other impatiently while Doris spoke to Johnnie's son, Derek, and arranged for them to come over that afternoon.

"Thank you so much," Gracie said when Doris hung up the phone.

"I'm as interested as you are. I didn't know I had my own little mystery when I came here to stay."

After lunch, Caroline helped Gracie with the inn's laundry. While they were folding towels, Caroline asked, "How's everything going with the house? Did you decide to get a loan or not?"

Gracie's shoulders sagged. "I'm not sure. I got the loan application but I haven't filled it out yet."

"If you're not absolutely certain about it, maybe you shouldn't do it. A bank loan is a pretty significant commitment."

"But I don't know if I can sell my house without fixing it up first. And I need a loan for that."

"But the loan is making you uncomfortable."

Gracie laid a towel down. "The truth is that I'm uncomfortable selling the house at all."

Caroline was silent. She'd been ecstatic when Gracie decided to move to Nantucket, but what if it had been a bad idea?

"I don't like the thought of strangers in my house. I know that sounds silly, but there are so many memories in that house. Strangers wouldn't know about those memories, but I do, and— I'm not making any sense."

"Oh, Gracie." Caroline put her arms around her sister. "Maybe you're just trying too hard."

"What?"

"You're thinking of taking this loan out, but have you given God a chance to work first?"

Gracie was quiet in Caroline's embrace. Then she gave Caroline a quick squeeze and pulled away. "It just seems—I don't know— irresponsible? To just step back and say, 'Okay, God, sell my house for me even though I know it needs to be updated.'"

"But God orchestrated your coming to live in Nantucket. If He wants you here, then surely He'd orchestrate the sale of your house for you, without a loan that makes you uncomfortable."

Gracie ran her hand back and forth over a stack of neatly folded towels. "Do you really think so?"

"I know God brought us to this inn for a reason. I know this deep in my heart. He won't leave you high and dry with your house hanging over your head."

"I'll have to think about it. And pray about it." Gracie reached for another towel to fold. "But I think you might be right."

"I'll pray for you too."

The sisters were ready to go when it came time to drive Doris to see her cousin Johnnie. She had already seen him several times while staying at the inn, but this time she seemed agitated about the visit.

"You don't need to do this," Caroline said to her when they all met in the parlor. "We don't want to be forcing you to ask questions you'd rather not." Even though she was burning with curiosity, she also didn't want to be bullying Doris into doing this.

"I want to know. Maybe it was all coincidence. But if it wasn't, I would rather know than have to wonder."

She directed them to Johnnie's son's home just outside of town, and Caroline suspected that Gracie drove the Packard a tad faster than normal.

The house was a charming modern home with simple lines and a shady front yard. As soon as they pulled up, Johnnie's son, Derek, opened the front door and waved to them.

Derek smiled as they trooped up to the house, his white-blond hair a striking contrast to his deeply tanned face. "Hi, Doris." He bent to kiss her cheek, and she introduced the Marris sisters.

"Go on in," Derek said.

They entered the living room, where Johnnie sat on a recliner, a stick of a man with Doris's blue eyes and his son's thick hair, although Johnnie's was more white than blond.

"How are you doing today? Thank you for agreeing to see us all." Doris spoke loudly.

Johnnie answered at a volume a little under a roar. "Oh, no trouble. I beat Derek at chess again, so he's sulking."

"Am not," Derek called from the front room, humor in his voice.

Caroline couldn't help but smile.

Doris and Johnnie chatted about family for a few minutes—his granddaughter's job at the hospital, his son's new business as a tour guide, which he'd just started after retiring from contracting a few years ago.

At last Doris said, "Johnnie, the reason we came is to ask you about my mother."

His eyes, weighted down with wrinkles, seemed to grow heavier. "Ah, I miss her. What about her?"

"Do you remember how she got the job at Montague House?"

He thought a moment. "She never wanted any other job."

"What do you mean?"

"As soon as we landed in Nantucket, she was inquiring about a job at that house."

Caroline reasoned that she shouldn't be surprised. After all, they'd suspected Doris's mother had deliberately gotten the position.

"Did she ever say why she wanted to work for them?"

"She didn't really explain to me. I was just a boy at the time. She was pretty determined. Maybe she somehow found out what they were paying their staff. She made friends with the other staff there and even spoke to the owners a few times. Finally she convinced them to hire her as a maid. And she didn't stay a maid for very long. When the cook was fired, she got promoted."

"What about my father?"

"They didn't hire him right away, but when the old chauffeur got sick, your mother managed to get the owners to hire your father."

"Did my father want to be hired by them the same way?"

"Not as I could tell. But he was right pleased to be hired as chauffeur."

Doris smiled. "Father liked his cars."

"Cars and roses. Those were what your father liked most to tinker with."

Doris chatted more with Johnnie, and he regaled them with some tales of the war. But he seemed to tire easily, and they left after half an hour.

In the car, Caroline opened up the conversation with, "I think Doris's mother knew about the connection between Hannah and the house. Do you think Hannah herself might have asked her to do something for her?"

"If she did, did she do it?" Gracie said.

Caroline remembered the secret room, stuffed with Hannah's things, and the unused ticket. "Do you think Doris's mother was supposed to find Hannah's things?"

"Her clothes, her mementos, her money." Sam nodded. "Maybe. But she never found it."

"If that money was from William, then it would make sense that Hannah wanted Charity to try to find it," Gracie said.

"But my mother never found it," Doris said.

"Maybe she looked but just couldn't find the opening," Gracie said. "After all, the only opening to the room that we know of is the panel that Sam found and dislodged by accident."

"It might also explain how Charity found the hidden passage to the basement," Sam said. "She was looking for secret doors because she was trying to find Hannah's secret room."

"But, Doris, she never told about this?" Gracie asked.

"No. Perhaps my great-grandmother Hannah asked her not to. I don't know if she told my father or not."

"I know this is all only speculation," Gracie said. "I guess we'll never know for certain."

When they were turning into the driveway to park the car in the carriage house, Caroline saw George's car in front of the inn. The sight of his handsome face and broad smile made her want to run into his arms, but she also felt a twinge of apprehension that he had another house he wanted her to look at.

She told herself to buck up. She knew George would only do what he felt God was telling him would be the best for both of them. She was determined to trust God and to trust George.

She was about to help Doris out of the car when Gracie waved her off. "We'll help Doris into the house. Go say hello to George."

Caroline headed down the driveway and met George halfway, as he was heading toward the carriage house. "Hello." He gave her a warm kiss.

"Did I forget an appointment we had?"

"No, but I do have a home I'd like you to consider."

She put her arm around his waist. "Sure."

However, he steered her toward the carriage house. To her surprise, Sam and Gracie were still near the car, and they were beaming at her.

George pointed to windows of the top floor of the carriage house, where the boxes in the loft apartment could be seen. "What do you say to that for our home?"

Caroline didn't understand what he was saying for a moment. Then she threw herself into his arms, making him stagger back a step.

"We'll live above the carriage house? Like Doris did with her parents?" She'd still be near her sisters, but they wouldn't be stepping on each others' toes. She'd still be in the beloved inn that her mother had wanted to run, that she had invested so much time and love into.

"We'll be able to renovate it."

Caroline was now doubly glad she had decided to scale back the wedding. She could use her money to help renovate the apartment.

George's eyes were twinkling brighter than stars. "And we'll probably need to clear out the boxes."

"I think the boxes add to the character of the apartment." Caroline winked at him. Then she turned around to look at where Gracie and Sam were standing. "Did you know about this?"

"George talked to me when you and Sam were out at the wedding consultant's office," Gracie said. "And I spoke to Sam about it later."

"We think it's a great idea," Sam said.

"So do I." Caroline gave George another kiss. It was a wonderful idea. It was the absolute best.

"Dad!" Evelyn rushed toward where her father was disembarking from the ferry, and he gave her a bear hug.

"Dad, I want a pony."

Brandon did a double take and then walked toward where Gracie stood with Evelyn's suitcase. "Is this your doing?"

Gracie laughed. "Sorry. She met a boy who owns a pony, and they've been having fun riding for the past week or so."

"Let me, uh, talk to your mother," Brandon said to Evelyn. To Gracie, he said, "I'm sorry to have to grab her and go, Mom, but I couldn't take much time off of work."

"I completely understand. It's been fun having her here."

Evelyn gave Gracie a hug. "Thanks for everything, Grandma."

"You're welcome to come back anytime." Gracie kissed her.

"Have you spoken to Paige lately, Mom?"

"No, not for a couple of weeks. Why?"

"Oh, no reason. Say good-bye to Grandma, Evie."

"Bye, Grandma." Evelyn gave one last hug, and then the two of them, Brandon carrying Evelyn's suitcase, headed back onto the ferry for its return run to the mainland. Evelyn's voice carried back to Gracie: "Dad, let me explain why I need a pony…"

Gracie was walking along the wharf, heading back to the car, when she got a call on her cell phone from Elizabeth Adams from the historical society. "Hello, Elizabeth."

"Hi, Gracie. I have some information for you."

"Oh boy. Do I have some information for you too."

"Really? What did you find out?"

Gracie explained about how they had found Doris's mother's Bible, and how she and her sisters and Doris were all descended from her.

"That's so cool." Elizabeth's voice sounded almost like a teenager's. "And that perfectly fits with what I uncovered today. Do you remember how I said there was a Nickerson family in Nantucket up until the 1850s? I discovered why they left Nantucket. There was a mutineer whose last name was Nickerson who was found guilty of killing several officers. One of those officers was an ancestor of the Elliott family, so there was a long-standing grudge between the two families."

"Do you think Jacob Nickerson was related to the mutineer? That would explain so much. Hannah's father had said that he hadn't wanted his daughter to marry a man who was unworthy for some reason. But from the note we discovered, it was obvious Hannah already knew Jacob Nickerson when he met her at the lighthouse the night before she disappeared. What if Jacob was the man Hannah had fallen in love with, but her father had disapproved of the marriage? He married her to Jedediah Montague instead. But when Jedediah died, Hannah had a chance to escape, and she did, and married Jacob after all."

"I don't know if that's really what happened, but it sounds romantic," Elizabeth said.

"It still doesn't prove if Hannah did or didn't steal the money from the lighthouse. I don't know that we'll ever discover that." Gracie looked out toward the ocean and felt the breeze tangling in her hair. She could stand out here on the wharf all day, discussing Hannah Elliott Montague Nickerson, but she had chores to do back at the inn. "Did Irene get back to you yet? She was going to look into Emmaline Nickerson, but I want to let her know what we just found."

"Why don't you shoot me an e-mail and I'll forward it to Irene?"

"Sure. Thanks, Elizabeth."

"Anytime."

Gracie was about to put her phone back into her purse when it suddenly rang again. It was her daughter, Paige. How odd, when Brandon had just mentioned her. "Hello, sweetheart. How are you?"

"Mom, did you sell the house yet?" Paige sounded slightly anxious.

"No, not yet."

"Good, because I want to buy it."

Gracie stopped strolling along the wharf, not sure she had heard her correctly. "You want to... Are you sure? Can you afford it?"

"Do you not want me to buy it?" Paige sounded unsure.

"Of course I want you to buy it." Gracie let out a huge breath. Hadn't Caroline told her to trust in God? "I'm thrilled you want to buy it."

"I couldn't stand the thought of some stranger in our house. I hadn't planned to buy a house for another couple of years, but I talked it over with Brandon, and he thought it was a good idea. He said he'd help me out financially so now I have enough for the down payment. And last week, I interviewed with a job in the Department of Justice as an ecologist, and I just got the offer letter today."

"That's wonderful! Congratulations." No wonder Brandon had asked her if she'd talked to Paige lately. "Oh, Paige." The bubble of joy in her throat made it hard to speak, but she was so happy she didn't care. "I'll be sure to give you a good price for it."

"That would help me out, Mom. But don't shortchange yourself. I know you need the money for yourself too."

"I don't care anymore." Gracie smiled at the busy wharf area, not caring who saw her grinning like an idiot. "God has been so faithful to me lately."

"God has been pretty good to me too. I'm glad I can buy the house from you."

"I'll get all the paperwork started."

"Good deal. Thanks."

Gracie stood there, her phone in her hand, the wind on her cheeks and the riotous color of the flowers along the wharf filling her eyes. She felt full. Her cup runneth over.

Thank You, Lord. Thank You.

Sam found she had tears in her eyes as she bent to hug Doris. "It's been so wonderful having you here."

"I've had the time of my life." Doris hugged Caroline also while Gracie picked up her suitcase and took it out to the station wagon, parked outside the inn's front door.

"You'll be back in September for the wedding, right?" Caroline asked.

"Are you sure you want me there? We're only distantly related."

"You're family. In truth, but also because of the time we've spent together these past weeks. Of course I want you there."

"You arranged for your granddaughter to pick you up when you disembark the ferry, right?" Gracie asked her.

"Yes, she called this morning to say she'd be there."

Sam and Caroline walked Doris to the car and waved as it headed down the street toward the wharf. "I'll miss her," Sam said. "I'm glad she'll be back in a few weeks."

"In the meantime, we've got work to do." Caroline turned back toward the house, and Sam followed. The contractors were arriving tomorrow to start work renovating the loft apartment, and they had to finish moving all the boxes out of the apartment. Gracie, not trusting their eye for antiques, had charged them not to throw anything away until she returned from taking Doris to the ferry.

Some boxes, from when the inn had been renovated in the fifties, were clearly trash, but Sam and Caroline dutifully set them aside just in case Gracie found some hidden treasure. The "possible trash" boxes were put in the parlor, while the few "keep" boxes were moved into the dining room.

"How did things go with Betsy at Sunday school yesterday?" Caroline asked. "I was so surprised to see her here to go to church with us."

"I was too, but I'm so glad she came. We had a lot of fun in the preschool class together."

"After that day she was in the kitchen with Evelyn, I would never have thought the two of you would start to become friends."

"Me too." Sam had been surprised to find that she and Betsy had worked well together in the preschool. She had invited Betsy to lunch with them after church, but Betsy had said she had to meet her family for lunch instead. However, Betsy had looked genuinely regretful that she couldn't stay, and before leaving, she'd wished Sam good luck on the baking competition on Saturday—and it looked like she really meant it.

The thought of the competition made her stomach twist, but Sam took a deep breath—of musty air—and reminded herself that it was in God's hands. She didn't need a blue ribbon in the contest to prove anything. She wanted to keep hold of her joy in baking and not lose it in the spirit of competition.

She may not be as knowledgeable about baking now as she wanted to be, but she would…someday.

Finally they had cleared all the boxes except the few pieces of furniture in the room—like Doris's family's desk—and the crates of the Montague brothers' things. They'd saved them for last because they also wanted to look through them. They carried the crates into the dining room and set them on the table, which they'd covered with newspaper.

"Look at this." Caroline held up a wrinkled, ruffled shirt. It had once been white, but there were large ink splotches all over the sleeve where there had perhaps been a mishap with a pen.

"It looks like one of the Montague brothers just wadded it up to throw into the trash."

Caroline shook out the shirt so they could get a better look at the lacy ruffles on the collar and cuffs, and a balled up piece of paper fell out of the folds of dirty cotton.

"What's that?"

Sam bent to pick it up from the floor. "More trash. Looks like scrap paper."

"Well, don't throw it away because it might be antique scrap paper." Caroline winked.

Sam uncrumpled it and discovered it was sheet music. "Were any of the Montagues musical?"

"Maybe. There's that piano."

"This says, 'For organ,' not piano." Sam scanned the rest of the page and almost dropped it. "Oh my goodness."

She thrust the page at Caroline and pointed to some printing at the bottom: "Property of Robert Fenton, Emmanuel Church."

"Robert Fenton? That name sounds familiar—"

"It's the lighthouse keeper from whom the money was stolen. He was an organist for Hannah's church, remember?"

Caroline gasped. "This is his sheet music, among the Montague brothers' things."

"How would they have his sheet music? They didn't go to his church, and in those newspaper clippings, they said they had never gone to the lighthouse."

"Because they lied. Because they stole that money. They must have told the newspaper all those things about Hannah because they were going to blame her for it."

"Do you realize this might be proof they stole it?"

"If it's not proof, it's close enough."

Sam traced the name written on the sheet. "Something just occurred to me. Where's the copy of the family tree that we got from Doris's Bible?"

"I put it in the library." Caroline went to get it, and Sam followed because what she was looking for was in the library too.

They had put some of the Montague brothers' crates in a corner of the library so Gracie could go through them at her leisure. Sam rooted through them until she found the blotter. She flipped to the page with Hannah's name and "I'm sorry" written on it several times.

Caroline showed her the photocopied page of the family tree, and Sam looked up at Hannah's daughters' names. The tree had been expanded by different family members, as could be seen by the different handwritings. Until she'd seen Robert Fenton's handwriting on the organ paper, she hadn't thought to compare the writing on the blotter with what she guessed Hannah's handwriting was.

"Look at how Hannah wrote her daughter's name, Susannah." Sam pointed to it. "Now look at the blotter."

"They're wrong. No, wait. The first 'Hannah Montague' is wrong, but the later ones are closer."

"Look at 'I'm sorry.' It's the same way. The first one isn't Hannah's handwriting, but the other ones are closer. The writer was trying to match the funny way she did her R's."

"They were trying to forge a suicide note," Caroline said.

"They were going to kill her." Sam was mildly horrified at this notion. "The suicide note would frame her for the money that they stole."

"But they didn't kill her. We know she managed to run away— and maybe that's why she did it. Maybe she found out they were going to kill her—she was coming back from church, and she might have overheard them when they were in the house and didn't realize she'd returned. So she ran."

"And she couldn't go to the police. That society matron's journal had mentioned one of the Montague brothers chatting with the chief of police, remember?"

"She must have been too terrified to try to get her things from the upstairs secret room, so she stowed away on a ship to Massachusetts that night."

"Wow," Sam said. "That was really brave of her."

They stared again at the blotter and the family tree, and then Sam set the blotter down on a table.

And then she giggled.

"What is it?" Caroline asked.

"I was thinking about Gracie." Sam grinned. "All I can think of is that she's going to be so disappointed we discovered all this juicy stuff without her."

CHAPTER
Twenty-three

The day of the Summerfest baking contest dawned a little cloudy, but the clouds burned away by nine o'clock, when Sam had delivered her blackberry cobbler to the judging tent.

She almost didn't want to release the Styrofoam container with her precious cobbler, and the woman behind the registration table had to tug at it to take it from her, giving Sam a strange look as she did so.

Sam gave a smile and a half shrug.

"Judging starts in fifteen minutes," the woman said. "But the awards ceremony won't be until one o'clock. Enjoy your day here at the Summerfest fair."

Walking away from the judging tent with Sam, Caroline rolled her eyes. "As if you can enjoy yourself while waiting to hear the results."

Gracie, walking on Sam's other side, asked, "What did Betsy enter?"

"She said she was going to enter a blackberry tart."

"She doesn't have a chance," Caroline said stoutly. "I admit I like her better now, but I still think you're the better baker."

Sam laughed. "Let's just enjoy the day."

They toured the craft tents, where various items had been entered for the other contests at the fair. They were torn about which they liked best from the quilting contest, but they all agreed the elaborate throw with the delicately crocheted flowers was the best in the crochet contest, and they couldn't choose between two specific lace shawls in the knitting contest.

Gracie got funnel cakes for all of them, and they happily got the blackberry topping all over their faces as they tried to eat them delicately.

Sam saw Betsy in the distance, standing next to a woman who was an older version of her. That must be her mother, Eloise Meyer. The woman had a hard mouth and deep-set lines of disapproval on her face, and Betsy looked slightly harassed. However, she saw Sam and waved cheerfully before returning her attention to her mother.

"Is that who I think it is?" Gracie said.

"I think so."

Caroline linked arms with her sisters. "I am very grateful for our mother and for both of you. Now let's get some ice cream."

They managed to while away the time until one o'clock, when they gathered outside the judging tent where a small stage had been set up. They had to wait while they announced the winners of the cake division and the cookies division before they moved on to the pies division, which Sam and Betsy had entered.

Gracie and Caroline both grabbed Sam's hand tightly as they waited. Her heart was hammering so hard she was afraid it would fly right out of her chest.

"Fifth place," the announcer said, "goes to...Samantha Carter, with her blackberry cobbler."

Sam felt her stomach drop one moment and then experienced a rush of elation as she realized she had won something out of all the contestants. What was there to be disappointed about? Gracie and Caroline were squealing with joy. Sam went up to collect her ribbon and certificate.

"Fifth place!" Gracie said. "And your first time entering!"

"Next year, first place," Caroline said, beaming.

They waited through fourth, third, and second place, and finally the announcer said, "First place goes to… Betsy Carlisle with her blackberry tart."

Sam was able to clap heartily for Betsy as she walked up to accept her ribbon. Betsy smiled for the photographer who took her picture, but surprisingly, Betsy's mother, Eloise, seemed more excited than Betsy herself about her win. Eloise was clapping hard and had thrust her chest out in pride.

Sam left Caroline and Gracie in line for kettle corn while she tried to speak to Betsy. She waited behind some other people who sounded like they were Meyer clan cousins, and finally she reached Betsy.

"Congratulations." And Sam meant it. She hugged Betsy, who hugged her back.

Betsy whispered in her ear, "Thank you."

"For what?"

"I know that this win won't necessarily improve things with my mother, but you and your sisters have helped me realize that God loves me no matter what awards I win or don't win. I want to bake because I enjoy it."

Sam squeezed her hard once and then released her to another person who wanted to congratulate her.

As she made her way back toward her sisters, Sam heard a voice call her name. She turned to see Lenora Worth, the teacher from Daley Academy, hurrying toward her with her face alight.

"Congratulations on your ribbon," she said.

"Thanks."

"I'm so glad I ran into you, because now I get to deliver my news in person. The school wants you to come in for an interview on Monday."

Sam felt a moment of elation, a rush of excitement at this new turn of events. But then she remembered the time she'd spent each morning the past week reading her Bible, getting back into her quiet times for the first time in years. And she knew this teaching job wasn't for her.

"I'm sorry, Lenora, but I think I'm going to withdraw my application."

"But why? You'd be such a good addition to the school."

"I've been praying about the job the past week, and I realize that it's not what I really enjoy doing anymore. I volunteer at the Sunday preschool, and that seems to satisfy me. I'd rather spend my days doing something I've come to delight in—my baking. I want to spend more time working at it and developing my skill."

Lenora sighed. "Well, I can't say I'm not disappointed, but I do understand. Congratulations again on your ribbon—that's fantastic!"

And as Lenora walked away, Sam knew she'd done the right thing.

Epilogue

The tourists had left the island a little after Labor Day, so the beach was almost empty except for the small gathering among the dunes.

Holding roses from their own garden in her hands, Caroline walked barefoot through the sand toward the two small clusters of folding chairs.

She walked slowly, savoring the moment. The wind ruffling through her hair, the salt air smelling like waves and seashells. The trailing end of her silk shawl, printed with pimpernels, billowed around her, and she felt like a scarlet flame.

Excitement made her heart gallop, but she walked sedately so she could smile at the people she loved so much, reaching out to touch hands when she drew close. Brandon and his wife Stacy with their wriggling three-year-old twins. Gracie's daughter Paige. Sam's daughter Jamie.

Shirley Addison had donned a white polyester pantsuit with a gigantic rhinestone elephant pin on the collar. Shirley gave a soft *humph* as Caroline approached, but Caroline saw her lips curl into a fond smile as she passed her.

Doris had come, accompanied by her granddaughter. They both had dressed in simple peach dresses; Doris's smile encompassed Caroline in warmth like a tangible hug.

Gracie had donned a pretty blue dress with matching scarf that made her eyes look like sapphires. Max sat at Gracie's feet, and next to her sister was Bill Dekker, his hair neatly trimmed. He looked handsome in a hunter-green short-sleeved shirt and khaki slacks. Gracie reached out to clasp Caroline's hand for a moment before Caroline walked on.

Sam had worn a vivid green shift dress that made her look elfin and mischievous, which was emphasized by the fact she looked as excited as her grandniece Evelyn, the flower girl, who stood next to her in a citrus-colored dress, holding the empty flower basket and beaming brighter than the sun above. Both reached out to touch Caroline as she walked past them, their touches full of love.

And then she locked eyes with George, and the world fell away. His smile made her heart feel full to bursting. He looked dashing in a red linen shirt and pants, the cuffs and legs embroidered with silver and white. The two of them gravitated toward each other like twin stars, and at the touch of his hand on her elbow, Caroline felt complete.

She heard Pastor Stan speaking, heard herself responding, heard George's rumbling voice. The silver and turquoise wedding band he slipped onto her finger gleamed in the sunlight.

"You may now kiss the bride."

And then George was kissing her, and she heard the applause and laughter and cries of joy of the people who meant so much to her.

They turned and walked back up the aisle amid more smiles, more hugs, more laughter. But Caroline paused when she caught sight of the Misty Harbor Inn in front of her, looking like it had its arms open wide to welcome her home.

It truly was home, now. Caroline and her sisters knew that Misty Harbor was meant to be theirs. It was part of their family history. A part of their mother's history.

And as the autumn sunshine caressed her face, Caroline felt sure that above, her mother, Rosalie—and Hannah—were smiling down on them.

ABOUT THE
Author

Evangeline Kelley is the pen name for the writing team of Patti Berg, Pam Hanson & Barbara Andrews, and Camy Tang, who collaborated to create Postcards from Misty Harbor Inn. Each of them has published novels individually, but this is their first series together.

A NOTE FROM
the Editors

We hope you enjoy Postcards from Misty Harbor Inn, created by the Books and Inspirational Media Division of Guideposts, a non-profit organization. In all of our books, magazines and outreach efforts, we aim to deliver inspiration and encouragement, help you grow in your faith, and celebrate God's love in every aspect of your daily life.

Thank you for making a difference with your purchase of this book, which helps fund our many outreach programs to the military, prisons, hospitals, nursing homes and schools. To learn more, visit GuidepostsFoundation.org.

We also maintain many useful and uplifting online resources. Visit Guideposts.org to read true stories of hope and inspiration, access OurPrayer network, sign up for free newsletters, download free e-books, join our Facebook community, and follow our stimulating blogs.

To learn about other Guideposts publications, including the best-selling devotional *Daily Guideposts*, go to ShopGuideposts.org, call (800) 932-2145 or write to Guideposts, PO Box 5815, Harlan, Iowa 51593.